MICKEY MANTLE DOESN'T EAT BROCCOLI

BY

PHILIP SCHLAEGER

Published in the United States of America.

ISBN-13: 978-1515383833
ISBN-10: 1515383830
BISAC: Fiction/Humorous

For anyone who's ever been a thirteen-year-old boy....

And for anyone who's ever known one.

1

HE WAS SUPERMAN in flannels and spikes, Hercules with a bat, the most idolized star who ever played the game. The Mick didn't just hit baseballs...he crunched them.

I was six when his tape-measure home runs first rocketed into my life. I'd gone in the kitchen to make some Ovaltine. Dad and Mr. Feldman were sitting at the table, playing gin and talking about this nineteen-year-old rookie at the Yankees' spring training camp. *Mickey Mantle*, they said his name was.

"Not even DiMaggio hits them like that," Dad was saying. "You seen those forearms, Nate? They're like Popeye's."

"Papers say he smashed one six hundred and fifty-six feet in an exhibition game," Mr. Feldman said. "*Six hundred and fifty-six feet!* That's farther than a football field!"

"*Two* football fields," Dad said.

"One field, two fields, it's still six hundred and fifty-six feet." Mr. Feldman snatched the pencil off the scorepad, broke the point off, and stirred his coffee. "Found out it tastes better lead-free."

Satisfied his coffee was now properly stirred, Mr. Feldman took a sip, smacked his lips, and put the pencil back on the scorepad. "Know what a Yankee coach told sportswriters? Told them when Mantle gets up to hit, guys get off the bench and elbow each other out of the way to get a better look. I'm telling you, Lou, hard as this kid hits the ball he's gonna be the first player in baseball history to kill somebody with a home run."

"Nate, Nate, you don't kill somebody with a home run." Dad picked up the ten of clubs Mr. Feldman had discarded and threw out the queen of hearts.

Mr. Feldman shook his head and grumbled. "First you throw out a king, now another queen. What, you think we should get rid of monarchies?"

Dad ignored the question. "All those home runs the Babe hit, none of them ever killed anybody. Ruth, Gehrig, Meusel, Lazzeri...none of those guys on Murderers' Row killed anybody. They called them *Murderers Row* because they murdered pitches, not fans."

Mr. Feldman drew a card and groaned. He switched around the cards in his hand. Then he re-switched them. Finally, he threw out the nine of diamonds and picked up a potato chip.

Dad ignored the chips and snatched the nine. "I'm knocking."

"You're knockin'?"

Dad laid down his cards and smiled. "On *seven*, Mantle's number."

Mr. Feldman grunted. "Two sixes, a three, and a jack...twenty points."

"Twenty-five," Dad said. "Jacks are ten."

Mr. Feldman waggled his finger at me. "You watch, Philip, he's gonna do it. Some poor guy walkin' his dog

2

down 163rd Street won't ever know what hit him. He'll be walkin' along and stop to let the dog do his business. Know what's gonna happen to him?"

I shook my head.

"He's gonna be drilled in the head, smack in the old noodle. And you know by what?"

I shook my head.

"A ball."

"A *ball*?"

"A baseball, Philip. Hit clear out of the Stadium by this Mantle kid."

Was Mr. Feldman serious? At six, I was old enough to know that no one had ever homered over the roof of Yankee Stadium—not even Babe Ruth. Anybody who could hit home runs all the way to 163rd Street, and lethal ones at that, had to be superhuman.

Mickey Mantle, I soon learned, was.

2

MY WORSHIP OF THE MICK began the next spring, even before we moved from the Bronx to Cincinnati, which was where Dad had met Mom when she came to town with the skating team from Oberlin College. Mom had gone to the school on a figure skating scholarship, and Dad had liked her figure. Two years later, Lou Kleinmann graduated from the University of Cincinnati with a double major in finance and marketing; Leah Friedlander, from Oberlin with a triple axel. They honeymooned along the Scioto River in Chillicothe the following summer.

The reason Dad sold his bar up on Gun Hill Road and we moved to Cincinnati was because Mom had accepted a lucrative job teaching remedial penmanship at UC. Mom was an expert in cursive writing, No one was better in closing *a*'s and *g*'s.

"You know what happens when you leave your *a*'s and *g*'s open, honey?" she'd lecture me. "People can confuse them with *u* or *y*, and then you know where you are?"

I'd shake my head.

"Guyana. Is that where you want to be? In South America, where you can't find good rye bread?"

I never had an answer for that.

We'd hardly unpacked from the move when my Cincinnati relatives decided my name wasn't working in family conversations since no one knew if they were talking about me or my cousin Philip in Baltimore—not that anybody in the family ever talked about him much anyway. Aunt Helen insisted they could put an end to all the Philip confusion at her Passover Seder if they stuck a nickname on me.

Aunt Tillie, who never agreed with anyone without putting in her own two cents, pointed out that in Judaism it's traditional to give someone the nickname of a beloved family member who has passed away. "That way you keep the nickname alive," she said. "That way you keep the nickname alive." Because she had three children and a husband who often acted like one, Aunt Tillie was in the habit of sometimes repeating herself.

Mom looked around the table. "So whose nickname do we keep alive?"

"I don't know, Leah," Aunt Sylvia said. She'd arrived late to the Seder, getting stuck in traffic on a one-way street near UC when a sudden epiphany told her she was stuck going in the wrong direction. "Seems to me everybody's accounted for."

"Well, there has to be someone we've missed," Mom said.

And so it was that I was nicknamed *Skippy* in loving memory of Uncle Nate's late Scottish terrier. *Skippy*—it was a nickname that seemed to work for both Aunt Helen and Aunt Tillie, everyone in the family but Grandma Bessie. Grandma Bessie was never certain whether they were talking about me or peanut butter.

Frankly, I'm not sure it was just the name *Philip* that had the family confusing me with my cousin Philip who lived in Baltimore—which, as I was to later learn from my book report on the first book in the *American Zip Codes* trilogy, was not Baltimore but Bellmore, and that Bellmore was on the south shore of Long Island. Aunt Tillie said we looked alike, that we had the same haircut and missing baby teeth. Since I hadn't met Cousin Philip in Baltimore, Bellmore, or any zip code for that matter, I couldn't tell you. And because all childhood photos of him vanished after his nose job, I have no idea what Cousin Philip looked like when he was six—other than his having a bigger nose, of course.

But even if we did look alike back then that's where the similarity ended. And it wasn't that Cousin Philip stubbornly insisted on saying *to-mah-to* when everyone else said *to-may-to*. No, it was far more serious than tomatoes.

It had to do with Willie and Mickey.

Cousin Philip idolized Willie Mays, worshipped the centerfield grass Willie played on in the Polo Grounds. I might have been able to live with that. But I could never forgive him for what he pulled at my bar mitzvah party, backing me up against a wall and jabbing his finger in my chest, screaming that Willie, not Mickey, was the best player in baseball. It was something you just didn't scream outside asylums.

I was twelve when Mickey had his monster season, the kind of season your average ballplayer only dreams about. He was a pinstriped nightmare, terrorizing pitchers with fifty-two home runs, the most anybody hit in the American League or National League in 1956. It didn't matter what they threw him—fastball high inside, curve on the outside corner—or if they threw right-handed or left. The Mick was a switch hitter, could slug tape-measure home runs swinging from either side of the plate.

Bob Lemon, Billy Pierce, Early Wynn...all the American League's top pitchers had stood alone on the mound, kicking the dirt, shaking their heads, spitting out a big stream of tobacco juice and a bigger stream of obscenities. There was no need to turn and see the outfielder completely helpless, no need to watch him just standing there as he looked up in awe. From Boston to Kansas City, pitchers around the league learned pretty quickly the sudden roar of the crowd meant another one of The Mick's rocket shots had disappeared over the wall.

No one had ever hit a baseball harder or farther than Mickey Mantle. And fast? Mickey was so fast he'd hit a ground ball and sometimes be called out even when he beat the throw to first base. Umpires couldn't believe anyone could speed down the line like that.

Mickey Charles Mantle was something else all right. Yet great as he was, he never tooted his own horn. He never looked down on rookie ballplayers— or cub reporters either. And no matter what city he was playing in, he never walked by anyone who had a hand out. Mickey had a heart as big as center field in Yankee Stadium.

The Mick was twenty-five going into the 1957 season with the Yankees, just starting to reach his prime. He already had Cooperstown written all over his muscular delts and lats. Featured stories were written about him in the papers. He was on the cover of magazines. Babies throughout America were named after him. He was the most-talked about man in sports. If you hadn't heard of him you were either dead or in a coma. He was young, blond, and handsome with All-American looks, the first telegenic baseball star in the new television age.

The Mick was who every boy growing up in the Fifties wanted to be. We wanted to talk like him, wear our baseball caps like him, run the bases like him…most of all, hit a ball like him.

I worshipped The Mick…oh, how I worshiped him! But I hadn't seen him hit even one home run in 1956. I hadn't seen him trot around the bases while the crowd went crazy. I hadn't seen him mobbed by teammates as he reached home plate.

I hadn't seen Mickey Mantle play one inning of his monster season.

3

I MISSED EVERY GAME The Mick played in 1956, and it was all because we were now living in what Aunt Tillie called the Sahara Desert.

I'd been eight, and Mickey in his second year with the Yankees, when we moved once again, this time from Cincinnati all the way out to the furthest reach of human civilization, where scorpions outnumbered rattlers and rattlers outnumbered people. *Tombstone, Arizona* was what townfolk called the place.

"Tombstone's supposed to be a healthy place to live," Dad said. "The dry air will be good for Mom's neuroses."

What Dad didn't say was that for years—going back before the Earps established themselves in town—newcomers had found Tombstone's dry air hard to breathe since it was often filled with lead. At the height of the claim-jumping season, one-way trips to Boot Hill had sometimes been undertaken daily.

But despite its frequent drop in population, Tombstone had lived up to its epithet as *The Town Too Tough to Die.* No longer a little one-hearse town, Tombstone's shot-up streets were now paved and curbed, its hitching posts now parking meters. By the time Dad moved us, Tombstone had become the cultural and culinary center of Cochise County. It had mock gun fights at high noon—in honor of

Gary Cooper—and the "world famous" OK Corral Diner, which boasted it had the only restrooms this side of Tucson deodorized with burning charcoal.

Yet Aunt Tillie remained unimpressed.

"You think the movie studios are falling all over each other to shoot Westerns there?" she told Mom. "Not any more, Leah…not any more, Leah. Not after what Tombstone did to Alan Ladd, Van Heflin, and Jack Palance. Not after what Tombstone did to Alan Ladd, Van Heflin, and Jack Palance."

The way Aunt Tillie explained it, *Shane* had been all set to shoot in town, but Paramount had been forced to look elsewhere when informed that a new ordinance prohibited bushwhacking inside city limits.

"But the bullets are blanks," the studio protested.

"Doesn't matter," said Mayor Earp, a great-great nephew twice removed of Wyatt. "An ordinance is an ordinance."

Yet despite its outlaw of bushwhacking, Tombstone's reputation remained intact. It was why every major league team shunned the town, even for spring training, and why I hadn't seen Mickey take the field with the Yankees.

To tell you the truth, even if the Yanks wanted to train in Tombstone—which they most assuredly did not—there was no place in town to play baseball. Oh, Slowdraw Field was big enough and kept up enough for a major league game all right. The problem was Slowdraw held the overflow from Boot Hill. You couldn't run the bases without tripping over tombstones…or an unfocused tourist.

Indeed, tourists were now coming to Tombstone by the handful. On a clear day there would be three or four of them up on Boot Hill. They'd whip out their Brownie Hawkeyes, pushing and shoving each other like third graders to see who got to pose for a photo next to the tombstone with the epitaph:

Shot for no reason at all

I'd never seen Mickey play on TV either. What few TV antennas there were in Tombstone never carried a Yankee game. Sure, there were midget wrestling matches from a TV station in Tucson and *Hopalong Cassidy* re-runs, but never a Yankee game. There was in fact only one TV set on our block on Gunslinger Way and it belonged to the McCrackins, who weren't exactly eager to share it—except on Tuesday night when Milton Berle was on.

Every Tuesday night was a block party at the McCrackins. "You bring the cakes and cookies," Mrs. McCrackin would tell Mom. "Shirley Stickler's making her jalapeño salad, Carol Fish is bringing Hebrew National hot dogs and creamed horseradish, and I've got Adrienne Cacciatore down for braised sauerkraut. Adrienne's also bringing her special lima bean chili."

So the women would bring their cakes, cookies, salads, hot dogs, horseradish, chili, anything they could carry across Gunslinger Way before a pack of wide-eyed neighborhood dogs jumped and slobbered all over them. The men would be sitting around the dining room table talking business, talking about pork bellies and the price of cactus futures. And we kids would be running around outdoors, squashing scorpions and counting down the minutes until we heard the familiar siren that meant the *Texaco Star Theatre* was once more on the air. Out would come Uncle Miltie in lipstick, dress, and high heels—looking more like Aunt Miltie than Uncle Miltie.

Tuesday night was the highlight of the week. The other nights we'd take our Red Ryder flashlights out in the back and watch the cactus grow. You know, cactus like you see in a John Wayne movie. Only how come John Wayne never falls off his horse, landing butt first in a bed of cactus? How come, of all the boys enrolled in Beginners Posse, it was me who got stuck with Punxsutawney Spill, the only horse in Greater Tombstone to ever get spooked by his own shadow? Fall off a horse anywhere in Tombstone and you know what you land in?

Prickly Pears.

Oh sure, they look innocent enough in those scenic photos you see today in *Arizona Highways*. But Prickly Pears have long, sharp needles that don't discriminate by age, race, or national origin. Trust me, I know. It's why I swore I'd never ride a horse again. For years afterwards the only horse anyone could get me on was the one on Coney Island's merry-go-round. But it had to be on a day when you couldn't see the merry-go-round's shadow.

No, I couldn't watch The Mick belt tape-measure home runs. But there was nothing about Tombstone to prevent me from reading about them. Once a week, I'd buckle up my holster, making sure my gun was loaded with enough caps in case there were kids in black hats crouching out there behind the Prickly Pears that lined the way to the mailbox.

I'd learned my lesson...and it had cost me Mickey Mantle.

4

THE HOLE-IN-THE PANTS GANG had
jumped me one morning as I did my John Wayne walk to
the mailbox to get *The Sporting News*. Unlike John Wayne
I wasn't armed, and the Gang knew it. They'd been lying in
wait, and I was out to lunch…well, actually I'd just had
breakfast and was daydreaming of Annette Funicello. Point
is, I wasn't watching where I was John Wayne-ing…and
they were.

The two of them were wearing black cowboy hats,
high-top black Converses with rubber spurs, and black
kerchiefs pulled up just under their eyes. The taller one
sneezed, his kerchief slipping down revealing his running
nose and identity. He was Clyde Zander, not even nine and
already the playground terror of every kid in kindergarten.

"This is a stickup! Hand it over!" Clyde pointed his
plastic-handled cap gun at me. "And why are you walking
like a sissy?"

I stopped singing *She'll Be Coming 'Round the
Mountain When She Comes.* "I'm not walking like a sissy,"
I said. "I'm walking like John Wayne."

"Looks like a sissy walk to me." Clyde's twin sister
Bunny could mask her face, but couldn't mask her whiny
voice. "Just hand it over, Kleinmann!" she whined.

"Hand over what?" I said.

"How am I supposed to know?" Bunny whined. "This is our first job."

"Whatever you've got." Clyde had wiped his nose. He sucked in his belly, which caused his pants to slip down, and blew into the barrel of his fifty-shot Bronco 44, the toughest cap gun in the world by far.

"But I haven't got anything," I said.

"Well, you're supposed to," Clyde said, flattening his lip over his front teeth. "You ever stand out in the rain with your guts beat out?"

He sounded exactly like Humphrey Bogart's double.

"Clyde thinks he does impressions," Bunny whined, twirling her gun. "You oughta hear him do Cagney's double."

"You rat…you dirty rat," Clyde pulled up his pants and sneered. "How can we rob you if you haven't got anything?"

He had a point. He also had a loaded cap gun aimed at my head.

"How about my Bazooka?"

Bunny stopped twirling "You're *carrying*?"

"Yeah, but I've only got one left."

"We'll take it," Clyde said.

So I reached in my pocket and pulled out my last Bazooka.

"Hand it over!" Clyde ordered.

"Better do it," Bunny whined. "He's run out of impressions."

But before I could hand Clyde the Bazooka, he snatched it from me. He unwrapped the paper, broke the bubblegum more or less in half, and gave the smaller piece to Bunny, who shot him point blank.

"Okay, you got what you want." I hitched up my pajamas. "Can I go now?"

"How do we know there's nothing else in your pockets?" Clyde said, rubbing cap gunsmoke out of his eye.

"Do it!" Bunny whined.

I turned the pockets of my pajama pants inside out. My good-luck rabbit's foot tumbled to the ground.

"Thought so." Clyde had a grin on his face.

"You satisfied now?"

"Take your boots off!"

"My boots?"

"You heard him!" Bunny whined. "Take 'em off!"

I pulled my boots off. Clyde took the left one, turned it upside down and gave it a couple of shakes. My treasured Mickey Mantle baseball card, the card I always carried with me, fluttered out. Clyde snatched it off the brown grass.

"Will you look at that? It's Mantle's rookie card!" Before I could protest, he shoved it into his pocket.

"Look at him, he's crying," Bunny whined. "Why are you crying like a sissy?"

"I'm not crying like a sissy," I sniffled.

"Looks like tears to me," Clyde said.

"Give it back," I said. "It's my only Mickey Mantle."

"Aw, too bad," Bunny whined.

Clyde grabbed Bunny's arm. "C'mon, let's get out of here before he starts bawling."

"In a sec." Bunny stuck her cap gun into my ribs and popped a bubble. "Just one more thing, Kleinmann. Stop

15

botching up *She'll Be Coming 'Round the Mountain.* It's 'she'll be driving *five* white horses,' not six."

I wasn't going to argue—not with a cap gun in my ribs.

5

I NEVER SAW that Mantle rookie card again. Nor any other Mickey Mantles. Every chance I got I'd buy a pack of Bazooka bubblegum, hoping this time The Mick's card would be one of the five inside. I'd get Nellie Fox, Al Kaline, Al Rosen, Warren Spahn, once even a Ted Kluszewski, but never Mickey Mantle.

Like I said, I'd learned my lesson the hard way. Which is why I never John Wayned out of the house in the morning again without my gun, always making sure it was loaded with caps. It was also why I never sang *She'll Be Coming 'Round the Mountain When She Comes* anymore.

Once a week I'd quietly tip-toe out to the mailbox, eyes darting between the Prickly Pears just in case Bunny and Clyde were out there. If I was lucky *The Sporting News* would be inside the mailbox, and I'd holster my gun and quickly snatch it. With a *Yippee Ki Yay,* I'd forget John Wayne and hurry back inside to read it.

Before reading the cover stories and the articles on each major league team, I'd turn to the Yankee box scores and check on how Mickey did. *How many did Mantle get this week?* didn't mean hits. It meant home runs.

Dad liked baseball too, but he didn't have time to be the kind of Mickey Mantle fan I was. Dad had gone into real estate development in Tombstone, which meant he was out in the desert half the day looking at lots, putting up *For Sale* signs with a note at the bottom that read in bold red letters, *WARNING: Do Not Hand-Feed the Scorpions and Gila Monsters.* When he wasn't restocking his first-aid kit, Dad was trying to figure out what kind of family was likely to move all the way out to Diamondback Hills sometime in the next decade. Much as he would have liked to, Lou Kleinmann didn't have time for baseball.

My grandfather was another story.

Grandpa Albert still lived back in Cincinnati, in Bond Hill, where he was semi-retired—meaning he wasn't selling used semis anymore—so he had a lot of time on his hands, time to see every Yankee game carried on NBC's *Game of the Week.* Grandpa Albert said the TV camera would close in on each Yankee hitter as he took his batting stance at the plate and that the camera would zoom in so tight on Mickey's arms you could actually see the muscles twitch.

Everyone in Bond Hill knew my Grandpa Albert. You could always recognize him by his golden tan, which went well with his *joie de vivre* and his brown fedora. Whatever the season, every morning, regardless of the humidity, Grandpa Albert looked like he'd stepped out of a Brooks Brothers catalog, his hand-painted, paisley ties always knotted in a perfect half-Windsor. Behind his wire-rimmed bifocals, his blue-gray eyes seemed forever twinkling, his whole face lighting up whenever he saw Linnie and me.

Grandpa Albert was only about five-foot-five, but no one stood taller in my eyes.

It was 1957, and I had just made it through my fourth year of side-stepping scorpions when Grandpa Albert called from Cincinnati with exciting news.

The call came in February when most of the scorpions in Tombstone were hibernating. Grandpa Albert said he'd decided what to do with the hundred gallons of Esso gasoline he'd won in a baseball contest in the *Cincinnati Enquirer.* He explained he'd studied a map of the Sahara and figured he had enough gasoline and purified water for Grandma Bessie and him to visit us and make it back to Cincinnati. A visit meant we'd talk about Mickey…and it meant presents for my eight-year-old sister and me.

Linnie, of course, isn't the same bratty Turkey Lips she was back then. With the passage of time, she's changed. She's become worse. It's why these days I only see her at family milestones—like readings of last wills and testaments.

But I digress. I was telling you about the visit that February from my grandparents.

I remember Grandpa Albert and Grandma Bessie brought Linnie a transistor radio and an obnoxious, self-absorbed doll she promptly named Linnie Junior. Little Linnie could drink out of a nursing bottle, wet her diapers, roll her eyes, and say things like *Ma-Ma, Da-Da,* and *I Love Lucy.*

I was luckier than my little sister, much luckier. Not only did I get the new Hardy Boys mystery, *The Ghost of Skeleton Rock,* but I got a pair of black, lizard-print Durango boots…and the Magic 8 Ball.

"Go ahead, ask it something," Grandpa Albert said. "But you have to shake it a couple of times before you do."

"Think maybe I should ask it something easy first?"

Grandpa Albert smiled. "Up to you."

"Okay, Magic 8 Ball….do your stuff." I shook it a couple of times. "What's my nickname?"

SIGNS POINT TO YES

Grandpa Albert chuckled. "You have to ask it a yes-no question."

"A yes-no question?"

"You know, like 'Is my nickname Skip?'"

I shook the Magic 8 Ball. "Is my nickname *Skip*?"

YES DEFINITELY

"Guess it's working okay," I said.

Grandpa Albert smiled. "Ask it something else."

"Can I ask it *anything?*"

"Well, as long as it's a yes-no question."

I gave the Magic 8 Ball a couple of quick shakes. "Will I ever meet Mickey Mantle?"

IT IS CERTAIN

6

EVERY DAY WAS SUNDAY with Grandpa
Albert around. He'd pile Linnie, Linnie Junior, and me into
his Olds, stop to load up on ice-cold Dr Peppers, and drive
us across the desert to the middle of nowhere and hang a
left. I'd sit up front with my trusty Red Ryder Daisy Air
Rifle, riding shotgun in case we came across a howling
band of marauding renegades or a hostile band of littering
tourists.

Turkey Lips rode armless. Not that she was a
paraplegic, you understand, it was just that she never
carried a weapon, not even a bobby pin. Linnie Kleinmann
knew no fear. When she was two, she'd walked off the high
board of the swimming pool...topless. At four, she was
going to bed with the lights off and the closet door wide
open. Linnie wasn't afraid of the family skeletons everyone
said were in the closet. She wasn't even afraid of a tag-
team spanking from Mom and Dad for biting me, even after
I'd explained to her most of the rubber scorpions were
dead. My explanation had got me nowhere. She'd bitten me
anyway.

Grandpa Albert would dote on Linnie, but I knew I was
his favorite. I was his first and only grandson, and he
simply couldn't spend enough time with me. We'd play
ball together, and he'd teach me how to switch hit just like

21

Mickey did. I didn't have a baseball back then, but luckily there were grapefruit trees in the neighbors' backyard. In a week I was able to splatter a pitch batting lefthanded or right.

Grandpa Albert would tell me about the Indians who used to live in Arizona—the Navajos, Hopis, Apaches, and the rest. I learned Tonto was a wuss compared to Cochise and Geronimo and that the only reason he got to be the Lone Ranger's "faithful Indian companion" was he had married into the family. Geronimo, on the other hand, was something else. Grandpa Albert said if Geronimo hadn't surrendered, the Army would never have gotten him and Arizona would never have become a state—which would have meant that Barry Goldwater couldn't be in the U.S. Senate and someday run for President.

And Grandpa Albert would talk baseball.

He'd tell me about Babe Ruth, the Bambino, and how his curse on the Red Sox meant Boston would never win another World Series. He said he'd been at Yankee Stadium the day the dying Gehrig stood at the mike and told the crowd he was *the luckiest man in the world.* Grandpa Albert said hearing Lou's words, grown men cried.

Grandpa Albert would tell me all about the great DiMaggio, how he'd hit safely in fifty-six straight games and that his record would never be broken. He'd talk about the crazy antics of Dizzy and Daffy Dean and the scrappy, reckless play of the Gashouse Gang. And he'd tell me about the beanings, spikings, insults, death threats, and countless humiliation Jackie Robinson endured, and how

Jackie integrated baseball without anyone swinging from a tree.

And always, always there were stories about "The Hebrew Hammer"—Hank Greenberg, the only one of Grandma Bessie's eighty-seven third cousins in baseball's Hall of Fame.

Then Grandpa Albert would take me down to the drug store on Doc Holliday Avenue and buy me the latest *Superman* and *Red Ryder* comic books. We'd grab stools at the soda fountain and sit there arguing who was better— Willie, Mickey, or the Duke. He'd order me a huge chocolate sundae and grin as half the chocolate syrup dripped down my new Mickey Mantle tee shirt.

But I didn't care.

One day Grandpa Albert told me the best story of all, the true, incredible story of how he met his hero, his idol...his Mickey Mantle.

7

IT WAS 1905, and Grandpa Albert was thirteen and studying for his bar mitzvah when he met the baseball legend who was arguably the most dominating pitcher of all time, the man they called Big Six. They called him that because he was six-feet tall in his stocking feet, tall in those days. Big Six had just led the Giants to the '05 World Series championship over the A's, pitching a record *three shutouts in six days.* It was a feat so unreal it would one day be selected by ESPN as the greatest playoff performance of all time.

Anyway, as Grandpa Albert told the story, it was just after the '05 World Series and he had taken the subway from his home in Washington Heights on the tip of Manhattan to his cousin Esther's Sweet Sixteen Party in the Bronx when it happened.

He was standing around at the party, talking with a few other boys about horseless carriages, vaudeville stars, and the '05 World Series. "Twenty-seven innings!" one boy said. "Twenty-seven innings and no runs."

"Twenty-seven innings *and* only one walk," chipped in Grandpa Albert, who knew Big Six's stats like the back of his hand. "Talk about pitching. Big Six is—"

"The best," interrupted a cute, little, freckled-faced girl in pink buttons and bows, who'd walked up to where the boys were talking. She looked straight at Grandpa Albert with her big, blue eyes and said, "Wow, listen! They're playing that new song, *Daddy's Little Girl.* Isn't it absolutely divine?"

Grandpa Albert wasn't sure exactly what to say so he just nodded.

"So would you like to dance?"

"I guess so," Grandpa Albert said.

"My name's Peggy."

"I'm Albert."

Now you have to remember Grandpa Albert was thirteen, meaning he didn't have much experience dancing with girls. Soon he was stepping on Peggy's toes. So Peggy, being the toe-sensitive girl she was, led him off the dance floor, and they sat down and talked. They talked about horseless carriages and vaudeville stars. Grandpa Albert said they had started talking about the '05 World Series when Peggy said, "Oops, it's time for me to go home. My dad's here." She grabbed Grandpa Albert's hand. "C'mon, I'll introduce you."

And that's how my grandfather got to meet the great Christy Mathewson, Big Six.

Grandpa Albert said he and Christy stood and chatted for a while, talking about the kinds of things idols and idol worshipers talk about, until Christy announced that his horseless carriage was double-parked and he had to run.

"Nice talking with you, Albert," he said. "Anything I can do for you?"

Anything he could do for me? Grandpa Albert said he gulped and asked Christy if he'd give him his autograph.

"Sure, kid." Christy reached into his jacket and pulled out a pen. "Got some paper I can write on?"

Grandpa Albert didn't. But all was not lost. Christy picked up a crumpled, stained napkin off a table, uncrumpled it and, between gravy stains, scribbled:

To Albert, who's taught me a lot tonight about horseless carriages. Never give up your dreams. And always have pen and paper with you—Christy Mathewson

And there the story ended.

Grandpa Albert told me it was a dream come true. There he was, Albert Kleinmann, thirteen and studying for his bar mitzvah, one moment stepping on toes at cousin Esther's Sweet Sixteen party in the Bronx and the next moment actually meeting Christy Mathewson. Grandpa Albert said he'd kept that uncrumpled, stained napkin all these years and that it was one of his most prized possessions.

What a story! My grandfather, the man whose pull with the tooth fairy had caused quarters to become half-dollars, had actually *met* Big Six! I told him my lifelong dream ever since I was six was to meet Mickey Mantle, that I'd give anything to meet The Mick and get his autograph, have him write something special just for me, that I'd treasure it forever.

"Forever?"

"Forever. I'll never lose it, Grandpa…I promise."

Grandpa Albert smiled.

"I won't," I said. "I'll keep it in my room…never let it out of my sight. You'll see."

Grandpa Albert took out his pipe and tamped the tobacco. Satisfied, he lit it. "You'll meet him," he said. "I met Christy Mathewson, and you'll meet Mickey Mantle."

"*How?*" I asked. "How am I supposed to meet him? The Yankees never come out here. And Yankee Stadium is 2,385.67 miles away."

Grandpa Albert chuckled. "You'll meet him, you'll meet him. Have a little faith." And he smiled that special smile of his, the one that meant grandfathers know best.

8

IT IS CERTAIN

I COULDN'T SLEEP. I lay in bed thinking about meeting Mickey Mantle. I knew the sheep thing wasn't going to help me fall asleep. I was never good with sheep. I'd always lose track of the number I'd counted and have to start all over again. I needed something I knew I could concentrate on.

So I started counting The Mick's career home runs.

I'd got to 121 when the alarm clock rang. That meant it was nine Saturday morning and meant every kind of weed known to mankind was outside waiting for me.

Back then, weeds weren't like they are today. Back then, weeds were *weeds.* You gardened a bed of roses when I was thirteen, and you took your life in your hands. You had the monstrous seven-foot tall burdocks and the even taller angelicas. You had the hideous-looking goatheads and the prickly Himalayan blackberries that some people said were really mutations from the Catskills. You had weeds that carried childhood diseases like mumps and whooping cough. You had weeds that refused to die.

There was no escaping pulling weeds. I'd tried everything I could think of, even feigning diarrhea. But it was useless. So I kicked off the sheets, got out of bed, pulled on my Durango boots, and—in a cloud of bedroom dust and a hardy *High Ho Silver!*—slid down the banister into the living room. Dad was sitting on the couch, holding and patting Mom's hand.

"Let's go into the kitchen," he said. "Don't want your mother to start crying again."

I started to tell him I was on my way to the kitchen anyway since I needed to eat my Wheaties, but I sensed whole kernels of wheat weren't on his mind right now.

I was right.

I followed him into the kitchen. Sprawled on the table from last night were Miss Scarlett, Colonel Mustard, and Professor Plum—Turkey Lips always got mad when anyone beat her. Dad pushed them aside and motioned for me to sit down.

"Can't make money in real estate development here," he said. "It's like I'm snake-bitten." He sighed. "And it's your mother too."

"Mom?"

He lowered his voice. "Her neuroses haven't gotten any better out here."

I nodded.

"We're going home, Skip."

"We're moving back to *Cincinnati*?"

"Cincinnati. Spinning Wheel Cafe's been up for sale. Grandpa Albert showed me the numbers, said it'd be a good move for us to go in together and buy it. So that's what I've decided to do....I'm sorry. I know you'll miss Tombstone."

Was Dad kidding? No more sitting out back watching the cactus grow. No more scorpions. No more riding lessons on Punxsutawney Spill.

"You'll make new friends," Dad was saying. "Remember the Farkises? Well, their son's your age."

Yeah, I remembered Fenny Farkis. He was a pretty good kid...even if he wore a Red Sox cap. And I hadn't forgotten some other kids too...like Elaine Novak. To be honest with you, I had a crush on Elaine in the second grade and used to dream of marrying her someday...until the first time I saw Annette Funicello.

There she was, in the TV department at Sears, standing in the middle of the screen singing *Who's the leader of the club that's made for you and me?* I was smitten. Not that there hadn't been other girls that caught my eye, you understand, but always, always I remained true in my dreams to Annette Funicello.

I fell on my knees. "Can we move next week, Dad?"

9

MOVING WHEN YOU'RE thirteen isn't the easiest thing in the world. Moving means leaving behind all your friends...though memories you're allowed to take with you.

There was Clifford teaching me how to yodel like Roy Rogers and punching me when I broke one of his new Elvis records. There was Johnny Pima, the toughest kid in the eighth grade, losing to me in thumb wrestling, a stunning upset even though he used his pinkie. There was Ricky showing me how to hold Damon, his defanged pet rattler, while Damon gummed the mice Ricky force-fed him.

I had to say *adios* to the Cisco Kid too. That's what we called Duncan Cisco, who liked to pretend he was Zorro. The Kid would tell me *That's-what*-la madre-*said* jokes that made no sense to anybody...sometimes not even to Duncan himself. We'd also bet on things. We'd bet on how many marshmallows we could stuff into our mouths. When that got old, we switched to jalapeños.

Leaving Tombstone also meant I'd miss my class reunion at Gene Autry School, where I'd come close to setting a new fifth-grade record for detentions. That I didn't was only because Miss Lindemuth went a whole week without catching me blowing bubbles in class.

Then there were Ozzie and Harriet. To each I'd be saying a tearful good-bye. Ozzie was my horny toad—honest, that's what they're called. I could hold Ozzie in one hand, turn him over on his back, and tickle his horns. Sometimes I'd stroke his belly until he dozed off. Harriet was even friendlier, the kind of pet tarantula that feels perfectly at ease sitting on people's shoulders. She also liked playing hide-and-seek with me when I came home after school. But Harriet was probably happiest in her own tank playing with her plastic toy spider.

Mom made me set Ozzie loose, saying horny toads had never lasted all the way to chilly Cincinnati, that they did best when in heat. So I carried Ozzie down to the little patch of desert next to Gene Autry, tickled his horns one last time, and let him go. I figured when he got hungry for peanut butter he'd make friends on the school playground.

As for Harriet, Mom said I could whine all I wanted but it was illegal to transport tarantulas across state lines… even if they were housebroken. Mom's ad in the classifieds ran two weeks before she found a good home for Harriet. The lady who wound up taking her said she had a dog that Louise could chase around the living room. She also promised to take Harriet in to the vet when her vaccinations were due.

No, moving wasn't going to be easy. Still, I knew it was worth it. Cincinnati wasn't New York, but it was at least a major league town. And I knew all the top players in baseball would be gathered there this summer to play in the All-Star game. The Mick would be coming to Cincinnati… and I'd be there to meet him.

10

BY THE TIME we'd resettled in Cincinnati and I'd given *The Sporting News* my change of address, I no longer had to worry about tripping over the bottoms of my jeans. I'd shot up more than two inches and now came up to Dad's mustache, that is when he was sitting in his favorite easy chair in the den, feet propped on the matching cracked vinyl ottoman. He'd sit there, glued to the TV, scribbling notes into a yellow legal pad as he watched 1956 episodes of *Father Knows Best.*

Dad didn't like being interrupted when he watched the reruns, particularly when Mom would remind him he'd best go out and water the lawn before the sun went down. Mom didn't like him out there alone watering in the dark.

"Anything could happen to you out there," she'd tell him.

You'd listen to Mom nag, and if you closed your eyes you'd swear she was Alice Kramden...you know, Alice Kramden on *The Honeymooners.* Not that Mom looked like Alice, you understand. If anything she could've passed for Lucy's pal, Ethel Mertz, though I personally thought Mom was more attractive...particularly when she wasn't nagging me. Dad was the spitting image of Spencer Tracy—same face, same stocky build. Only thing different was Dad's mustache and that he never fell for Katherine Hepburn, not even in *Woman of the Year*. Dad's taste ran more toward Ethel Mertz, which, of course, was a good thing for Mom.

"Suppose there's a weed out there, Lou, and you don't see it and you trip over its roots? You could fall down and hit your head and then what happens? Suppose while you're lying there in a coma some vine comes along as big as an anaconda and strangles you?"

Mom said she had read in *Readers Digest* that it could happen.

"Why do you have to worry me to death, Lou? Can't you see you're setting a bad example for your son?"

To Dad's credit, he didn't blow his stack at Mom, like Ralph Kramden would've at Alice. Dad had slept on the couch enough to know jumping up and hollering *One of these days, POW! right in the kisser!* didn't cut it with Leah Kleinmann. So he held his tongue and hurriedly leafed through the pages of notes he'd taken on *Father Knows Best* to see how Jim Anderson had handled Margaret when she accused him of setting a bad example for Bud. But Dad never found even one situation. Nor did he find any mention about Margaret being written out of the show because Jim had worried her to death.

He was on his own.

"Did you hear me, Lou?"

"Yes, dear…yes, dear…right away, dear." And he bit his lip and reached for another legal pad, no doubt thinking *Bang! Zoom! Straight to the moon!*

"Look what he's picking up from you! He's already leaving the toilet seat up!" Mom had gone to all-out nagging. "Suppose Linnie gets up in the middle of the night, falls in, and we don't hear her cries for help?"

34

Dad looked at me and sighed. Without saying a word, he got up and turned off the TV. My father was no dummy. He'd been married long enough to know it was useless to tell Mom she was being neurotic when she was already well in stride. That's why he now made sure he had the lawn watered before dark so he could watch *Father Knows Best* in peace. He also made more of an effort to put the toilet seat down.

But I digress.

I was talking about how much I'd grown. And it wasn't just physical. Not to brag, but I was already showing signs of being a mathematical genius. In fact, I'd been the only one in my grade in Tombstone who could divide decimal numbers by decimal numbers without ever having once paid attention in class. I was fast becoming a geographical whiz too and could recite the names of all six states in New England, and do it in reverse alphabetical order.

You try it.

Meanwhile my jeans kept getting shorter.

There were people Mom would run into when she was dragging me through the Boys' Department at Shillito's— people who hadn't seen me since we'd moved to Tombstone—who couldn't get over how much I'd shot up. Some went as far as saying I looked older than my years even though I acted much younger. Aunt Tillie, who never missed a chance to gossip, told her mah-jongg group I bore a striking resemblance to both my parents, that I'd inherited Dad's sinuses and Mom's big mouth.

Other than my sinuses and mouth, everything about me was pretty much average. I looked just like any other thirteen-year-old-boy who happened to bear a slight resemblance to

Ricky Nelson. Except Ricky didn't have zits…at least not on camera. Ozzie wouldn't have allowed it.

11

YOU MAY RELY ON IT

"HE SAID HE SAW it where?" Mom asked.

"*Readers Digest*," I said. "Fenny said he saw it in his grandma's *Readers Digest*. He was staying with her last night. The TV wasn't working, and there was nothing else to read while she was taking a bath."

"And it was a doctor's finding on the cause of zits?"

"Not just one doctor," I said. "*Nine* of them." I told her Fenny said he read in *Readers Digest* that nine out of ten leading dermatologists agree that the leading cause of zits is broccoli.

Mom raised her eyebrows. "And the tenth?"

"He said the leading cause is Brussels Sprouts."

"PHILIP MORRIS KLEINMANN!"

It was Thursday night, which meant we were having meat loaf, mashed potatoes and gravy, and broccoli for dinner. Mom always made meat loaf, mashed potatoes and gravy, and broccoli on Thursday. Sometimes on Monday too.

I stared at the broccoli on my plate. They looked disgusting...maybe more than disgusting. I don't know who invented broccoli, but whoever did should be stood up against a wall and shot. And not with a Daisy Air Rifle.

"Mom, do I have to eat them? Dad hasn't had any."

"That's 'cause he's not here, stupid," Linnie said.

Mom shook her fork at Linnie. "Didn't I tell you not to call your brother names?"

"But he calls me names. He calls me Turkey Lips."

Mom dropped her fork into her mashed potatoes, splattering gravy on the table. "You call your sister *Turkey Lips*?"

"Only to her face," I said.

Mom shook her head. "Linnie, get me a clean sponge. They're in the second drawer, right behind you."

"Where?"

"Second drawer...one down from the first."

Linnie's search for the sponge left her near-empty glass of milk on the table unattended. Mom quickly filled the glass almost to the top, then put her finger to her lips. "You say one word to your sister," she whispered, "and you're getting a second helping of broccoli."

I got the message.

"Which sponge?" Linnie asked.

Mom turned from the table. "What do you mean, 'Which sponge?'"

"Well, there's a blue one and a green one. Which one would you like?"

"'Which one?' Linnie, the one that goes best with brown gravy!"

"Take the blue," I said, winking at her.

"Here," Linnie said, handing Mom the green sponge. "Can I go feed my dolly now?"

"Not until you finish your milk."

"I did finish my milk."

"Then what's that in your glass?"

Linnie looked at her glass. "But I—"

"Drink it!" Mom said.

"So where is Dad?" I asked.

"Down at The Spinning Wheel," Mom said. "His night bartender called in sick, so Dad's working late tonight. He'll probably be starved when he gets home."

"He can have my broccoli," I said.

Mom exploded. "That's enough out of you! Eat them or else!"

"What about the field research study?"

"What field research study?"

"The one that's proved there's a link between the forced eating of broccoli and juvenile delinquency."

"EAT THEM! YOU KNOW THE RULE."

Yeah, I knew Mom's rule. I tried to tell her *Eat it or no dessert* was in violation of my civil rights. I'd watched enough educational programs on TV, like *Perry Mason,* to learn forcing a minor to eat broccoli, Brussels Sprouts and cauliflower—asparagus too—ran against the Eighth Amendment, which flat out prohibits cruel and unusual punishment.

Problem I had was Mom was the kind of mother who didn't like Raymond Burr's looks, and so she didn't watch *Perry Mason.* When I tried to explain the Eighth Amendment protected me from eating broccoli, Brussels Sprouts, cauliflower, and asparagus, she threatened to take away my baseball cards and incarcerate me in my room…with no dessert.

Breakfast was a different story. No one had to tell me to eat my Wheaties. I ate them every morning for breakfast just like the big orange box said Mickey did, often adding strawberries and bananas. M&Ms too. As sloppy as I ate,

Mom never had a problem with the M&Ms. She knew if I spilled them they wouldn't melt all over the kitchen table and floor. Besides, anything Ronald Reagan said to eat for breakfast, with or without M&Ms, was fine with Mom. She'd happened to catch the Wheaties commercial on TV and saw that Ronald Reagan was no Raymond Burr. Ronnie's looks made him her kind of guy, and it would remain that way until he came out of the closet and announced he was a Republican.

"Your broccoli's getting cold. You better eat them right now, buster. They'll make you strong."

"Mom, *spinach* makes you strong. Broccoli makes you fart."

Mom shook her head. "Why do we always go through this? I bet Mickey Mantle's mother didn't have to tell him to eat his broccoli."

"Mickey Mantle doesn't eat broccoli."

"How do you know?" Linnie asked.

"You've seen the Yankees play on TV, haven't you?"

"Of course, silly."

"Ever see Mickey do a post-game interview?"

"Yeah, so?"

"You ever hear him fart?"

12

WITHOUT A DOUBT

"SO HOW YOU G-G-G-GONNA meet him?" Fenny Farkis looked up from a big bag of Fritos he'd been munching since we got on the bus.

Fenny Farkis was my age, but didn't look it. Not with a face like that. What he looked like was Desi Arnaz. Fenny was wearing a long-sleeved tee shirt with broad blue and white stripes and a pair of lightweight tan corduroys—his mother wanted him to look presentable since we were going downtown. On his feet were his new pair of Buster Brown shoes—his mother not too happy about them being already scuffed.

"You forget, Skip?" Fenny said. "The Yankees don't c-c-c-come to Cincinnati to play the Reds. They're in the *American* League. Only chance you have is the All-Star g-g-g-game. But that's not till July…light years away."

"I know, I know," I said. "Got any ideas?"

"Meeting M-M-M…him?" He pushed his bangs out of his eyes and scratched his head. "Maybe you c-c-c-could write Ann Landers for advice."

When I confided I wasn't sure what to write to a woman old enough to be my mother, Fenny told me not to worry, that he'd help me with the letter. Yep, Fenny was a pretty good kid all right. Which was why I was curious.

"So what kind of dog was it, Fenny?" I asked.

"What kind of d-d-d-dog?"

"You know, the name *Fenny*. They nicknamed me after a Scottish terrier. What kind of dog were you nicknamed after?"

"You think I g-g-g-got my nickname from a *dog*?" He laughed. "It started with my d-d-d-dad. Dad's from B-B-B-Boston and bleeds Red Sox. He wanted to name me after Elden Aucker, his favorite pitcher, but Mom talked him outta it."

"Good thing too."

"And Mom didn't like T-T-T-Ted Williams....so Teddy was out. They wound up naming me Fenway Farkis.... When T.T. learned to talk he c-c-c-couldn't say *Fenway* and it c-c-c-came out *Fenny*...."

He stopped and lowered his head, frustrated. "I'm sorry. Sometimes I have trouble g-g-g-getting words out. Takes me too much time to t-t-t-talk and say what I want to."

"It's okay, Fenny," I said. "Take your time to talk. I have time to listen."

Fenny looked up and smiled. He passed his bag of Fritos to me. I reached in and took the last handful.

"Thanks to my little b-b-b-brother everyone started calling me *Fenny* and it stuck."

Fenny and I were stuck with T.T. and there wasn't a thing we could do about it. Fenny's mom had made it perfectly clear we couldn't go all the way downtown to Fountain Square by ourselves unless the two of us became the three of us. And since Fenny and I were dying to see *Legend of the Lost*, the new John Wayne movie at the Grand, we were stuck taking Fenny's little brother to

McAlpin's first so he could wait in line with a thousand other kids for a coonskin cap autographed by Davy Crockett, who in real life was McAlpin's Santa Claus.

T.T. was the nickname Fenny and I had hung on the little Farkis. Everybody thought T.T. stood for Tyler Taylor. To Fenny and me, T.T. meant *Tattle Tale.* When T.T. was around you could hardly do anything without him tattling. You couldn't leave wet towels on your bed, you couldn't lick icing off the cake baked for the Canasta game, you couldn't short-sheet Linnie's bed. Heck, you couldn't even fart.

T.T. had been tattling ever since he was old enough to cry, *"Mommy, Fenny hit me!"* It didn't matter Fenny was three miles away at school. It was *"Mommy, Fenny hit me!"* By the time he was four, T.T. was beginning to hit his stride. He'd gone from tattling on Fenny to tattling on the other kids at nursery school. *"Miss Maitland, Barry's playing with himself again!"* T.T. was now seven, but you knew, you just knew he would be the snitch of his generation.

So there we were, Fenny and I with T.T.—yellow-and-green striped tee shirt sticking out of the back of his red overalls—on the Roselawn-Bond Hill 43. We were bouncing down Reading Road, spit-balling all the way downtown to Fountain Square and the largest collection of pigeon shit west of the Alleghenies. Fenny was talking about Willie Mays being better than Duke Snider, I had my eyes closed, picturing Annette Funicello, and the little Farkis had just now gone to telling the bus driver Fenny and I were spit-balling all over the bus and that one had just hit him in the nose.

T.T.'s tattling about our spit-balling drew the attention of the bus driver away from the highlighted route map that hung on the sun visor next to a state roadkill license. As the bus driver turned to give us a dirty look, the bus, which was now bouncing up the driveway of St. Aloysius Orphanage, suddenly veered up on the sidewalk narrowly missing half the student body. Hats, bags, trash, newspapers, and a dirty diaper were flying all over the bus.

That's when we saw it.

It was right there in the Sunday comics, now strewn all over an empty seat across from us. For the moment we forgot all about *L'il Abner* and *Steve Canyon, Flash Gordon* and *Tarzan,* even our favorite, *Little Orphan Annie,* who, unlike Madeline Schwartz, was sexy despite her flat chest—word around school was crazy Harvey Meshugana had cut Annie out of the comics and pinned her up on his closet door.

Staring right at us in the Sunday comics was a huge line drawing of Mickey Mantle in a full-page promotion for *Esso's Mickey Mantle Tape-Measure Home Run Derby.* The Mick was kneeling in the on-deck circle, bat over his shoulder, ready to step into the batter's box and swing away. Kneeling next to him was the Yankees' batboy.

Below the drawing were the rules and entry form for the first week of the contest. Entry was limited to boys and girls twelve through sixteen. The rules weren't terribly complicated…unless, I guess, you happened to be crazy Harvey Meshugana. To win, you had to pick the total number of home runs Mickey would hit each week. That wasn't too bad. Thing was, you also had to put down the distance of his longest home run. And to make sure even

Harvey understood how it worked, they had an example below:

Mickey's home runs...3
Longest home run...413 (feet)
Entry...3-4-1-3

Each week whoever came closest to being correct would win fifty dollars cash—ten times the weekly allowance I got for pulling weeds. Right before the end of the season there'd be an awards luncheon for all the weekly winners. There'd be one baseball question, just one question, with fifteen seconds to write down the answer. Whoever came closest to the right answer would get to be the Yankees' batboy for the last home game of 1957...and also win a year's supply of Esso gas.

Batboy for the Yankees! I'd be kneeling with Mickey in the on-deck circle, ready to take the fungo bat from him as he strode toward the plate to take his stance in the batter's box. I'd be wearing a Yankee uniform with a big number *+/-O* on my back. Me, Skip Kleinmann, batboy of the New York Yankees! Eighty thousand eyes would be on me, watching me pick up every bat flung from the on-deck circle. Every cool-looking girl in school would know who I was, think I was out of sight, and beg to go out with me, even offering me their book reports. Our phone wouldn't stop ringing.

"Skip? I'm sorry he's not here," Linnie would say. "He's still out being fawned over."

But first I had to be one of the weekly winners. That would put me into the finals with a shot at being the Yankees' batboy for the last home game of the season, where I'd be handing bats to The Mick!

45

The rules said you had to fill out the entry blank and deposit it at any Esso station before six P.M. each Saturday for the following week. If you mailed your entry in after six, it wouldn't be accepted.

Fenny looked at my Mickey Mouse watch, which I wore as a tribute to Annette Funicello. "The deadline's six P. M....c-c-c-can we make it?"

I told him it was no sweat.

13

WE WERE SWEATING...crowded elbow-to-elbow, shoulder-to-shoulder, armpit-to-armpit with half the perspiration in Greater Cincinnati. We were all squeezed, single file, into a parented line of screaming, coon-skinned kids that snaked across and through the third floor of McAlpin's up to a table to get Davy Crockett's autograph. McAlpin's was charging two dollars for Davy's *X*, with half the money to go to the Alamo Widows Fund.

It was Davy Crockett Day at McAlpin's, and it wasn't even Davy Crockett's birthday. No matter to McAlpin's. They'd set up their own Frontierland, stocking it with everything they could think of that would make a kid look just like the King of the Wild Frontier himself.

A dollar got you a tee shirt with a life-like print of Fess Parker disguised as Davy. You could buy a genuine leather belt made from the pelts of genuine guinea pigs, or a pair of hamster-suede moccasins with bright yellow laces and genuine foam-rubber insoles. The spikes made the hamster moccasins "perfect," claimed McAlpin's, "for sneakin' up on sleepin' Injuns." If lacing up your spiked hamster mocs to catch hostile-snoring redskins red-handed wasn't your thing, you could buy a flintlock pistol that could shoot two single-shot caps in succession. It was supposed to be a model of the kind the pioneers used, except the pioneers didn't shoot caps—at least not those who lived to the end of the Oregon Trail.

"Davy/Davy Crockett/King of the Wild Frontier…"

Davy's ballad, now in its umpteenth-and-a-half week as the Number 1 song on the *Hit Parade*, was on McAlpin's loudspeaker…and it was on nonstop. Nine thousand kids were singing along—except T.T., who was getting more and more impatient with each chorus.

"Davy/Davy Crockett/King of the Wild Frontier…"

"Do something!" he whined at Fenny and me. "Do something…or I'm telling!"

I wanted to smack him, but I knew if I did it would cause a chain reaction with whining kids being smacked up and down the line.

"Davy/Davy Crockett/King of the Wild Frontier…"

"Do something!"

"HEY KID, PUT A LID ON IT, WILL 'YA?"

It came from a woman up ahead of us who looked the spitting image of Ernest Borgnine. T.T. ignored her, stuck his chin out, and opened his mouth. "Do—"

"I said *PUT A LID ON IT!*"

T.T. put a lid on it.

"Thanks, lady," I said. And my words were echoed up and down the line as we slowly snaked across the third floor of McAlpin's, eating up more and more valuable time.

Time, in fact, was taking its toll on most of the line, particularly on those not potty trained. The floor was getting wetter and slipperier by the minute. Forget the spiked hamster-suede moccasins, McAlpin's would have really cleaned up if somebody had thought of selling Davy Crockett water-proof wading boots...and nose plugs.

A few armpits in front of us, a young mother was shaking her head and rolling her eyes. "I've been in this frigging line since...since I don't when," she said, obviously pissed by her kid. "I know I was here when Davy and Mickey Mantle were arm wrestling. I think Mickey let Davy win."

That got my attention. "The Mick was here? At McAlpin's?"

"He was sitting up there with Davy Crockett for a while. He was autographing his baseball card for kids with one hand and arm wrestling with the other. Kids were going crazy. It was a madhouse."

"Holy bull shark! Mickey Mantle was here?"

"Bull shark?"

"He was here? Signing his baseball card?"

"He was in town to help Glen Sudek celebrate his divorce."

"Who's Glen Sudek?"

"Glen Sudek? Mickey Mantle's cousin...second cousin, I think. He's the floor manager of the third floor. He and Mickey are supposed to be very close. They say Mickey came all the way in from New York for Sudek's last divorce."

"Davy/Davy Crockett/King of the Wild Frontier..."

Fenny grabbed my wrist and looked at my watch. "We're not g-g-g-gonna make the deadline, are we?"

I repeated that it was no sweat. What I didn't tell him this time, was I was beginning to get nervous.

14

I MISSED THE MICK. I missed John Wayne. And now it looked like I was going to miss the deadline for entries in Esso's Mickey Mantle Tape-Measure Home Run Derby. It was five-forty, and the only Esso station downtown was a good three Skyline Chili parlors away.

Chili is to Cincinnati as chowder is to Boston, cheese steaks are to Philly. Chili is Cincinnati's unofficial heartburn and is probably why every new antacid is always rolled out first in the Queen City. Three-Ways (chili and spaghetti topped with a huge pile of grated cheese), Four-Ways (add chopped onions), and Cheese Coneys (hot dogs with chili and a glob of grated cheese) are eaten for breakfast, lunch, and dinner. Sometimes too as a bedtime snack.

Skyline's chili is the people's #1 choice. They say that *yumstasticalicious*—derived from the words *yummy*, *fantastic,* and *delicious*—was first used to describe it.

I'm not sure how chili got to be so big in Cincinnati. If you believe Uncle Harold, Cincinnati chili, in all its gobs of shredded cheese and onion forms, began with the arrival in town of a hungry Greek immigrant named Zorba, who was fleeing the Polynesian wars. Uncle Harold said not knowing anything about making pizza, Zorba opened a chili parlor downtown on Government Square and named it after his wife. Word quickly spread through the Federal Building that Empress chili was something else. Soon everyone in town was flocking to Empress to get their chili fix. Before you knew it, every Greek immigrant worth his feta was opening up a chili parlor. Or so it seemed.

Anyway, there we were, Fenny and I desperately racing to the closest Esso station with T.T., coonskin cap on his head, in tow. We jay-raced across Vine, across Walnut, with tires screeching, horns honking, and T.T. wailing. Suddenly, T.T. stopped wailing and tugged on Fenny's arm. We'd reached the first Skyline.

"I wanna Coney," he whined.

"Not now," Fenny said. "We haven't g-g-g-got time."

"I wanna Coney!"

Fenny and I both glared at him. "No!"

"I'm telling."

Fenny looked at me, and I looked at Fenny.

"I'm telling!"

We had no choice. We had to get the little Farkis a Coney. But we soon found out getting a Coney at Skyline wasn't as simple as getting a Coney.

"With onions or without?" asked the Skyline girl behind the counter. She had a blue Skyline baseball cap atop her head and was wearing a blue Skyline tee shirt that said *Skyline Chili, Yumstasticalicious.*

T.T. wasn't listening. He just stood there at the counter, his grubby little fingers playing with the box of foil-wrapped, two-cent, chocolate mint patties Skyline had stacked up by the Rolaids. T.T. was helping himself to two handfuls of the candy, being careful to take them from the bottom of the stack. Chocolate mint patties were falling all over the counter and on to the floor.

"With onions or without?" the Skyline girl repeated.

Fenny looked at T.T. I looked at my watch.

"Onions."

"You want mustard on it?"

T.T. just stood there, unwrapping the foil.

Fenny poked him. "The g-g-g-girl's asking you a question."

T.T. looked at the girl and nodded.

"One squirt or two?"

"B-B-B-Better give him one," Fenny said.

"I want *two*. I want *two*!" T.T. whined.

"One, T.T. Just one squirt's enough," Fenny said.

"*Two*...or I'm telling!"

T.T. got two.

And so it went. Relish or no relish...large Coke or small Coke, or no Coke...ice or no ice...hot dog rare, medium, or well done. T.T. greeted each question with a thoughtful answer, then would change his mind...twice. The look on the little Farkis' chocolate-smudged face told me he relished changing his mind about relish.

We didn't have much time left. And we hadn't even got to *box or bag?* Fenny grabbed my wrist-watched wrist and winced. "We're not g-g-g-gonna make it, are we?"

I told him we weren't going to make it. Not unless Superman suddenly staggered out of the telephone booth with Lois Lane's lipstick on his face, put us on his back, flapped his cape, and flew us to the Esso station.

Fenny bit his lip, turned, and glared at T.T. The little Farkis had taken one bite out of the Coney and stopped.

52

"I don't want any more." T.T. handed the messy, once-bitten Coney to Fenny. I thought Fenny was going to kill him...and he almost did.

"I'm telling!" T.T. screamed, as one of the Skyline girls scraped relish, onions, two squirts of mustard, a partly eaten bun, and a glob of grated cheese off his face, and another Skyline girl took half a hot dog out of his nose.

"I'm telling!"

I grinned at Fenny, who grinned back. He picked two of the mint patties off the counter, unfoiled one and handed me the other.

"I'm telling!" T.T. whined.

"Telling what?" said a big, tattooed guy sitting on a stool at the counter. He untied the bib Skyline had given him to protect his black leather motorcycle jacket, then wiped the chili off his Harley-Davidson sunglasses. He looked up and winked at us.

"You all saw what they did!" T.T. whined.

"What *who* did?" came a woman's voice. "I didn't see anything!" She was sitting in a booth up front, the sun beams through the window highlighting her tinted blue hair. She'd put on her bifocals and looked across the table at her companion, who looked wrinkled enough to be her husband. "Did you see anything, honey?"

"What was that you said, dear?"

"DID YOU SEE ANYTHING, HONEY?"

"Nope, didn't see any bunny. Did see a chipmunk though." His dentures flashed as he stuck his fork into a glob of her uneaten shredded cheese.

"Me neither. I didn't see anything," chimed in a waitress who looked like she could have been Rocky

Marciano's sister...or brother. "And I sure didn't see no chipmunk."

She turned her head, staring at T.T.—still sitting in a pool of relish, onions, and mustard—while trying to balance three trays of Four-Ways, Three-Ways, Coneys, French fries, and Cherry Cokes, all ordered by a couple of Phi Rho pledges at a corner table. Somehow Marciano made it to their table, drawing applause from around the room for staggering only twice before dropping just one tray. The Phi Rho pledges stood and whistled.

"I'm sorry, boys," she wailed, staggering again, "but we're out of Rolaids again."

Turned out not one person in Skyline had seen anything.

Still, Fenny and I weren't taking any chances. We'd been victimized by T.T. too often. So we took sworn statements from each customer, as well as from Marciano, who was now sprawled on the floor. The boys from Phi Rho had reached *five* when she threw in the towel.

15

Dear Ann Landers,

I'm thirteen and when I play baseball with the other boys I always pretend I'm Mickey Mantle even though I haven't hit any home runs batting left-handed. All my life I've been dying to meet Mickey, but couldn't since we lived in the middle of the Saharra Desert. Now we live in Cincinnatti, Ohio. That's why I need your advice. How am I supposed to meet Mickey Mantle this year like my Magic 8 Ball says when the Yankees don't play in Cincinnatti and there's no way the Reds will be in the World Series?—signed STRIKING OUT IN CINCINNATTI

"THERE, THAT SHOULD d-d-d-do it," Fenny announced, admiring his two-finger typing. "You satisfied now?"

I made him check the spelling of *Saharra* in the dictionary and, grumbling, he crossed out the second *r*.

"Anything else?"

"Did you have to put in that I haven't hit any home runs batting left-handed?"

"Well, you haven't," Fenny said. "When you bat lefty you strike out a lot."

"I do not!"

"Oh yes you d-d-d-do."

"Well, The Mick strikes out too."

"Yeah, b-b-b-but he hits home runs."

Fenny's dad was in court, and with Mr. Farkis downtown we'd gone into his study to use his typewriter to peck the letter to Ann Landers. The study looked like it was paneled in oak, maybe pine…though it could have been weeping willow. Understand I wasn't good on trees.

Fenny was sitting at a fancy old desk. It was the kind of desk Queen Victoria must have carved *Q.V. x P.A.* into when she was writing love letters to Prince Albert. Fenny's dad didn't have anything carved into his desk, but he did have a hand-carved ash tray on top of it. A polished brass lamp with green glass shade and a Remington Rand Letter Riter were next to it.

I was standing behind Fenny's shoulder, watching him type. "Only one *t* in Cincinnati," I told him.

"You sure b-b-b-bout that?"

I nodded. While he fixed it, I eyed the built-in book shelves to my right. Fenny's father had put a couple of framed photos on the second shelf. One was a family photo at Fenway Park with the Green Monster in the background. The other was a photo of Mr. Farkis shaking hands with a man I recognized from the papers as Cincinnati's chief of police. The rest of the shelves were filled with volumes of the Ohio Criminal Code.

Fenny had assured me we could get in and out of his father's study without getting into any trouble. Besides, he said, assistant DAs usually don't prosecute their son.

"*Usually?*"

"Well, at least n-n-n-not on first offense."

With the letter to Ann Landers written and edited, Fenny wiped the keys on the keyboard with his shirt. "D-D-D-Don't wanna leave prints," he explained.

I nodded. I knew my *Dragnet*. I watched it every week and seen that with fingerprints, Joe Friday could solve a case in just thirty minutes…maybe twenty if you cut out the commercials.

"Look, Skip, m-m-m-makes you happy, we'll delete the left-handed sentence." Fenny had an eraser in his hand.

"Nah, forget it," I said. "She's probably not into switch hitting."

"Yeah, probably not." Fenny had found an envelope and handed it to me. "G-G-G-Got the address?"

I did.

"G-G-G-Good. When you get home, stick the letter in it, write the address, and slap a two-cent stamp on."

"That's it?"

"Well, you have to m-m-m-mail it of course."

Fenny finished wiping, satisfied he'd taken care of each and every fingerprint. "There, that oughta do it," he said. "Now let's get out of here before my dad walks in and c-c-c-calls the police."

16

IT WAS THE THIRD day of the rain when I got the erection. Mom had seen me coughing and sneezing and didn't want me walking home five miles through the rain again, particularly when I had a bar mitzvah lesson that night. So with help from the neighborhood handyman, she'd put up the top of her garaged '57 Buick Riviera convertible and driven to my school to pick me up.

The Riviera had Lockheed-inspired fins and white-wall tires. It had a two-tone blue and white body, though the hood was a creamed coffee splashed on by the neighborhood handyman. Mom had bought the car after the dealer explained the only Buick model she could get without portholes was an Olds. The Riviera was ninety-nine percent brand new—the left tail-light having been replaced after Mom broke the original backing out of the Buick dealer's parking lot.

We were driving up Losantiville, a block or two from the country club, and the rain was coming down pretty hard. The windows were fogging up, but you could still make out the kids sloshing up the sidewalk. And that's when I saw Madeline Schwartz, the skinniest, most homely-looking, most flat-chested girl in the entire eighth grade. Madeline had a big crush on me, even though I was never going to kiss her because her mouthful of braces had bits of broccoli caught in them. Anyway, there was Madeline Schwartz right up ahead sloshing. She was struggling with her books, and it looked like she about to lose the struggle.

Mom had seen her too. "Honey, that skinny little girl up there sloshing, the homely-looking one struggling with her books, isn't she in your class?"

"You mean Madeline?" I pushed down the button that locked the door. "No, Mom."

Mom looked at me puzzled, shrugged, and cut off a taxi. The cabbie blew his horn and held it. Mom paid no attention.

And then we both saw another girl up ahead. It was never hard to recognize Elaine Novak, even in a rain storm, because she had the biggest boobs in the entire eighth grade. I knew from diligent scientific observation hers were the biggest because she sat one row up and to my left in Biology and wore tight sweaters that made me forget all about amoebas, paramecium, and all those weird-looking unpronounceable things.

Mom didn't need to ask if Elaine Novak was in my class. She already knew because Elaine's mother, recently overruled as PTA Parliamentarian in a luncheon coup, was in the group that played Canasta with Mom once a week. Mom pulled over and stopped the car, honked and Elaine, hair all dripping wet, got in. She wiggled in next to me in the front seat, her wet thigh innocently pressing mine.

That's when it happened.

Elaine acted like she didn't see anything, but I knew she did because her eyes got as big as saucers. Mom's eyes were glued on the slippery road ahead so she didn't see the problem that was literally rising. Instead, she began peppering Elaine with the kind of questions grown-ups always ask kids.

First, came the questions about how Elaine's family was. After all, Mom hadn't seen Elaine's mother, Mrs. Novak, since the coup that day.

"How's your mother, Elaine?" Mom asked.

"Fine, Mrs. Kleinmann."

"Your father?"

"He's fine too," Elaine replied, shaking her wet hair on me.

Mom honked at the car ahead, which had stopped at a yellow light. The driver rolled down his window, Mom rolled down hers, and it became a contest to see who gave the best finger.

"Your grandmother…how's she doing?" Mom rolled her window back up, satisfied she'd won.

"She still misses him," Elaine answered.

"Your grandfather was a good man."

"It's her cousin Eddie she misses. But I think he's up for parole in a couple of years."

Some mothers would have stopped right there. Not mine. Leah Kleinmann wasn't a quitter. She moved from asking Elaine how her family was to a whole new subject of interrogation.

"What about boys, Elaine? I bet there's a boy you're stuck on."

"Well, I really like Randy Wolf—"

"That's nice."

"And Kenny Niederman—"

"Two is nice too," Mom said, making a right turn on two wheels.

"And Andy Mayerson...and Sammy Hopovich...and Stevie Kapinsky...and Jeff Rosenfeld...and Corey Steiner...and Philip Schlaeger...and Lenny Gordon...and Chuckie Goldenbladder...and Hughie Koncusion...and Philip Schlaeger...and—"

"I think you already said Philip Schlaeger."

"Sorry...and Peter Carella...and Khadijah Goldstein."

"*Khadijah* Goldstein?"

"His parents wanted a girl."

Mom didn't know what to say. So she didn't. But Elaine did.

"Oh, and Barry Klopnick and Larry Klopnick."

That Elaine liked both Barry and Larry was clearly befuddling Mom.

"Uh, Elaine, aren't Barry and Larry brothers...identical twin brothers? How can you be stuck on identical twin brothers? I don't know if that's kosher."

"But they're not completely identical, Mrs. Kleinmann," Elaine said. "Barry has more zits."

I could tell Mom was flabbergasted. I mean, who wouldn't be? Face it, Elaine Novak just plumb-out liked boys—either that or she planned to someday go into dermatology. She was stuck on just about all the boys in our class but crazy Harvey Meshugana and me. Mom must have realized it too.

"Is there anyone you've, ahem...*skipped*?" Mom asked, figuring Elaine would get the hint.

"I like Cubby too."

"Cubby? Who's Cubby?"

"The cutest Mouseketeer. I love the way he sings *M-O-U-S-E*. I get goose bumps."

Uh-oh. Kill the boys and go on to something else. When all else fails—and with Elaine, all else was obviously failing—grown-ups always, always bug you about how you're doing in school.

"How are you doing in school?" Mom had started the bugging.

Elaine said she was doing fine in English, Spanish, and Biology, but was having a lot of trouble in Mathematics.

"I wish I knew math like Skip does," she said, glancing at my crotch.

"So, why don't you help Elaine?" Mom said to me. "Look, honey, you're good in math. You're always figuring out the batting averages, slugging percentages, and...what's that thing you do for pitchers?"

"Earned run average."

"Earned run average," Mom repeated. "That's it, earned run average. So will you do it?"

"Do what, Mom?" I said, my eyes glued to Elaine's chest.

"Will you go over to Elaine's sometime and give her a hand? How about it, Elaine? Wouldn't you like Skip to help you out?"

"I guess so," Elaine sighed, seeing that I'd lost my erection.

"Good," Mom said, slaloming pass a Rambler and an Eldorado. "Then you two kids should pick a time to get together."

I wasn't about to protest. Thanks to Mom, I was going to spend time with Elaine Novak. I was going to spend a few hours with just her and her boobs.

17

I SWALLOWED THE GIRAFFE before I translated....

"For the horses of Pharaoh went with his chariots and his horsemen etcetera into the sea, and—"

"Hold it! Hold it right there, Skip. You're reading the wrong passage."

Myron jumped from the armchair, spilling the box of broken animal crackers he'd been munching. A hippo, a headless gorilla, and a two-legged elephant tumbled to the floor.

"That is *not* what you're supposed to be reading from the Torah. *Exodus 37.1*...that's your passage."

Myron Finkelstein was my bar mitzvah tutor, and he'd been sitting across from me in the dorm room at Hebrew Union College that he shared with Maimonides, his goldfish. Though a school dropout, Maimonides had fish-bowl smarts and always knew when his water needed changing. He'd backstroke until Myron got the message.

Myron must have been about six-three or so, a walking, talking beanpole with a full head of Brylcreamed black hair—which being religious, he never combed on the Sabbath. On his forehead were black horn-rimmed glasses. The glasses were supposed to make him look like a

Talmudic scholar, but made him look more like Buddy Holly.

Myron was a third-year rabbinical student at HUC. Actually, he was now in his third year of the first year of the five-year program. At the rate Myron was progressing in his studies, HUC figured he'd be ordained a rabbi in another fifteen years, which meant his eligibility to play baseball—he was the team's backup pinch runner—would be used up way before then. With his athletic scholarship withdrawn, Myron, who blew a mean *shofar* or ram's horn, was now playing gigs at youth group conclaves and tutoring bar mitzvah students to help make ends meet.

I explained to Myron the passage I was reading about the horses and chariots etcetera of Pharaoh was a whole lot more exciting than the passage Rabbi Breitzig had given me for my bar mitzvah.

"Doesn't matter," he said. "You have to read the Torah portion of the week. Your week is *Exodus 37.1*—Bezalel and the building of the ark. It's important. Acacia wood is something you don't see every day in houses here."

"Like linoleum?"

"Like seeing linoleum."

So there we were, Myron and I, volleying back and forth over the Torah passage for my bar mitzvah. He was Pancho Gonzalez; I was Sancho Panza. I told him memorizing all those specs for the ark, the atonement cover, and the lampstand—to say nothing of the exact metric weight of the cherubim—was out of the question.

"And there aren't any Cliff Notes available," I said. "At least not in transliterated Hebrew."

"Doesn't matter," Myron said. "And there's no etcetera in the Torah either."

He bent down to scrape the animal crackers off the floor. He wiped off the elephant with his shirttail and offered it to me. I declined.

"Myron, isn't Temple Mechiah supposed to be a Reform temple?"

"So?"

"So can't I ask Rabbi Breitzig to reform the passage for my week?"

"Nope. The passage that week is the passage that week."

"Then let's change the week," I said.

"Let's change the topic," Myron said. "You like hippo?"

It was Rabbi Breitzig who'd suggested Mom hire Myron Finkelstein to be my bar mitzvah tutor. The Rottenbergs, the Shmedriks, the Fishbeins, the Pockmarks, the Sterns, and the Kreplachs had already booked their tutors. So too had the O'Neals, who had Americanized the family name from O'Neil with an *i* to O'Neal with an *a* upon their arrival from Ireland. (The O'Neals/nee O'Neils had hitched their wagon and set sail from Dublin, immigrating to New York after hearing the streets of the city were paved with French Fries. That it was two years after the potato famine was over didn't matter to the O'Neils, who loved French Fries.)

Anyhow, Mom had gone ahead and hired Myron as my bar mitzvah tutor. Aunt Tillie thought it was because Mom was impressed with Myron's knowledge of Hebrew, which he could stammer in either a Sephardic or Ashkenazi accent. But Aunt Tillie was wrong. What had impressed Mom about Myron was that with the Rottenbergs, the Shmedriks, etcetera. already having plucked every tutor on Rabbi Breitzig's *A* and *B* lists, Myron was the only one available on the *Others* list.

Myron had grown up in Brooklyn and had spent his summer vacations fishing unsuccessfully for sheep in Sheepshead Bay. He was fourteen when he was told there were no sheep's heads in the Bay, though he might find the head of a *Mafioso*, and that *sheepshead* was the name of a fish that resembled a lamb chop.

It was from this ichthyologic lesson that Myron had begun scrutinizing fish for wool, once having a fit after finding a hair in the gefilte fish Mrs. Finkelstein always served the family on Friday nights. Myron had refused to touch gefilte fish again unless it was first sheared.

With Myron showing obsession with anything ovine, his father decided it was time to start his son on the *shofar*. The ram's horn had come naturally, of course, to Myron, and in no time he'd broken centuries of tradition by ad-libbing the *shofar*'s calls to standing-room-only congregations. It was Myron's ability to master the horn— the first on the High Holy Days to hit high C in *Te-Ru-Ah*—that had won him an award of $753.50 by the local Hadassah chapter to attend HUC. They'd also planted a tree in Israel in his honor.

"Too bad your bar mitzvah's not on *Rosh Hashana*," Myron said. "I could teach you how to blow a mean *shofar*."

"Yeah, too bad, Myron," I sighed.

"Okay, let's try it again." Myron's hands were folded across his lap, and he seemed to be studying his toe nail. "From line ten. *Ve'asu aron....*"

"Ve'asu aron...."

"Keep going."

"Oh-say shitim amatayim—"

"Not bad. But it's *AT-zei* not *'OH-say.'* Oh say is how you start off singing *The Star Spangled Banner*."

"Like before the game at Yankee Stadium?"

"Before they announce the starting lineup." Myron cleared his throat and, in a voice that sounded like it was over the Yankee Stadium P.A., thundered, *"BATTING FOURTH...batting fourth...IN CENTER FIELD...in centerfield...NUMBER SEVEN...number seven... MICKEY MANTLE...Mickey Mantle...MANTLE."*

"NOT BAD...not bad," I said. "But Yogi bats fourth, not Mickey. The Mick bats third."

Myron ignored the correction. "And you need to chant it."

"Chant it?"

"Yep, chant it. You're supposed to chant it."

"The Yankees' starting lineup?"

"Your bar mitzvah portion."

"Do I have to?"

"Nope. Not if you don't want to max out on bar mitzvah presents."

I told Myron I'd chant it.

18

CANNOT PREDICT NOW

"RANDOM," THE SCHNEID WAS saying. "The answers are random. They've got nothing to do with what you ask it. Don't be silly, you're not going to marry Annette Funicello someday."

"Why not?"

"Don't you read *TV Guide*, Felipe? Annette admitted Mickey is more than a mouse to her."

The Schneid had come over after school to watch *The Mickey Mouse Club* show with me. It was something we did every Wednesday afternoon. We called it "Annette Funicello Day."

Stuart Schneider was what you might call a little pudgy. He had chipmunk cheeks with a growing complement of zits, squinty eyes, and a porcine nose. Some said he resembled a sawed-off Orson Wells, but I couldn't see it. To me, he looked more like Lou Costello—you know, of Abbott and Costello. The Schneid had an encyclopedia mind and, without any hesitation, could give you, in fluent eighth-grade Spanish, the batting average of any ball player since 1942, the year we both were born. He knew the annual rainfall in Brazil, the population of East Berlin, and the second largest city of each state...in Mexico.

Me, I was lucky if I remembered anybody's birthday.

The Schneid was also an expert on what Uncle Harold called *jean alley.* He'd traced his family tree and shown me the traced copy to prove he was related to Amelia Earhardt on his mother's side and that he was the only family member in the eighth, ninth, or tenth grade who knew what had actually happened to his cousin.

"Just before Grandma closed her cataracts for the last time," said The Schneid, getting choked up, "she took my hand in hers and told me...she told me Amelia...had starved to death in New...New Guinea...when ringing...."

He stopped, blew his nose, and sobbed. I'd never seen him cry before. Not even when he got stiffed Trick-or-Treating on Halloween.

"It's okay," I said. "Ringing what, Schneid?"

"Ringing bells..." he sniffled, "and shouting *'AVON CALLING!'*"

"Amelia Earhardt worked for Avon?"

The Schneid pulled himself back together. "That's what Grandma said. What, you don't think Amelia Earhardt would be selling Fuller Brush, do you, Felipe?"

"Guess not."

"May I continue?"

"Sure, Schneid."

The Schneid said his grandma had told him Amelia had come to this one split-level hut where there was a loud party going on.

"Grandma said it was so loud that you could hear it all the way down the block to the crocodile pond."

I told him I'd never heard of a crocodile pond—duck pond and maybe a pond with Rhino drain, but never a crocodile pond.

"Doesn't matter," The Schneid said. "Do you want to hear the story or not?"

Knowing The Schneid as I did, I knew he'd take my no as an insult. So I nodded.

"Anyway, Grandma said Amelia stood on the doorstep ringing the bell. She didn't know everyone was downstairs in the rec room cannibalizing. Grandma said Amelia could get pretty obstinate at times."

"She'd get her dandruff up?"

"What are you talking about? Amelia used Head & Shoulders. It says so right in the flight manifest."

I told The Schneid I was sorry, that I wasn't thinking. "Forget I mentioned dandruff."

The Schneid ignored my apology and went on to explain that Amelia had stood on the doorstep ringing the bell, not realizing no one was about to leave the feast and come to the door.

"Grandma said for a week Amelia kept ringing the bell and ringing the bell until she had no more strength to ring it."

I shook my head. "Guess that would get her pretty weak."

"That was it," The Schneid said. "She was gone."

"Amelia Earhardt?"

"No, Grandma."

"I don't know, Schneid," I said. "What makes you think the answers are random?"

"Because inside the Magic 8 Ball is a plastic icosahedron floating in a sea of blue liquid."

"Icosa...what?"

"Icosahedron. It's a polyhedron. You know what a polyhedron is, don't you, Felipe?"

"Of course," I said, though I had no idea what he was talking about.

"Well, the Magic 8 Ball has a polyhedron that's an icosahedron. It's floating in blue dye."

"Floating? A floating icosa…hedron?"

"Yep, floating. Stanley Kaplan and I dissected a Magic 8 Ball for our Science Club project."

The Schneid explained the icosahedron had twenty sides, with a different answer on each side—ten positive, five non-committal, and five negative. "When you turn the Magic 8 Ball over, one of the answers shows up in the window. It could be any one."

"That doesn't mean it's random," I said. "Watch." I shook the Magic 8 Ball a couple of times…. "Magic 8 Ball, am I going to meet Mickey Mantle this year?"

YES DEFINITELY

"See, Schneid, what did I tell you?"

"Random," The Schneid said.

"Okay, I'll shake it and ask it again….Magic 8 Ball, am I going to meet Mickey Mantle this year?"

WITHOUT A DOUBT

"Still think it's random, Schneid?"

"Random."

I handed the Magic 8 Ball to him. "Go ahead, you ask it a question."

The Schneid sighed. "I can't believe I'm doing this."

"Just ask it already."

The Schneid shook the Magic 8 Ball a couple of times…. "Will I ever miss making honor roll?" He turned it over.

YOU MAY RELY ON IT

"See, Felipe, it's random. If it's accurate it would have said MY REPLY IS NO or maybe DON'T COUNT ON IT."

"Well, maybe you *won't* make honor roll next time. Maybe you'll get a *C* on your report card."

The Schneid glared at me. "Don't be stupid." He thrust the Magic 8 Ball back to me.

"Watch, Schneid, I'll ask it again….Will I meet Mickey Mantle this year?" I handed the Magic 8 Ball back to him. "Here, you look."

The answer that had floated to the window was IT IS DECIDEDLY SO.

19

THE YANKEES HAD TAKEN two of the three games from the Red Sox—and at Fenway Park no less. The season was now into its fifth game and The Mick had yet to hit a home run. Yankee fans had started switching from Bronx cheers to clamoring for his scalp.

Frankie the Dickhead knew scalps. He was probably the best barber in the area, but he was a Dickhead just the same. Frankie was arrogant, he was a wise ass, and he hated kids. He would gleefully intimidate anyone under the age of sixteen.

"Got a driver's license, kid?" he'd snap. If you didn't have a valid driver's license to prove you were sixteen, you were done for. You were scalped.

The Dickhead was short and squat with beady, dark eyes, yellow teeth—which you'd seldom see since he seldom smiled—and straight black hair drooping across his forehead. He'd snipped off most of his mustache and now looked like a short, squat copy of his idol—though I'm not sure the *Führer* was ever caught on camera picking his nose with his little finger. And the Dickhead hummed. He hummed *Lili Marleen* while he cut your hair, and he hummed *Lili Marleen* while he cut you to pieces.

Why we went to Frankie the Dickhead, I'm not sure. Maybe it was the manicurist. She'd sit there on her little stool, the top three buttons of her dress unbuttoned, giving you a good look at the Promised Land whenever she leaned over to buff your nails. Some men went to Frankie's twice a week just to get a manicure. One man I knew went three times a week, the third trip to enjoy the glorious benefits that came with a thirty-minute pedicure.

Dad had taken me to Frankie the Dickhead's because Mom made him. It was all because I was going over to the Novaks' to help Elaine with her math. Mom said I'd better look at least halfway presentable because she didn't want to be embarrassed at the next Canasta game if Mrs. Novak stood up and announced to everyone that I was over her house helping Elaine with her math and that I definitely needed a haircut.

"Next!"

"Haircut and a shave." Dad sat down in Frankie's chair and strapped himself in. "But don't make it too close."

Frankie shot him a look. "Why are you interrupting? Can't you tell I'm humming?"

I buried my face deep in the sports section of the *Post*, reading Pat Harmon's column. I was hoping Frankie wouldn't spot me when I heard that unmistakable voice of the Dickhead.

"Are you shittin' me, Charlie? Mickey Mantle better than Duke Snider?" Frankie held his side, laughing his jackass laugh. I prayed he'd split his gut laughing.

"Mickey Mantle?" He stopped trimming Dad's sideburns, pointed the scissors at Charlie, and grinned.

"Duke Snider...now *there's* a center fielder. Mickey Mantle can go back to them mines they got in Oklahoma. Can't hit his way out of a paper bag...strikes out with

runners on base…can't run without hurting himself….
MVP, my ass. If the Yankees were smart, they'd trade that
bum for somebody who can play baseball."

I clenched my teeth. Frankie was stropping his razor,
looking at Dad's neck, and humming again. It sounded like
he was trying to hum *Deutschland Über Alles*. Which was,
of course, stupid of Frankie since he was second-generation
Italian.

Dad gulped as the razor, in one quick stroke, passed
over his throat, slightly nicking him.

"*Mantle*? This is what I think of Mickey Mantle."
Frankie grinned at everybody, stuck one finger up high, and
farted.

I'd had it. Frankie was finished…finished nicking Dad,
finished knocking The Mick. Finished with a capital *F*.

"Frankie," I said, "you know what everyone at school
calls you?"

"What's that, kid?"

"*Dickhead*."

"Dickhead?" Frankie threw his head back and laughed.

"Yeah, *Dickhead*." And then I hit him with it. "And
half the men in the neighborhood say the reason you act
like a Dickhead is because you know you have the smallest
wiener in town."

The manicurist gasped, the men in the barbershop
exploded with laughter, and I ran out the door as Frankie
went ballistic.

MICKEY MANTLE DOESN'T EAT BROCCOLI

20

I WASN'T THINKING about Mickey Mantle. I should have been thinking about how I was going to meet him, but I wasn't. Right then I was thinking of boobs, deeply cleavaged boobs.

I was, in fact, head over heels in love. Put cleavaged boobs right smack in front of a thirteen-year-old boy and it's inevitable. And Elaine Novak's boobs were definitely cleavaged. We were sitting out by her pool, and she was wearing one of those little one-piece, terry-cloth playsuits. She had a puzzled look on her face. I had a smile on mine.

Elaine had honey-colored hair, which she wore in an updo like Doris Day. She had the legs of Cyd Charise, the boobs of Jayne Mansfield, the face of Grace Kelly, and the sunglasses of Sophia Loren.

She also had the mind of Gracie Allen.

Elaine had brought out a pitcher of lemonade and a couple of metallic-colored aluminum cups and set them by her feet. "Want some?" she asked.

I nodded.

She poured the lemonade into the two cups. "Which one, red or silver?"

"Silver," I mumbled.

She pouted. "I was hoping you'd mumble red."

I told her red was fine.

"You sure?"

"Well…"

"No, go ahead. You're my guest."

"Okay, I'll take silver."

"Take the red." She leaned forward and handed the red cup to me, giving me a deeper view of her cleavage.

I took a sip and gulped. I could see below the freckle line.

"You can have more." She smiled at me, and I prayed I wouldn't get an erection.

She leaned forward again. I gulped again.

Elaine stopped smiling and resumed pouting. "I still don't get it," she said, playing with the silver Star-of-David chain around her neck.

"Get what?" I said, my eyes glued to the little beads of sweat that were dripping down her cleavage.

"You really think you're going to meet Mickey Mantle this year? You *really* do?"

"That's what the Magic 8 Ball keeps saying."

"You have a Magic 8 Ball?"

I explained to her that every time I ask the Magic 8 Ball if I'm going to meet Mickey Mantle this year it never answers *no*. "I asked it before I left for school this morning and know what it said?"

"You forgot your lunch bag?"

I stared at her …and this time not at her cleavage.

"Elaine, did the nurse ever drop you on your head?"

"Don't be silly. We couldn't afford a nurse then. My mother had to drop me."

I didn't know what to say to that—other than "Say goodnight, Gracie." So I said nothing. She looked at me, not understanding my silence.

"Magic 8 Balls are icky."

"Icky?"

"Icky," she repeated, and she scrunched up her face. "It's that icky blue stuff that oozes out when you crack the ball. It makes you puke." Elaine said she'd seen it when she was baby-sitting for a little boy.

"He was playing with his Magic 8 Ball when I told him it was time to go to bed. He asked the Magic 8 Ball if he had to, and it said **YES DEFINITELY**. Then you know what Stevie did?"

I told her I had no idea.

"He asked it if he could crack it open and drink the stuff inside, and it said **WITHOUT A DOUBT**. He puked all night."

She leaned over to pour some more lemonade, and I leaned forward, trying to look down her cleavage, hoping she wouldn't see my erection.

"Want to talk about it?" she asked.

I blushed.

"I just don't understand."

I lowered my eyes and told her I was sorry.

"So why is interest simple?"

"Oh, that…. Simple," I said, my interest now on the heaving freckles on her chest.

"You're making fun of me, aren't you?"

I wanted to assure Elaine I wasn't interested in making fun of her and that my interest was simply on her cleavage. But I knew if I did, she would tell her mother I was a pervert, her mother would tell mine, Mom would tell Dad, and the next thing I knew I'd be sent to reform school with no hope of seeing the Yankees play. And I knew by the time they let me out of reform school, The Mick would be retired.

Best not to say anything about Elaine's cleavage. Or my erection.

"What don't you understand about simple interest?" I asked, squirming in my lawn chair.

"Everything."

I sighed as she sighed, causing her chest to rise and fall.

"Skip, you paying attention?"

I sure was, but I was afraid to say so. Instead, I started explaining the concept of simple interest to her. When I told Elaine it all had to do with money, her eyes lit up. At least I think they did. I couldn't be sure because she had sunglasses on. I told her when money is borrowed, interest is charged for the use of that money for a certain period of time. She smiled, so I plowed ahead.

"When the money is paid back, the principal—"

"The principal?" She took off her sunglasses to reveal a pair of almond-shaped, golden-brown eyes. "Mr. Winetka?"

"The amount of money that was borrowed."

"Ohhh."

"You take the amount borrowed, multiply it by how long you borrow it for, multiply that by the interest rate, and you've got the interest."

"Ohhh."

She smiled again, and I could tell she had no idea what I was talking about. But that didn't stop me. I ventured on, equations dancing in my head. I switched from interest to negative integers and from negative integers to metric measurements. I'd worked my way to ratios, and she was still smiling—with no idea what I was talking about.

Suddenly, she was no longer smiling. She was licking her lower lip and those gorgeous, golden-brown eyes were peering intently into mine. I knew she was getting serious.

"Earned run average," she said.

"Earned run average?"

"Earned run average." Her eyes double blinked. "How do you earn an average?"

"You don't earn an average," I said. "Let's say the Reds are playing the Pirates and Klippstein is pitching—"

"We're in trouble."

She was right, of course. But I thought it best not to get her started on the Reds' pitching, which was causing Birdie Tebbetts, the Reds' manager, to run out of Rolaids.

"Reds are playing the Pirates. Klippstein's pitching. Okay?"

"Okay." She doubled blinked again.

"Let's say Klippstein gives up three solo home runs—"

"All in the first inning?"

"Doesn't matter. Klippstein gives up three solo homers, and then Jablonski makes an error which causes another run to score. Klippstein's only credited with those first three runs that were his fault."

"They sure were!"

"So of those four runs the Pirates score off Klippstein, one isn't an earned run."

She smiled then wrinkled her nose. I couldn't tell whether she got it or not.

"So how do you get it?" she said.

"Get what?" I asked, staring at her now glistening cleavage.

"Earned run average. Pay attention."

"I am," I said, my eyes riveted to her heaving chest.

"So what's an earned run average?"

I took a deep breath. "You take the total number of earned runs divide that by the total number of innings pitched multiply that number by nine and *whazew* you've got the earned run average."

"Whazew?"

"Okay, no *whazew*."

"That's better." She smiled and I could tell, like interest and ratios, she had no idea what I was talking about.

"Anyway, that's ERA, earned run average. That's it."

"That's it? Why isn't there an unearned run average? Why don't they figure out URA?"

"They just don't."

"But they should," she said. "It's only fair. If there's an earned run average, there should be an unearned run average."

I knew it was useless to try to argue Elaine out of unearned run averages. She was getting pretty worked up about it, and I could picture her marching downtown, carrying a big sign that read *SUPPORT URA!*

So I did the smart thing. I said nothing. I just nodded, focused back on her cleavage, and smiled.

21

OUTLOOK GOOD

IT WAS THE END of April and neither The Mick nor I were doing so well. Mickey had hit just two home runs for the Yankees, and I was still stuck on zero in Esso's weekly Mickey Mantle Tape-Measure Home Run Derby. Which was the same number as the times I'd beaten The Schneid in playing *HORSE.*

The Schneid could beat me ten times out of ten with my own basketball, but he'd still sucker me to play him for a dollar. No matter how much I tried I could never resist him, and he knew it.

The Schneid was very methodical when he played *HORSE.* He'd always bounce the ball three times with his left hand, three times with his right, and wag his tongue before he called each shot. If he made it—and he usually did—I'd have to make the exact shot he did. If I didn't—and I usually didn't—I'd get a letter hung on me.

"Left handed from here, swish into the net."

He made it, of course...and I missed it, of course.

"*H....*" The Schneid started his dribbling routine again when he suddenly stopped. "You get a good look?"

"A good look at what, Schneid?"

"Boobsville. You were over at Elaine's house, weren't you?"

So I had to tell him all about Elaine Novak and her cleavaged boobs. Then I had to repeat it. Only then was he ready to focus back on basketball. He bounced the ball three times with his right hand, three with his left and, for good measure, once off his right knee.

"Reverse layup, switching from right hand to left in midair." He stopped dribbling. "Oh, and no backboard."

He made it, of course...and I missed it, of course.

"*H-O*....One-four-two-one. That's what I'm going with this week. One home run, 421 feet. What about you, El Felipe?"

"Three-four-three-one."

"*Three? Three* homers for The Mick? No way. Paul Foytack's going for the Tigers on Saturday, and Frank Lary's pitching Sunday. Mickey never hits them."

"He will this time."

"We'll just have to see." The Schneid bounced the ball three times with his left hand. "Hook shot off the light above the garage, bounce off the rim, then drop through the net."

He made it, of course...and I missed it, of course.

"*H-O-R*....Yeah, yeah, nobody hits 'em farther than Mickey. But, Felipe, you got to admit The Duke's a more consistent home run hitter."

"Why do you say that?"

"Look at the last four years—'53, '54, '55, '56...." The Schneid bounced the ball again as he rattled off numbers. "Mantle: 21-27-37-52. Now here's Snider: 42-40-42-43. Four straight years of forty or more homers. *That's* consistent."

He stopped bouncing. "Need I say more, Felipe?"

The Schneid did a reverse tongue wag. "Left-handed discus throw, rattle three times around the rim, bounce up and hit the light, then swish through the net."

He made it of course...and I missed it of course.

"*H-O-R-S*...."

"Yeah, but Ebbetts Field isn't Yankee Stadium," I said. "You put The Mick in that bandbox, and he'd hit fifty each year. You lose a ton of home runs when you hit to center field in Yankee Stadium. They don't call it Death Valley for nothing. What's it to center at Ebbetts?"

"Straightaway center? Three-ninety-three," said The Schneid, who knew the distance to ballpark fences like he knew the population of East Berlin.

"And in Yankee Stadium?"

"Four-sixty-one."

The Schneid bounced the ball again. "Okay, the fences are closer where Snider plays. I'll give you that, Felipe. But the pitchers the Duke has to face in the National League are a lot tougher than the ones The Mick sees in the American League."

I had to admit The Schneid had a point. And he was about to have another. He licked his finger. He was actually going to test the wind.

"From here. A 360-spin, cross-over dribble, throw the ball off the backboard, catch it between the knees, and underhand it into the net. Wagging your tongue is optional."

He made it of course....This time I wasn't even going to try.

"*H-O-R-S-E.*"

I shook my head and handed him a dollar bill.

85

"*Gracias, amigo,*" The Schneid said in perfectly fluent eighth-grade Spanish.

It was the kind of statement you'd expect from someone on the honor roll.

22

YOU MAY RELY ON IT

IT BEING TUESDAY, Myron had not only combed his hair, he'd also showered—the shave would come Friday. We were sitting in his room , and he had a big smile on his stubbled face. He always smiled like that when I handed him a check from Mom for tutoring me for my bar mitzvah.

Myron was wearing his best pair of ink-stained Levis and a frayed *Skyline Chili* bowling shirt, neither of which seemed particularly rabbinical. He'd kicked the loafer off his left foot and wiggled the toes sticking out of his sock.

I'd taken the bus straight from school, which was why I still had my khaki pants on. You didn't wear jeans to school back in the Fifties. If you did, you were sent home with a note to your mother. You did it again, and a registered letter was sent home to your father. That always did it. I'd dipped into the hamper that morning and put on my favorite shirt, the yellow button-down, highlighted last night with lemon meringue pie. The spaghetti sauce was new, splattered on during today's lunch. Mixed with the lemon meringue stains, it gave the shirt a Jackson Pollock effect.

"Barnum oughta make Baseball Crackers," Myron said, finishing up a box of animal crackers. "They'd really make money. Ever read the *Boston Record*? They've got people up there given half a chance would bite Ted Williams' head off."

I rolled my eyes.

"Think I'm kidding? That guy they got who writes sports, he's always ripping Williams."

Myron reached down and rubbed the big toe sticking out of his sock. "Hey, you're not a Red Sox fan are you?"

"Yankees," I said. "Like my Uncle Harold in New York."

"Hope he doesn't live in Brooklyn. Not if he's a Yankee fan."

"Nope, he lives in New Rochelle." I told Myron that Uncle Harold had spent five years as a pitcher in the Yankee farm system.

"*Five* years?"

"He made it to Class D…in Poughkeepsie, I think."

Myron shook his head. "Class D's about as low as you can get and still be in the minors. Nobody spends five years in Class D. He should've given up on baseball."

"I know," I said. "But Uncle Harold can be pretty stubborn. He told everybody it was only a question of time till he got called up by the Yankees."

"Giants," Myron said. "I've always been a Giants fan. Cost me too."

He leaned forward and pushed up his glasses. "See this nose? Got it broken twice, and that's when I was still in grade school. *Twice,* Skip. That's what happens when you grow up in Brooklyn rooting for the Giants."

I peeked at the clock next to Myron. Less than ten minutes to go. The Yankee game started in fifteen minutes.

"You know on Flatbush Avenue they actually think Duke Snider is the best center fielder in baseball." Myron shook his head. "He isn't."

"I know," I said.

"I just don't get it. How can anybody who knows anything about baseball think Duke Snider is better than Willie Mays? Snider can't carry Willie's glove. Willie could run circles around him and *still* catch the ball. And he's a better hitter too."

"Not like Mickey Mantle."

"Really?"

"Question I keep asking is *Will he be able to make it? Think he will?*"

"Make what?" Myron had turned the empty box of animal crackers upside down and was shaking the crumbs into Maimonides' goldfish bowl.

"The party. I'm going to address the invitation to Yankee Stadium. Do you think he'll get it and come?"

"Do I think *who* will come?"

Who? Was he kidding me? "The Mick, Myron. I checked and the Yankees have the day off. So do you think he'll come to my bar mitzvah party?"

23

AS I SEE IT, YES

"YOU'RE NOT INVITING MICKEY MANTLE!"

"But Mom…"

"You are not inviting Mickey Mantle to your bar mitzvah party!"

"Why not? Uncle Harold thinks it's a good idea."

"Uncle Harold thinks diet water is a good idea."

Mom and I were sitting at the kitchen table, and she was showing me how to fold laundry while she talked about the chosen people. These were the people she'd chosen to receive invitations to my bar mitzvah party. I offered to trade Uncle Nate and Aunt Tillie for The Mick.

"What did I just say? No Mickey Mantle. And stop making that face at me."

I wasn't giving up. I knew Mom could sometimes, given the right situation, be reasonable. After all, she was practically a Libra, and they're supposed to be practical. So between sneezes from the lint I explained I'd already told Fenny that Mickey was coming, that Fenny had told Harriet Linzer, and that Harriet had made an announcement in her homeroom, which Jill Eichorn had heard and told the PA announcer.

"Mom, the whole school thinks Mickey's coming! And it'll be on Al Schottelkotte at eleven too!"

"*Philip Morris Kleinmann!*"

Mom gathered up some lint and handed it to me. "Here, take care of it."

I started to fold the lint and stopped…. "*Aachoo!*"

"*Gezundheit.*"

"Mom, I'm not kidding. Barry and Larry Klopnick told their cousin Natalie…you know, the Natalie who used to be an information operator at Cincinnati Bell. Natalie called *WCKY News* and left a message for Schottlekotte."

But it was no use. Mom wasn't one of those moms who give in to whining, pleading, or horoscoping. She rose from her chair, brushing lint off her apron. She gave me one of her *What did I just say?* looks and pointed up the stairs. She didn't need to say anything. I knew the routine. Mom called it being grounded. I called it being incarcerated.

Incarceration. It was a fate worse than broccoli. You couldn't go out. You couldn't bike, or shoot baskets, or camp under the picnic table. No phone calls. No TV. No radio. Which meant I couldn't listen to the Yankee game, and I had a lot riding on it.

It was the last game of the week, and The Mick was way overdue for a home run. I had him at one for the week, and I knew he had a good shot at making it. After all, The Mick was…well, The Mick. Besides, he'd always hit well in Comiskey Park. The Yankees would be facing Billy Pierce, the ace of the White Sox staff. Pierce had a nasty curveball, but Mickey hit Billy like he owned him.

"*I Love Lucy…I Love Lucy….*"

It was an all-too familiar voice, and it was coming next door from Linnie's bedroom.

"*Ma-Ma...Da-Da...I Love Lucy...I Love Lucy....*"

Great, that was all I needed. It wasn't enough I'd been incarcerated and couldn't listen to the game on the radio. Now I couldn't even slump at my desk and bemoan in peace. Was I going to have to hear Linnie's stupid doll go on all night?

Not if I could help it.

I banged on the wall.

"*Ma-Ma...Da-Da...I Love Lucy....*"

I marched angrily into Linnie's bedroom.

She was standing there with her transistor radio held up to her ear, kicking her right foot out then bringing it back.

Turkey Lips was short and slight for her age, with a mop of stringy, mousy brown hair hanging around her stupid face. She was missing her two front teeth—neither of which I was responsible for—which made it hard for her to whistle. It also gave her trouble in pronouncing the letter *s*.

"Linnie, what *are* you doing?"

"What doth it look like I'm doing? I'm lithening to my tranthitor radio. Thhhh, *Uncle Al* ith on. I think little Linnie Junior had thomething thuck in her voice. She kept thaying *I Love Luthy...I Love Luthy,* but I gave her Milk of Magnethia and burped her and everything ith okay now."

"*Milk of Magnesia?*"

"It'th okay. I'm not thupid, I checked. There'th no ethpiration date."

"But Milk of Magnesia doesn't—"

"Thhhh, don't bother me." And with that, she shook her leg at me and sang *"...and you thake it all about...."*

I looked at my Mickey Mouse Club watch, which, as you know, I wore as a tribute to Annette Funicello. The game had started fifteen minutes ago.

"Linnie, what *are* you doing?"

"The Hokey Pokey." She kicked her left leg out, then turned herself completely around. *"And thath what ith all about!"*

But Turkey Lips wasn't finished. She stuck her butt out and shook it at me.

"Linnie!"

"Quiet! I can't concentrate!"

And then mercifully she stopped and clapped her hands. That's when it hit me.

"Quick, Linnie, let me have your transistor." I explained I needed to listen to the Yankee game.

"Uh-uh."

"Linnie, I'm serious. I've *got* to listen to the game!"

"Grandpa and Grandma gave it to *me*, not you."

"Linnie!"

"And you can't have it."

The game had to be in the second inning by now, and I had no idea what the score was. I was desperate with a capital *D*. I needed Turkey Lips to give me her transistor for a couple of hours, and I was ready to do anything to get it.

"Two hours," I said. "Two hours and I'll give you a quarter."

She shook her head. Linnie Junior cried and Linnie picked her up.

"Okay, make it fifty cents. That's a good deal. Fifty cents for just borrowing it."

"You going to give me intereth?"

"Interest?"

"Yeah, you do know what intereth is, don't you, Penith Breath?"

I was ready to kill her on the spot. But I knew if I did, Linnie Junior would be an orphan and that it's hard seven months before Christmas to find people willing to adopt a stupid-looking, self-absorbed doll with a voice box often stuck on *I Love Lucy*.

I fell on my knees and begged.

"How do I know I'll get it back in exactly the thame condition I gave it to you?"

"I promise, I promise."

"You promith to baby-thit her? Will you give Linnie Junior her bottle and change her diaper? You promith and you can take the tranthitor radio."

24

I SHOULD HAVE known better. Never again would I beg Turkey Lips to give me her transistor radio—or anything else for that matter. Never again would I get on my knees and promise to baby-sit her obnoxious namesake.

For seven innings I'd nursed my emergency M&Ms. I'd listened as Turley mowed down the first six White Sox batters, listened as the Sox took a 1-0 lead in the third on a sacrifice fly by Minoso, listened as Chicago tacked on a run in the fifth on a two-out walk to Nellie Fox with the bases loaded, listened as Skowron came through with a monstrous shot in the sixth to cut the lead to 2-1, listened as Luis Aparicio walked, stole second, and rode home on McDougald's throwing error, this one putting the White Sox up 3-1 in the seventh.

The game had now gone into the top of the eighth. Time was running out on The Mick...and on me. The Yankees would be sending Bauer and Martin up to the plate, followed by Mickey. If he was going to hit one out, this was his last chance to do it.

That was when Turkey Lips' little transistor radio went out. I shook it, banged it on the floor. Nothing. Livid, I stormed into her room.

"Thhhh, you'll wake her up. Can't you tell the baby ith thleeping?"

"*Linnie, I swear—*"

"Will you pipe down? Whath your problem anyway?"

I clenched my teeth and counted—*1...2...3...*. I know I should have counted to *10*, but I couldn't make it past *3* before I exploded. "THE BATTERY IS DEAD!"

"Then you'll just have to replace it." She stuck her tongue out at me.

"Me? Me, replace *your* battery?"

"You promith. You thaid I'd get my tranthitor back exactly like it wath when I gave it to you. And when I gave it to you the battery wath working. So, Penith Breath, you'd better hop on your bike and run down to the thore right now."

"Can't," I grinned. "I'm grounded."

"You're going to be more than grounded. Wait till I tell Mom you broke the rule on being grounded!" She sucked her thumb, a contented look on her stupid face.

"You wouldn't dare!"

"Watch me." She strutted to the bedroom door, still sucking her thumb.

"*SCHITT!*"

She turned, her thumb popping out of her mouth. "You thaid a four-letter word!"

"Did not!"

"Did tho! And you thaid it in front of Linnie Junior!"

"Who can't hear anyway."

Turkey Lips glowered at me and hissed—though it came out more like a *hith.* "Just becauth dollth are thleeping dothn't mean they can't hear four-letter wordth."

"Look, I said '*schitt.*' It's a six-letter word. *S-C-H-I-T-T.*"

"That ith *not* how you thpell it."

"In the King James version of the thesaurus it is."

"Whoth King Jameth?"

This required some creative thinking on my part. "You don't know who King James is?"

"No. Never heard of him."

"I'm not surprised."

Linnie stuck her tongue out at me again—I'm pretty sure it was a move unrecognized by The Hokey Pokey Federation.

"You gonna tell me who King Jameth is?"

"King James is the English king who...who enacted the dipsong." There, my brain had come through once again.

"You mean *diphthong*, don't you, thmarty?"

"No, *dipsong*."

"What's a *dipthong*?"

"A dip that sings *The Hokey Pokey* song," I said, a big grin on my face.

I must have hit a nerve because she threw a pillow at me and stormed to the door.

"Hey, Turkey Lips, wait a minute!"

"Now what?"

"Don't slam the door," I said. "You'll wake Turkey Lips Junior up."

25

"EXTREMELY MALEVOLENT OR malicious... *malignant...M-A-L-I-G-N-A-N-T.*"

Miss Tsuris nodded approvingly. "And can you use *malignant* in a sentence?"

"A muscle that is susceptible to malignant hyperthermia contracts more frequently."

"Very good, Stuart Schneider. Nice use of *contract.*"

Miss Tsuris had been teaching for twenty-some years and had eyes in the back of her head. She didn't miss a thing. Like the flashing of Jeannette Moskowitz's hand mirror. Jeanette sat in the back row flashing and putting on a fresh coat of lipstick.

"Okay, Jeannette, you're next. *Emancipate.*"

Jeanette stood up, blotting her lips with a tissue. She wadded it and tossed it to Alex Bulgatski, on whom she had her monthly crush. "To free from restraint, influence or bondage...*emancipate...E-M-A-N-C-I-P-A-T-E.*"

"And in a sentence, please."

"He insisted the proletariat could not *emancipate* itself through the use of state power."

"Nice, Jeannette," Miss Tsuris said. "Maybe we should get you a subscription to *Pravda.*"

It was the first class after lunch, and we were regurgitating our Latin lessons. Miss Chastity Tsuris was our teacher. *The Pain*, as she was known as before and after class, should not be confused with Miss Tsuris *The Agony*, who was our social studies teacher—though it was hard not to mistake them since Miss Tsuris and Miss Tsuris were identical twins, and the only way you could tell them apart was by their growls. The Pain had gone to an exclusive prep school in New England and matriculated with a distinctive preppy growl cultivated at Cape Cod clam bakes when there weren't enough clams to go around. Agony, who was home-schooled and weaned later than her twin, had a daintier growl that was actually more of a debutante gargle. Of course, anybody who was stuck with both Pain and Agony as teachers had double trouble.

Like me.

Actually, Social Studies wasn't entirely bad as long as you knew your Great Lakes and which capital cities were on which rivers. It was just when you were given a history quiz on American presidents, you had to remember Tsuris The Agony thought Lincoln was overrated. She'd crossed him off the list of our country's greatest chief executives, replacing him with Millard Fillmore. Miss Tsuris said "Jilted Millard" was more deserving since he'd been a man and delayed the Civil War. The way Miss Tsuris explained it, "Jilted Millard" delayed it because he knew he hadn't gotten over his fiancé breaking their engagement and thus was in no shape to emancipate anybody.

Latin was something else altogether.

In Latin you didn't have anyone emancipating slaves. But you did have irregular verbal conjugations to worry about. And if you couldn't rattle off your *veni, vidi, vicis*—which no one could except Stanley Kaplan—you'd suffer unrelenting Pain. Tsuris The Pain would have you stand on one foot in front of the whole class and recite some stupid Latin ditty you'd never hear on *The Mickey Mouse Club Show.* You'd have to do it seven times. And if you put your foot down after six, she put down hers.

So there I was, sitting at my crib-noted desk, minding my own business, sneaking a blow of Bazooka, my bubble-gummed face buried in my notebook. I'd stuck the latest issue of *The Sporting News* inside it and was working on my entry in Esso's Mickey Mantle Tape-Measure Home Run Derby, poring over the ERA of the pitchers Mickey would likely be facing that week. I should've been paying attention to the struggle Hughie Koncusion was having conjugating, but I wasn't. And The Pain knew it.

I never saw her coming. Believe me, if I had I would've closed the notebook before she caught me with *The Sporting News.* But like I said, I wasn't paying attention...or I wasn't until I heard the roar. It was unmistakably The Pain's, and it was directed right at me.

"PHILIP MORRIS KLEINMANN! WHAT DO YOU THINK YOU'RE DOING?"

I told Miss Tsuris I was conjugating pitching staffs. And I started regurgitating. "To start for the White Sox Saturday against the Yankees at Comiskey Park...*Dick Donovan...D-O-N-O-V-AN...*. Hoping not to give up a home run to Mickey like last time he faced him at Griffith Stadium... *Pedro Ramos...R-A-M-O-S....*"

"THIS IS *NOT* WHAT WE'RE DOING IN CLASS!" The Pain roared. "WE'RE CONJUGATING *VERBS,* NOT PITCHERS. DO YOU HAVE AN EXPLANATION?"

An explanation? For why Dick Donovan was starting Saturday? I didn't know what to say. So I didn't.

The Pain folded her arms across her chest and tapped her foot. "I'M WAITING!"

So I told her all about Esso's Mickey Mantle Tape-Measure Home Run Derby, and how I was trying to figure out how many home runs Mickey was likely to hit next week.

She growled and snatched *The Sporting News* from my notebook. Before I could say anything, *TSN*—the revered *Bible of Baseball*—was drawn and quartered.

"I'm sending a letter to your parents," The Pain said with a muted roar. "I'm going to tell them what you've been conjugating in class and that you should *not* be allowed to enter the Mickey Maris Tape-Measure Home Run Derby."

"It's *Mantle*," I said. "Mickey *Mantle*."

"ARE YOU CONTRADICTING ME, PHILIP?"

"No, Miss Tsuris."

"I'm telling your parents you should not be allowed to enter the..." she paused and huffed, "*The Home Run thing*."

"For how many weeks?"

"HOW MANY WEEKS? HOW MANY WEEKS? *THE REST OF THE SEASON!*"

26

ASK ME AGAIN LATER

THE PAIN came Saturday, shortly after lunch.

"You want to explain this?" Mom held up the letter from Tsuris The Pain.

"On a full stomach?" I said. "Shouldn't we wait a couple of days?"

"I think you better go in the furnace room," Mom said, adding that Dad was down there already steaming. "You know your father. Will he talk to a repairman? Oh, no, not your father. But he says he wants to talk to you."

"Now?"

"Now!"

I was sweating, and I hadn't even walked into the furnace room yet.

"DAMN THIS FURNACE!" Dad yelled from downstairs. "IS HE COMING OR NOT?"

Mom turned her head to the stairs. "KEEP YOUR SHIRT ON, LOU! HE'S COMING! AND STOP YELLING…YOU'LL WAKE ME UP!"

I tip-toed down to the basement—this was no time to do my patented head-first slide down the stairs. Muttering 'Yea though I walk through the valley of death… ' I walked into the furnace room.

"About time you got here," Dad said, putting his shirt back on. "And why are you acting like a praying mantis? Here, hold the wrench."

"You want me..." I stammered, "to hold...the wench?"

"Did I say *wench*? What are you, tone deaf? Take the dang *wrench*."

I took the dang wrench.

"Not between your knees!"

I told Dad my hands were full. And indeed they were. Mom had shoved the letter from Miss Tsuris into one of my trembling hands and the number for H&R Heating into the other.

"Let's have it," Dad said.

I stuck out my knees to him.

"Your hands!" Dad said, ignoring the wrench which had dropped on the floor.

I held out both hands to him. He looked at them and shook his head.

"Look at you. *Thirteen* and still biting your fingernails. When are you...." He stopped before he could say *stop*. "All right, let me see that letter." He reached in his shirt pocket for his reading glasses, which he didn't particularly like to wear unless he was examining the pictures of native girls in *National Geographic*.

"Uh, Dad, maybe you want to read the H&R number from Mom first?"

"Harrumph," he harrumphed, snatching The Pain's letter from my sweaty hand that wasn't holding the number for H&R.

I asked him if he wanted to trade Miss Tsuris' letter for the phone number for H&R Heating.

"No, I don't want to trade with you. Think you should explain this."

So I told Dad the whole story behind the letter: How The Schneid had contracted malignant in Latin class, how I hadn't seen The Pain coming because I'd opened my notebook to *The Sporting News* and was conjugating ballparks, how I'd explained to Miss Tsuris I was using *TSN* to figure out how many home runs Mickey Mantle would hit next week in Esso's Mickey Mantle Tape-Measure Home Run Derby, how, though it was Latin, she roared in English she was going to send a letter to my parents saying that because I wasn't paying attention to the conjugaling going on in class I should *not* be allowed to enter the Home Run Derby for the rest of my puberty which meant that I'd have no chance to be the Yankees' batboy for the last game of the season and kneel in the on-deck circle with The Mick. I left out the part about me blowing bubble gum because I knew Dad didn't like the idea of me carrying around my Bazooka in school.

"And all this is because of that Mickey Mantle Tape-Measure Home Run Derby?"

I nodded. "She called him Mickey *Maris*."

Dad laughed. "And if you win you get to be the Yankees' batboy for the last game of the season?" He set the letter down on top of a storage box. "Wow, wouldn't that be something!"

I nodded. "But what makes it really hard, Dad, is you have put down how far he'll hit his longest home run that week. That's why they call it the *Tape-Measure* Home Run Derby. Last week I had *2-3-9-7*. I had the 2 home runs right, but the 397, wasn't close."

"How far did he hit one?"

"Four twenty-one. It was off Ramos."

"And now your Latin teacher says your mother and I shouldn't let you enter the contest anymore."

I nodded.

"Hmmm, Latin….What was that thing they used to say when I was a kid? Oh yeah, I remember. 'Latin is a language / as dead as it can be/ it killed the ancient Romans / and now it's killing me.'"

He paused and I knew it meant he was reflecting.

"Latin? You'd be better off learning Finnish or Bengali. Only thing I remember in Latin is *Latin odi*."

"What does that mean?"

"I hate Latin."

"Me too," I said.

Dad put his hand on my shoulder. I knew it meant only one thing. There'd be no punishment. You don't punish a chip off the old block.

27

YES

THE SCHNEID AND I were lunching in the school cafeteria with some other kids in our class, all of us trading sandwiches and baseball cards. Danny Rifkin and Nick Kaufman were trading Moose Skowron for Dee Fondy, Philip Schlaeger was trading Eddie Mathews to get Al Rosen from Frank Gifford—the student council rep, not the football player—and The Schneid was trading his PB-and-J sandwich for Barney Levine's tuna on rye. No one was trading his Hostess cupcake.

Through it all, Ziggy Zagsky sat with his baloney sandwich. He'd eaten half and had a hyena on his face. That's what we called Ziggy's smile.

Ziggy had on a sky blue Izod shirt that went well with the glob of Russian dressing dripping down the alligator. Running down his right cheek was a thin scar. He looked a little like Al Capone...a young Al Capone with an Ibold wrapper, instead of a diamond ring, on the pinky finger of his left hand.

Sigmund "Ziggy" Zagsky was probably the shrewdest trader of baseball cards in the whole school, maybe the whole city. You had to be careful with Ziggy or he'd wind up with both your Roy Campanella and Whitey Ford, and you'd be left holding his Hubie Suvpansky. We called it *getting Zig-Zagged.*

Ziggy had Mickey's '51 rookie card, the one with The Mick's stats in his first season, the one I'd lost back in Tombstone to the Zanders. Ziggy knew how badly I wanted it. He knew too that Mickey Mantle rookie cards were no longer in print.

"So what will you give me for this '51 Mantle?" Ziggy asked no one in particular, holding the card up for all to see. "Look, his signature is printed right on it."

He sounded sort of like Edward G. Robinson in *Little Caesar*.

"Six, Ziggy," I said. "I'll give you Six."

Six was the nickname given Al Kaline, the twenty-one-year-old phenom who played right field for the Detroit Tigers. He was called *Six* because that was the number on the back of his uniform. It was the ultimate accolade one baseball player could give another. Like *That's some hot babe you got there, Twenty-Nine!*

"No deal," the Zig-Zag said. He took a bite out of the other half of his baloney and flashed the hyena.

"Spahn," I said. "I'll give you my Warren Spahn."

"Got it already."

"Scooter. It's Rizzuto's 1953 card."

He shook his head.

"The Barber...you can have Maglie."

"Nope." He slowly took another bite, his eyes darting between The Schneid and me.

I was getting more and more exasperated. I tried two- and three-card combinations—Antonelli and Fox...Ashburn and Adcock and Schoendienst—and still Ziggy wouldn't budge.

"Okay, Zig," I sighed, "I'll give you the Dodgers' starting infield from last year. Gil Hodges…Junior Gilliam…Pee Wee Reese…Randy Jackson."

"You forget Jackie Robinson?"

"He's retired," said Bernie Levine, who'd polished off half the PB and J that The Schneid had given him.

"So what?" Frank Gifford said. "His card's still good."

"You want Jackie? You can have Jackie too, Zig," I said.

Ziggy shook his head. He curled his tongue and licked the zit on the tip of his nose. He had me zagged and he knew it.

"What *do* you want for the '51 Mantle?"

Ziggy finished the rest of his sandwich. He licked his fingers and leaned back in his chair, the hyena again on his face. "You want Mickey Mantle's rookie card, Kleinmann? You *really* want it? What I want is one of Elaine's bras."

"What?"

"You hard of hearing? One of Elaine's bras."

It was incredulous, incredulous in capital letters— maybe more than INCREDULOUS if there's such a thing.

"You'll give me your 1951 Mantle if I give you one of Elaine Novak's bras?"

"I've started a collection. I've got a padded A, a strapless B, and a black underwire C. I need a D cup. You get me Elaine's bra, I'll give you Mantle's '51 card."

"How am I supposed to get Elaine's bra?"

"You want the card or not, Kleinmann?"

"You know I want it!"

"Then you better figure a way to get Elaine Novak's bra."

I was Zig-Zagged and I knew it.

28

IT IS DECIDEDLY SO

"TO LOOK SHARP...every time you shave/To feel sharp...and be on the ball/To be sharp...use Gillette Blue Blades/It's the quickest, slickest shave of all!"

Fenny and I were camping out...well, sort of camping out. We were sitting under the picnic table in our backyard. We'd spread a sheet over it and draped it down, giving us a makeshift tent. It was a great place to go when you wanted to get away from the sun...or the rain. We'd gone there with two fresh C batteries and Fenny's portable radio to listen to the Yankee game. I'd brought my toy soldiers, and we'd set them up, re-enacting the Battle of Bunker Hill. Except there wasn't any hill because the picnic table was set on flat ground. So we were calling it the Battle of Bunker Flatland, which gave the battle a whole different perspective.

"Hello again, everybody! This is Mel Allen here in the Gillette broadcast booth, with today's pivotal game between the New York Yankees and the Boston Red Sox...."

It was the end of May, and The Mick had been on a tear. He now had ten home runs. The Yankees as a team were doing well too, leading the league with a 22-17 record. Me, I hadn't come close to winning the weekly Mickey Mantle Tape-Measure Home Run Derby. And to top things off, I hadn't figured out a way to get hold of

Elaine's bra to trade to Ziggy for Mickey's rookie baseball card. It was beginning to get to me and it showed.

"Skip, Skip, relax. You'll d-d-d-do it."

"How? What am I supposed to do, Fenny? Walk up to her and ask for it? 'Excuse me, Elaine. If you're not using that bra, can I have it?'"

"Yes, the umpires have held up the start of the game...from here in the Gillette broadcast booth it looks like a passing tsunami...."

Fenny laughed and moved a column of infantry behind a weed. "No one does a g-g-g-game like M-M-M-Mel Allen."

And indeed Fenny was right. Mel Allen was a baseball institution—born, The Schneid said, with a baseball in his mouth. Since 1940, Mel had been the *Voice* of the Yankees, taking over for Garnett Marks when he'd twice mispronounced the name of the Yankees' sponsor at the time. When Ivory Soap became *Ovary* Soap, Garnett was fired and Mel was given the nod to replace him.

Mel Allen's voice was unmistakable. One of the twenty-five most recognizable in the *world*, *Variety* magazine said, right up there with Churchill's and Sinatra's. To men who followed sports, Mel's baritone voice was as holy as the Pope's. To women around the country, it had the charm of Rhett Butler's. They sent him passionate love letters, called him at all hours, asked him to parties, invited him to weekend get-aways in the Hamptons. None of it mattered. Through it all, Mel managed to remain unmarried and unattached, a testament to his total devotion to baseball.

During rain delays, The Voice would dip into his vast memory of Yankee heroes, telling stories about Gehrig, DiMaggio, Rizzuto, and the rest. We'd sit there, clinging to every word of Mel's rhapsodies, not caring that a thirty-minute rain delay had become an hour.

But today I wasn't clinging to Mel Allen. I was thinking more of Elaine Novak and her D-cup bra.

"Well, folks, the umpires have sloshed back onto the field...they've conferred at home plate...What will they do?...Yes, it's going, go-ing, gone!...The umpires have called the game...How 'bout that!"

"That's just great," I said to Fenny. "I figured The Mick would hit one today, and they call the game off. There goes my chance of winning this week."

"Mine too," Fenny said. "Well, at least you c-c-c-can now focus on Elaine." He smiled and wheeled around his artillery. "It shouldn't be a problem. Elaine's b-b-b-boobs are easy to focus on."

He was right of course. "I know, I know," I said. "I need to keep focused."

While I was trying to focus on Elaine and her D-cup, Fenny had brought up his reserves. I saw too late my men were surrounded like the 101st at Bastogne.

"Wanna g-g-g-give up?"

"Nuts!"

"So whatcha g-g-g-gonna to do about Elaine's b-b-b-bra?"

"I don't know, Fenny. I just don't know."

"Look, why don'tcha just b-b-b-buy a bra, and tell Zig it's Elaine's? How's he g-g-g-gonna know the difference?"

Fenny had a point. Yet the last thing I wanted to do was to go shopping all by myself for a bra, particularly a D cup. But who could I get to go with me? Fenny wouldn't, and I wasn't about to risk a tongue lashing by The Schneid, who was dead set against girls wearing bras.

What I needed was somebody who knew about bras, someone with hands-on familiarity.

29

HE MUST HAVE STOOD...oh, about five-eleven, give or take a few inches depending on whether or not he had both feet on the ground that day. And he was thin, maybe a hundred and forty-five pounds soaking wet, which invariably happened every time there was a thunderstorm. People said he must have thought he was another Gene Kelly because he would go dancing down the street at the first clap of thunder. Only unlike Gene Kelly, he never danced with an umbrella, which was why he was soaking wet every time it rained.

He had a high forehead and receding hairline, his hair made shiny with black Shinola shoe polish, which he brushed into his scalp in a vain attempt to cover the encroaching gray. Above his upper lip was a pencil-thin mustache that he claimed often caused girls to mistake him for Clark Gable—not that Clark Gable frankly gave a damn. The mustache was graying too, but he'd refused to apply Shinola, saying he was afraid he'd miss a spot and wind up with black shoe polish on his lip. Several front doors had been slammed in his face before he'd realized most girls didn't want to kiss a man with Shinola shoe polish on his upper lip.

Harold Greenberg was Grandma Bessie's kid brother. Hal Green was the name he went by when he played pro ball, pitching in places like Chillicothe, Hackensack, and Poughkeepsie. He got as far as Class D before his arm blew out one night while he was sitting at the bar, ordering a drink for some blonde bimbo in high heels and a higher skirt. That's when her husband walked in. Uncle Harold's pitching arm never was the same after that night.

Not that it bothered him. Oh, he'd sometimes talk about it, telling whoever he could get to listen that he could've been right up there with Bob Feller, that he could have been a contender...for the Cy Young Award, but that was the breaks. And literally it was. But Uncle Harold didn't let the unlucky break bother him. He'd moved to New York and had gone on to better things.

He became a specialist.

His first job was as an elevator operator in the Empire State Building, specializing, he said, in taking people all the way up to the observation deck on the 102nd floor. It lasted two days before his acrophobia set in.

His second job was in the copyediting department of the *Herald Tribune*, specializing in copyediting obituaries, It lasted till lunch. He'd just sat down with his tossed sardine salad sandwich when he was quietly called into the office of the obituaries editor, who told him that he really didn't need a copyeditor who was dyslexic and had 81-year-old people dying at age 18.

Next, he worked at the Bronx Zoo, specializing in cleaning up the elephant pen. But Uncle Harold found pachyderm dung wasn't to his liking, and so he had simply walked out one afternoon to the chagrin of the assistant zookeeper, who blackballed him from working in other zoos on the East Coast.

He was now, he said, the assistant baseball coach at Hebrew Union College's branch in Greenwich Village, specializing in teaching the rabbinical students how to steal.

Uncle Harold had given up an opportunity to spend the weekend with his weekly bimbo and flown to Cincinnati a couple of months early for my bar mitzvah, saving money by flying stand-by from New York to Washington and Washington to New York before changing planes at LaGuardia for a two-stop flight to Cincinnati with a layover in Minneapolis.

"I think they have a special this week on falsies," Uncle Harold said, his New York accent noticeably jet-lagged after flying two weeks. "J.C. Penney, that's where we'll go."

I was about to tell him what I needed was a good buy on a natural D cup, not falsies, but it looked like his mind was elsewhere.

"Just you leave it to me, Skippy," he said. "I know my away around bras."

30

UNCLE HAROLD MAY HAVE known his way around bras, but he sure as heck didn't know his way around Penney's. We'd taken the elevator to the second floor and were standing there in Ladies' Dresses. Not that Uncle Harold was into cross-dressing, you understand. The second floor was where ladies dresses were, though I don't know why they called it *Ladies* Dresses. Other than the store in Greenwich Village, there was no *Men's* Dresses in Penney's.

"Bras? We don't have bras on the second floor," said a snooty sales lady, who looked like she could've used a more uplifting one. She was a little on the heavy side, though it was nothing that thirty-six hours in the sauna wouldn't fix. "You want *Lingerie*...third floor."

"Third floor?" Uncle Harold said.

"Third floor. Third is one floor up from second."

So up we went to the third floor, one up from second, or so I thought. Problem was Uncle Harold never pressed the elevator's *3* button. His eyes were riveted on the shapely-legged salesgirl standing next to me. She was perfectly curved and coifed and wearing a mid-thigh, black smock with brass-like buttons and a white collar. Her deep blue eyes were large and made to look even larger by her makeup. Her skin had a healthy glow, the kind of skin you get from drinking chocolate milk at bedtime and omitting uncooked vegetables from your diet.

The doors opened on the first floor, and out walked Shapely Legs. So did Uncle Harold, following her to the perfume counter, where three other salesgirls were standing.

"I would switch around those two sprays on the counter," Shapely Legs said to them. "Here, let me show you what I mean." She moved the two-ounce bottles of Shalimar in front of the Channel No. 5, then carefully angled the whole row. Satisfied, she turned and smiled at us.

"I'm Estee," she said, offering a well-manicured hand, her fingernails glittering with some shade of orange polish, which matched her heels. She pointed out the other salesgirls. "This one's Helena, this one's Hazel, and she's Elizabeth."

Like Estee, Helena, Hazel, and Elizabeth had on similar short, black smocks and orange heels. Helena and Hazel were blonde and Elizabeth, a statuesque brunette.

Uncle Harold grinned. "Hi, girls!"

Helena, Hazel, and Elizabeth flashed us Miss America smiles. Then, taking their lead from Estee, they each asked *"May I?"*

Uncle Harold momentarily forgot about D cups. Putting his best foot forward, he nodded to Helen, Hazel, Elizabeth, and Estee to *spritz* us...twice if they wanted.

We'd gone through the *spritzing* twice when Uncle Harold nudged me. "Let's do it a third time. I think Miss Estee is beginning to like me. Third time's the charm."

He winked at Estee, grabbed my arm, and together we vamped a gauntlet of mascara.

Uncle Harold was ready to vamp again, but this time I grabbed his arm and back to the elevator we went. It didn't take much time for the elevator to reach the third floor and for us to walk through the door, smelling like we'd fallen into some new concoction of toilet water.

"Get a whiff of those two!" one dowager said to her friend, who was admiring a girdled mannequin. Her friend said she'd rather not.

Uncle Harold paid them no attention. His mind was back on D cups. He was, in fact, already rummaging through the clearance rack, looking for a bra that would do.

"I think this is too big," he said, holding the cups of a bra up to his chest.

"Need some help, gentlemen?"

Uncle Harold's modeling was interrupted by a J.C. Penney sales associate. Her hair was thin and graying, her shoes clunky. She looked old, maybe forty-five. Her nametag said *Gertie, Sales Associate*. Nothing on the nametag said *Smirking*. It was obvious it was implicit.

"We need a bra," Uncle Harold said.

"For yourself, sir?" Gertie asked, her smirk now explicit. "I think you're holding a double D. What you need is a 40, maybe a 42, double A. There's a dressing room if you'd like to try both a 40 and a 42 on. Do you want me to help you?"

Uncle Harold's face turned tomato red. He gulped, speechless.

"Why does he want a bra?" Gertie asked me.

"No, it's for me," I said.

"Aren't you a little young?"

"I'm thirteen. And you don't understand. I need a bra for my—"

"No need explaining." Gertie handed Uncle Harold a lacy black bra. "Would you like matching panties to go with it?"

Uncle Harold's reddened face went from tomato to beet. He turned and raced cross-legged through the clearance bras to the elevator. *"Gotta go!"*

"What's the matter with him?" Gertie had stopped smirking.

"Oh, it happens all the time."

"What does?"

I watched as Uncle Harold barely made it to the elevator as the doors closed.

"He's always making a mad run like that for the bathroom," I explained. "When Uncle Harold's gotta go, he's gotta go."

31

YOU MAY RELY ON IT

A GIANT PRAYING MANTIS had thawed from the Arctic ice and was starving for human flesh. It was now devouring its way south. I'd called The Schneid and told him if we waited much longer we'd miss seeing it.

"It's open!" The Schneid yelled from inside the kitchen door.

I shook out the umbrella, a big golf umbrella Dad no longer used since he'd given up the game, and ducked inside. The Schneid was sitting there at the Formica kitchen table, still working on his stamp collection. Next to annotating the centerfold in a new issue of *Playboy,* it was his favorite thing to do on a rainy afternoon.

"I don't like bug movies," he said.

He licked the back of a stamp and gently pasted it in place. Satisfied, he smiled. "Seventy-Fifth Anniversary of the Thirteenth Amendment to the Constitution...issued in 1940. It goes into the commemorative book."

Commemorative stamps were The Schneid's specialty. He had the 1940 stamp commemorating the 50th Anniversary of the State of Idaho, the 1951 Diamond Jubilee of the American Chemical Society, the 1948 Centennial of the American Poultry Association, and the 200th Anniversary of the Birth of Betsy Ross issued in 1952.

"I thought you liked *THEM!*" I said.

The Schneid shook his head. "You see one bug movie, Felipe, you've seen them all. The bugs start off minding their own business, not bothering anybody. Then something always happens to them, and they go on a rampage. What do you expect them to do when they mutate into giants? All those bug movies are the same."

He held up a purple three-cent stamp that had a covered wagon on it. "Stamps are different. This 1947 Utah Centennial isn't the same as other state centennial stamps."

"All bug movies are *not* the same," I said. "*THEM!*'s about ants and *Tarantula*'s all about...." My voice cracked.

"You miss Harriet don't you, Felipe?"

I sniffled. "You blame me? Wouldn't you miss a pet tarantula?"

The Schneid cocked his head, squinching his face. "Not me. I wouldn't be caught dead with one."

The Deadly Mantis was the name of the movie, and it was the main feature at the Monte Vista's Saturday matinee. The Monte Vista was up on Montgomery Road and was your classic neighborhood theater. It had been around since 1929, though renovations had been made. In 1938, they repaired the largest holes in the screen. In 1943, they put in a projector that didn't snap the film. In 1951, they did the seats, sandblasting off twenty-two years of gum stuck underneath.

Fifty cents got you into the Monte Vista on a Saturday afternoon, and a quarter got you enough popcorn to sit there in the first couple of rows and throw it at the screen. You could yell and scream and throw all the popcorn you wanted, and there'd be no parents to haul you up the aisle and out the door.

The matinee usually started with a Loony Toons cartoon. Bugs Bunny was our favorite, with Daffy Duck a close second. Sylvester was cool too—though Tweety was even cooler. Porky, we never went for. It's hard enough to get excited over a pig, let alone one that's a sissy. Which is no doubt why, in 2010, Porky was rated forty-seventh in *TV Guide*'s top fifty cartoon characters of all time.

After the cartoon there'd be a comedy short. If we were lucky, it'd be Laurel and Hardy. If we were unlucky, it'd be something stupid like *Snow White Frolics With the Three Stooges*. The Stooges were supposed to be funny, but to me getting smacked for saying something stupid was nothing to laugh about.

Next, would come a grainy, black-and-white serial cliffhanger like *Flash Gordon*. Flash always seemed to have his hands full with either the evil Emperor Ming or the luscious Dale Arden. Ming must have been jealous of the attention Flash gave Dale. That would explain why he sent Flash to the arena to fight a Tournament of Death against a masked opponent—a killer that wouldn't be unmasked until next week's chapter.

Flash was played by Buster Crabbe, who'd won an Olympic gold medal in swimming. I'm not sure why Buster got the part since you'd be hard-pressed to find an Olympic pool on the planet Mongo. Besides, Buster didn't look anything like the Flash Gordon we all knew from the comics. The studio knew it too, which is why they ignored Buster's protests and had him dye his hair blond. Buster must have been very self-conscious about being a golden blond because he kept his hat on in public at all times. The Schneid said he did it to keep men from whistling at him.

"You really want to see this?" The Schneid said. "A movie about a *praying mantis*?"

"Not just any mantis," I reminded him. "This one's a giant and it's deadly. It's been trapped in polar ice since prehistoric times Now it's untrapped and flying around eating human flesh."

"Can you blame it?" The Schneid said. "It hasn't eaten in a million years. You don't eat for a million years, you want something more filling than ants."

He shook his head and zipped up his wind- breaker. "Who writes these things?"

32

THE CARNAGE HAD ended. The mantis had met its doom, gassed in the Manhattan Tunnel, Colonel Parkman, the ace pilot, had saved the screaming girl photographer, and all was right in the world…until next week.

"Got any Jujubes left?" The Schneid asked.

"That's *all* you've got to say? Tell me you didn't like the movie."

"I didn't like the movie."

As the lights went up, I saw Danny Freyer running up the aisle. *"FREYER!"* I yelled. *"FREYER!"*

With my second *Freyer!* the theater erupted in pandemonium. Kids were yelling and screaming, pushing and shoving, scrambling over seats to get to the exit.

The Schneid turned and glared at me. "You nuts? You can't yell *Fire!* in a crowded theater!"

"I didn't yell *Fire!"* What I yelled was *Freyer!"*

It sounded like *Fire!"*

"No, it was *Freyer!* That was Danny Freyer running up the aisle. He owes me a dollar."

The Schneid sighed heavily. "Let's get out of here while we can."

With The Schneid leading the way, we somehow managed to weave up the aisle and through the lobby, stepping on just two fallen bodies in the mad scramble for the doors.

We were standing outside under the marquee, shirts streaked from three or four spilled drinks, as kids kept pouring out of the theater. The rain had let up, but the mad rush out hadn't.

Neither had the sirens.

"I can't believe you!" The Schneid slowly shook his head. "Now look what you've done!"

"*Freyer*," I said. "I yelled *Freyer!* not *Fire!*"

"Ohio Revised Code 2917.31," The Schneid said. "Inducing panic. Want me to quote it for you?"

I didn't, but I nodded anyway. I knew The Schneid, and I knew if I said *no* he'd be insulted and never let me copy his homework again.

The Schneid shut his eyes, concentrating. "*No person shall cause the evacuation of any public place, or otherwise cause serious public inconvenience or alarm, by initiating or circulating a report or warning of an alleged or impending fire, explosion, crime, or other catastrophe, knowing that such report or warning is false.*"

"You sure of that, Schneid?"

He opened his eyes. "You questioning me?"

"Uh-uh," I said, thinking of Latin homework.

"What 2917.31 means is that if people get injured because you cause a panic by falsely yelling *Fire!* you can be arrested and charged with a felony in the fourth degree."

"*Fourth* degree?"

"Six to eighteen months in prison."

"You're kidding!"

"No."

"Well, Fenny's father wouldn't prosecute me."

"He'd have to, Felipe. It's the law."

Three firemen jumped off the truck even before it came to a complete stop in front of us. Two of them quickly pulled out a giant hose and hooked it up to the fire hydrant. The third, undoubtedly the chief by the star on his ten-gallon helmet, John Wayned up to the marquee, cigarette dangling from his mouth. He stopped in front of the growing crowd of kids and flicked his cigarette to the sidewalk, stomping it out with a rubber boot. He smiled at us, a smile that looked grafted on.

"SMOKE...WHERE'S THE SMOKE COMING FROM?"

"There *is* no smoke," The Schneid said.

The chief tipped back his helmet with a heavy glove. "How can there be a fire without smoke?"

"There is no fire." The Schneid said.

"Well someone yelled *Fire!* We got a call!"

"He yelled *Fire!"* Some kid standing to our left was pointing straight at me.

The chief glared at me through his goggles. "What's wrong with you? You can't yell *Fire!* in a crowded theater!"

"I did *not* yell *Fire!* I yelled *Freyer!"* I looked at The Schneid. "Right, Schneid?"

The Schneid shrugged his shoulders as if to say *what can I say?"*

"He owes me a dollar!" I explained. "Danny Freyer...I saw him and yelled *Freyer!"*

The chief shook his head. "In a crowded theater? You yelled...*Freyer!?*"

"The theater wasn't crowded," I said. "There were empty seats on the right."

The chief whipped off his goggles, raking me up and down. "What are you, a smart guy?"

"Well, except for Biology."

"And you?" The chief was looking straight at the winking Schneid. "You a smart guy too?"

"Actually, yes." The Schneid pointed out that he got straight *A*'s. "Plus I know all the capitals..."

"In Mexico," I added. "And he speaks fluent eighth-grade Spanish too."

The Schneid nodded. *"Mucho si!"*

"You boys know what can happen to you if you yell *Fire!?*"

The Schneid nodded. *"Section 2917.31... Subparagraph 1."*

The chief clenched his jaw, then his teeth. "I oughta run you two down to the station! You do it again and I will!" Fuming, he jabbed his finger at me. *"Got that?"*

We nodded. "Got it, chief," I said.

"I am *not* a chief." He pointed to his shoulder. "See these stripes, kid? Know what they spell? *S-A-R-G-E-N-T!*"

"Actually it's spelled *s-e-r-g-e-a-n-t*," The Schneid said.

"Maybe it would be a whole lot easier if they made you fire warden," I said, trying to be helpful. "Warden's easier to spell."

"Fire warden? You think I'm a...fire warden?" Spittle was gushing from his mouth. *"Do I look like a fire warden*

to you?" He wiped his lip, all the while glaring at us. He started to say something, then caught himself and stomped away fuming.

"You see that look on his face, Schneid? How was I supposed to know he got demoted?"

"We're lucky he's not a chief and that we're in America," The Schneid said. "In Venezuela, a fire chief can order a firing squad."

I could see myself lined up against a wall, six rifles aimed at my heart, and they weren't Daisy Air Rifles.

The Schneid must have seen the sweat dripping from my forehead down into my quivering lips.

"Felipe, you okay?"

"I need a drink!"

"Me too," The Schneid said. "Slotnick's is the closest."

33

WE WERE LUCKY. Slotnick's was on the next block, and their soda jerks made the best phosphates in town...well, at least east of Vine Street. Since none of us spent much time west of Vine Street we didn't know where to get a good phosphate over there for fifteen cents.

A good phosphate is made with just the right mixture of seltzer water and flavored syrup—like chocolate, lime, or cherry—in a glass filled with ice. Add milk on top, and you've got an egg cream. Why it's called an *egg cream*, I don't know since no one in their right mind would put an egg in their cream and drink it. Besides, eggs are expensive—actually so is cream for that matter. But an *egg cream* is what they call a phosphate in New York City. No egg, just a little milk on top of your phosphate... *whazew*, you have an egg cream. Go figure.

Anyhow, Slotnick's soda jerks didn't make egg creams. They made phosphates, and I usually went for their chocolate or lime.

We'd stuck Dad's umbrella in the umbrella holder inside Slotnick's smudged glass door and were sitting on the floor by the magazines. The new issue of *The Sporting News* had just hit the stands, and I was reading the cover story on The Mick—The Schneid had already finished reading the cover story in *Modern Archaeology.*

"Cherry," he was saying. "Definitely cherry."

"Huh? What are you talking about, Schneid?"

"Beitler and Novak." He grabbed my shoulders and turned me toward the counter. "Look what they're drinking, Felipe. Tell me that's not cherry." He shook his head. "I've never known Beitler to order cherry. Novak, yes, but not Beitler."

Beitler was Diane, whose dad had done at least half the noses in last year's graduating class—this year Dr. Beitler was aiming for two-thirds—and Novak was...well, you already know about Elaine.

The Schneid was right, there was no mistake about it. Diane and Elaine were sitting at the far end of the fountain, swiveling on their stools, and what they were sipping through their straws definitely looked like cherry phosphate. Diane was wearing a light pink sweater that did nothing for her chest, green shorts that did nothing for her legs, and glasses with gray plastic frames that did nothing for her eyes. Elaine was wearing her cleavage.

"So why do you think they're drinking cherry, Schneid? Maybe they're out of lime?"

"And orange and strawberry too? At *Slotnick's*? Not likely."

Elaine must have spotted me shrugging, because she stopped swiveling, smiled at me, and waved. She whispered something to Diane, who giggled.

"Why don't we grab those stools next to them?" I said to The Schneid.

The Schneid wagged his tongue, following me over to Elaine and Diane.

"Hi," I said.

Elaine smiled and squished her straw wrapper into what looked like a squished worm. Diane burped.

"Excuse me," she said, blushing.

"Can I join you?" I asked.

"*May* I join you?" Diane said.

"I asked first!" I said.

Elaine put her hand on the stool next to her. "I guess so, but you can't sit there. She just went to the bathroom...should be right back."

The Schneid snickered. "Depends on which number she went for."

"That is *so* gross," Diane said.

The Schneid smiled at her. "I know."

I moved over one stool. The Schneid did the same. We signaled Timmy, the soda jerk, who was busy snapping his fingers and singing along with Little Richard on the radio.

"She's the gal that I love best..."

"Hey, Timmy!"

"Tutti frutti..."

"TIMMY!"

"WOP BOP A LOO BOP A LOO BAM BOOM!"

The *bam booms* finished, Timmy finally realized he had two new customers who were banging the counter. He duck-walked over to us, strumming an imaginary guitar. I wasn't about to tell him he was doing Chuck Berry, not Little Richard. Instead, I ordered a chocolate phosphate. The Schneid ordered a lime.

"Two straws or one?" Timmy asked. "You get two cents off if you use just one."

"One," I said.

"I brought my own," The Schneid said. "That should be four cents off."

"What are you a wise guy?"

The Schneid turned to me. "Didn't we just go through this?"

I nodded.

"And no ice, Timmy." The Schneid explained to me ice cubes take up half the glass. "No ice cubes means to fill the glass they have to give you more phosphate."

"Really?"

"Read Galileo."

Elaine must have heard The Schneid's ice cube proclamation, because she said she liked to suck on ice cubes, particularly ones that had holes all the way through them like the ones Slotnick's put in their Cokes. It looked like she was going to demonstrate, but instead she suddenly swiveled toward me. "I heard you wrote to *Ann Landers*!" You *really* did?"

I nodded.

"Well, what did she say? Tell me, tell me!"

"There's nothing to tell."

"He hasn't heard from her," The Schneid interjected.

I was about to say something about the letter to Ann Landers, but blanched. For at that moment, the stool next to Elaine was reclaimed…by *Madeline Schwartz*.

"Hi, Skip!" she cooed through her braces.

"Hi," I mumbled.

"You and Schneid get caught in the rain?" she asked, noticing our wet shirts.

I shook my head.

"We got drinks spilled all over us at the bug movie," The Schneid explained. "Mine's Pepsi, his is root beer."

"The bug movie?"

"We saw *The Deadly Mantis*," I said. "It's at the Monte Vista."

Madeline smiled a mouthful of braces. "So what did you think?"

The Schneid said he liked the newsreel, particularly the part that showed President Eisenhower signing a bill that conveyed property to Panama.

"*That's* what you liked?" Diane exclaimed.

"Well, the shot of Mickey Mantle being handed the home run trophy and holding it up high for everybody to see at the press conference…that was good too."

"I meant *The Deadly Mantis*," Madeline said. "What did you think of *The Deadly Mantis*?"

"Deadly stupid." The Schneid pushed the straw wrapper halfway up his straw and blew it at me. I ducked and he missed, hitting the middle of Boobsville. Elaine seemed unaware the straw wrapper had landed in her cleavage, and I wasn't about to tell her I could read the *Coca-Cola* on the wrapper.

"Stupid," The Schneid repeated. "All of a sudden this giant praying mantis wakes up, roars and, surprise, surprise, starts flying south."

Diane had set her phosphate down and was nibbling on a fingernail. "You think maybe he's tired of being hit by Eskimo snowballs?"

"*South?*" The Schneid shook his head. "Where else is the mantis supposed to fly? You can't blame it for wanting to fly to a warmer climate."

"Oh, c'mon, Schneid!" Madeline said. "It's a movie."

"Yeah, but it's a stupid movie. The mantis is supposed to be flying south? Then explain why it's flying from Washington, D.C. to New York. New York is north of Washington."

"It is?" Elaine said. "I thought it was east."

The Schneid rolled his eyes. "Look, the mantis started out up in Canada, right?"

"Right," Diane agreed.

"How did it cross the border into the U.S.? How did it get through Customs?"

"Who cares?" I said. And I went back to blowing bubbles into my phosphate.

"It's a movie!" Madeline said.

But The Schneid wasn't to be denied. "And what does it do when it gets to New York? Does it sit on top of the Empire State Building, ducking machine gun bullets like King Kong would? Does it take the bridge to sightsee Brooklyn? No, it takes the 'Manhattan Tunnel.'"

"So?" Madeline shrugged.

"It takes the tunnel? A manti*s* takes the *Manhattan* Tunnel?"

"So, maybe it wasn't smart enough to figure out which subway to take," Madeline said.

"Which subway do you take?" Elaine asked.

I rolled my eyes. The Schneid did too. "It could've asked which subway," he said. "It's not that hard to ask somebody."

"Unless you're a praying mantis," Diane said.

The Schneid ignored her comment. "You're missing the point. How can it take the Manhattan Tunnel? There is no *Manhattan* Tunnel!"

"So what? There's no Santa Claus either," Madeline said. "It's a *movie!*"

Elaine had been watching me blow bubbles into my phosphate. She stopped giggling. "There's really no Santa Claus?"

Diane laughed. "You *still* believe in Santa Claus?"

Elaine looked like she was about to cry. I took her hand and held it in mine. She sniffled.

"It's going to be okay, Elaine," I assured her. "And trust me…you can take the *D* to Brooklyn."

"I can?"

"Kings Highway…Sheepshead Bay…all the way to Coney Island."

She looked up at me and smiled. "I like the Tunnel of Love best."

34

NO DOUBT ABOUT IT

IT WAS SOMETIME in the middle of the night when The Mick died.

He'd been sitting at a soda fountain in the Bronx with Whitey Ford and Billy Martin—the three of them celebrating the Yankees' sweep of the Red Sox—and must have had one chocolate egg cream too many. He never saw the moose in the rear-view mirror. When the police found his dark blue, '57 Thunderbird wrapped around a flag pole in front of a post office on the Grand Concourse, they did what they were trained to do. They lowered the flag to half-mast.

I sat up in bed screaming.

Mom came rushing into my room. She sat on my bed, stroking my hair and sighed, not missing a stroke. "Tommy Salamo with the headlock and body slam again?"

I shook my head.

"That skinny, little thing with the bits of broccoli in her braces? Was she kissing you? Was that it?"

"Even worse." I pointed to the photo next to the alarm clock. "The Mick, Mom. They found his car wrapped around a flag pole."

Mom stopped her stroking. "Mickey Mantle?"

"He was on his way home after having a few egg creams in the Bronx. A moose ran a red light and rear-ended him."

"Honey, there are no moose in the Bronx."

"I don't know, Mom. It was a big moose. He had watery eyes and a big hump and was chewing his cud."

Mom said it sounded like what I saw what was a camel.

"No, it was a moose," I said. "Definitely a moose."

Mom fluffed my pillow. "Sweetie, the only moose I've ever seen in New York was that one at the Natural History Museum." She rubbed the back of her neck. "Well, I guess it could have wandered off into the Bronx."

"A stuffed moose?"

"Maybe it wasn't stuffed. Maybe it was still hungry." She glanced at my alarm clock and shook her head. "Two o'clock in the morning. Look, Philip, it was a nightmare, that's all. A moose did *not* hit Mickey Mantle."

"But it was so real!"

Mom sighed and reached for the Magic 8 Ball on my night stand. "You don't believe me? Here, ask it."

I took the shiny black ball from her hand. "Magic 8 Ball," I said, shaking it a few times, "was Mickey Mantle rear-ended by a moose in the Bronx?"

The message floated up into the plastic window...

CONCENTRATE AND ASK AGAIN

So I concentrated as hard as I could, shook the Magic 8 Ball a few times, and asked again, "Was Mickey Mantle rear-ended by a moose?"

VERY DOUBTFUL

"Then I can still meet him? I can still get his autograph?"

IT IS DECIDEDLY SO

35

SIGNS POINT TO YES

I DON'T KNOW when synagogue auctions first started. If you believe Uncle Harold, they go back to the weekly mah jongg game on the *Mayflower*.

Uncle Harold said the Pilgrims were supposed to land on Ellis Island, but there was a long waiting line to get in and you had to have a ticket. Since it was December and cold, he explained, nobody wanted to wait to get on Ellis Island, especially with Chanukah around the corner.

"Then Mrs. Standish said there was this nice Indian neighborhood up past the Bronx...good schools and all that. So they backed up the *Mayflower*, signaled a U-turn, and landed at the corner of Plymouth and Rockdale."

According to Uncle Harold, the problem was the congregation didn't have enough money to build a synagogue, so they auctioned off their muskets, Chanukah menorahs, and gefilte fish cleavers to the Indians, who would, of course, eventually use the cleavers against them.

Now I didn't know that much about early American Jewish history, but I knew enough from my bar mitzvah lessons with Myron to doubt there was a Jewish congregation on the *Mayflower*—maybe later on the Staten Island ferry, but not the *Mayflower*. What all this means is I can't tell you for certain what congregation held the first synagogue auction. I just know while it's possible there was a Jewish deli, there was no temple at Plymouth Rock.

Point is synagogue auctions have gone on to become a way to raise money for important synagogue things, such as the building fund and Hebrew school. They're also a way to get rid of some things the synagogue board doesn't want around anymore, like framed autographed photos of the last rabbi, who had this thing going on with the vice president of the sisterhood—even on the Sabbath, when you're supposed to rest and not do anyone.

The way the auction works is simple. You just write down your bid on a sheet of paper next to the item being auctioned, and the person with the highest bid wins. That's pretty much it.

The list of bids for a practically new Sears potty seat was already long and getting longer, but Linnie kept pleading with Mom, telling her it would be perfect for Linnie Junior. Finally, to stop Linnie from tugging on her arm, Mom entered a bid of $3.50, which temporarily put her third on the list.

And then I saw *the* list, the only list I wanted to be on. It was for two box seat tickets to the All-Star game in Cincinnati. The seats were in the row right above the American League dugout, which meant The Mick would be just a handshake away!

I knew box seats like that would cost $3.25 at Crosley Field's ticket window— a lot of money in those days since the minimum wage was about seventy-five cents an hour, and you were lucky if you made over $5,000 a year. Of course, your money went a lot further then too. Gas cost about twenty-nine cents a gallon. Nowadays, twenty-nine cents won't get your car backed out of your garage.

"Can we, Dad?" I dropped to my knees. "Can we?"

"How much? And get up. You'll get your pants dirty."

"So far the highest bid is eight dollars."

"For two box seats? And why are you still on your knees?"

I stood up and, brushing my pants with my hand, told him the money was for a worthy cause.

"And what would that be?"

I had to think fast. "Finding a new rabbi to replace Rabbi Breitzig?"

"Let's do it," Dad said. "And you can stop kissing my hand."

36

YOU COULDN'T BLAME me for hating Mr. Salamo. We were all set to claim the All-Star tickets when, at the last minute, he had to go in and top Dad's bid of eighteen dollars. And Mr. Salamo wasn't even a member of the Temple. Not only that, he wasn't even Jewish. Harry Salamo was our representative to the state legislature and a Republican at that.

Like I said, I hated Mr. Salamo. But I hated his son even more. And to make things even worse, Tommy Salamo hated me.

Tommy wanted to be a professional wrestler. That was his goal in life. One simple goal. He saw me as the first and second steps he had to take to get there, which was why he liked to step all over my face. Tommy's eyes would light up whenever he saw me. It meant a chance to practice.

Today, it was a new body slam. I should have seen him coming, but I didn't. I was on my way to the Boys' Room, daydreaming about winning the Mickey Mantle Tape-Measure Home Run Derby and being the Yankees' batboy, daydreaming about Annette Funicello, daydreaming just about everything but Tommy Salamo.

"*Well, look who's here!*" he whooped, a half-chewed candy cigarette dangling from his candy-stained mouth. *"CALL FOR PHILIP MORRR-ISSS!"*

Standing right in front of me, blocking the door to the Boys' Room and whooping manically, was all six-foot-three, three hundred and thirty pounds of Tommy "The Nose Hold" Salamo. He had a cauliflower nose that was running to his chapped lips, and his blackheads looked like he hadn't picked them in a week. His hair was Mohawked like Don Eagle's, and he pranced around me like a teenaged Gorgeous George in combat boots. He sneered at me, sneezed at me, then unbuttoned his fringed polyester Davy Crockett shirt, revealing a black tee shirt with *REMEMBER THE ALAMO!* blazed across the chest in blood-red, sequined letters. He had that look in his eyes I knew all too well, the look that meant my blood would soon run freely.

"Freeze!" His eyes crossed as he growled. "Don't make a move, Kleinmann!"

I wanted to tell him it was physically impossible for me to make a move if frozen, but thought better of it. Tommy Salamo wasn't the sort of zit-faced Neanderthal to take constructive criticism in the right spirit. Correcting Tommy "The Nose Hold" could be very painful...for me.

So I froze. Only then did I not move.

The Nose Hold wasted no time. He dropkicked me in the jaw, but he was just warming up. Before you could count *1-2-3* he had me in a nose hold, followed by a Boston crab, a Bayou crawdad, and what he called a Salamo butt bounce. Then he picked me up like I was nothing—and to him, that's what I was—lifted me high over his head and spun around, faster and faster like a 330-pound figure skater, shouting "*Ohhh yeahhh!*"

I knew what was coming next...but I was wrong.

With a high-pitched scream, Tommy Salamo dropped me. I landed smack on top of what was now the flatter flat chest of Madeline Schwartz, she of the broccolied braces. I looked up at The Nose Hold. He was bent over, holding his nuts and howling in pain.

Madeline had kicked him.

Tommy Salamo staggered into what he thought was the Boys' Room. But Tommy wasn't too bright and the kick to the nuts had just about turned his one light out. There were loud shrieks, followed by a high-pitched howl...and still another. The Nose Hold had staggered into the Girls' Room, and his nuts were paying the price.

I was still lying on top of Madeline, whose chest I'd flattened even more. Madeline didn't seem to mind too terribly, especially since my lips had landed on top of hers. She smiled in anticipation, and I could see her braces gleaming. Then I felt her lips press against mine. She tasted like broccoli.

"Wow! That was something! Thanks, Madeline!" I said. I could tell by her blush she thought I was talking about her kiss. I was about to tell her she misunderstood, that it wasn't her lips I was thanking her for, but my butt, which she'd saved in the nick of time. However, since I owed her my life, I thought it best not to disillusion her. So instead, I stammered out, "Wow... that...was some...kick, Madeline!"

And in truth it was. Madeline, who was probably no more than four-eight and eighty-five pounds, had leaped high into the air, spun around three hundred and sixty degrees, and executed a perfectly placed kick to Tommy

Salamo's scrotum. A black belt couldn't have done any better.

"Aw, it was nothing." She blushed again. "Just your basic *ushiro mawashi sushi*. We practice it all the time."

"Well, whatever it was, it was in the nick of time. You saved me, Madeline, you saved me. What else can I say?"

"You can say *yes*."

"*Yes* to what?"

"Box seats to see the game."

"The *game?*"

"The Yankees are playing the Clippers in an exhibition game in Columbus Saturday. You don't know that?"

The Columbus Clippers played in the American Association and were the Yankees' top farm team. I'd forgotten the game was Saturday afternoon...and I wasn't even thirty when you start having senior moments.

"Box seats?"

"My parents and their friends have four," Madeline explained. "Sixth row, behind the Yankee dugout. They can't make it Saturday and neither can their friends. So they gave two tickets to my big brother and two to me. Larry's driving. Want to go?"

This required some quick thinking. Me, sit in a car two-and-a-half hours, all the way to Columbus, with Madeline? The skinniest, most homely-looking, most flat-chested girl in the eighth grade? Madeline with those broccolied braces?

"Box seats?"

"Uh-huh."

"Sixth row, behind the Yankee dugout?"

"Uh-huh."

"Six rows from the playing field? Behind the Yankee dugout? Close enough to see Mickey Mantle's eyes?"

"Uh-huh. Uh-huh. Uh-huh."

She had me and she knew it. She put her hands on her curve-less hips and peered at me. "Well? What do you say?"

37

ASK ME AGAIN LATER

"HOW COME I CAN'T be Sitting B-B-B-Bull? Why do you get to be?"

I couldn't believe my ears. Fenny was actually taking on The Schneid. Fenny wasn't about to give up Sitting Bull sitting down.

"Cause I'm the head of this group," The Schneid said. "That makes me chief. Besides I'm related to Sitting Bull...on my mother's side."

"That's bull!" Jeannette Moskowitz said. "That's bull, Stuart Schneider, and you know it!"

Jeannette, Nancy Zimmerman, Lenny Gordon, Fenny, The Schneid, and I were all at Jeannette's house, munching the chocolate chip cookies Jeannette had baked while we struggled with our group project for Social Studies. Miss Tsuris The Agony had decided it would be a wonderful learning experience for the class—and a wonderful teaching break for her—by having us do group projects. We were studying the unsettling of the Indians as Americans settled the West. Our group project was Custer's Last Stand, and we'd decided to re-enact it for the class.

Nancy was the only one in our group who'd seen *They Died With Their Boots On* three times. She knew the final scene cold. Each time she saw it, she was so moved it brought tears to her eyes. "They've killed Errol Flynn!" she'd cry. "They've killed Errol Flynn!"

Since she was obviously crazy, Nancy was a natural for Crazy Horse.

Jeannette, who was the controlling sort and liked to give orders, decided she'd be General Terry, who was Custer's boss. Since it was Jeannette's house and Jeannette's cookies, we weren't about to tell her she couldn't be General Terry.

The Schneid suggested since Fenny couldn't be Sitting Bull, he play Rain-in-the-Face, who did the dirty work for Sitting Bull—unclogging toilets and all that kind of stuff.

Lenny, who looked like he was using chocolate chips as war paint, wasn't saying anything, and I knew he wasn't going to. Lenny wanted to be a mime when he grew up, which was why he was always practicing keeping his mouth shut.

"So what now?" Jeannette asked.

Lenny eyed the plate of cookies, rubbed his belly, licked his lips, and grabbed a handful of cookies. We figured he had a lot of gall, so that's who he became…Gall, the fierce Sioux war chief.

That left me as Custer.

General Terry gave Gall a playful whack on the head as he reached for another handful of the chocolate chips, then headed back to the kitchen, Gall following her. I was now surrounded by Crazy Horse, Rain-in-the-Face, and Sitting Bull. They looked at me, then looked at one another and grinned. They had me, and they knew it. Rain-in-the-Face was first to attack.

"I can't b-b-b-believe it," he said. "I can't believe you're d-d-d-doing it. Ugh."

"Believe what?"

"It," Rain said.

"He's talking about your date with Madeline," Crazy Horse said. "Madeline told Maureen Levenson you're going with her to the Yankee game in Columbus. Maureen told Stevie Berman, Stevie told Harriet Linzer, and now everybody's talking about it...well, just about everybody but Lenny."

"*I do not* have a date with Madeline!"

"Sure you do," Rain said. "You're in d-d-d-denial."

They all started whooping it up, except for Sitting Bull who'd been bull dozing.

"If I were you, I'd wear sunglasses so nobody recognizes you," Crazy Horse said.

"Yeah, the d-d-d-darker the better," Rain said. "You d-d-d-don't want anybody from school to see you with her."

"But it's a night game," I said. "You don't have dark sunglasses on at a night game. Nobody does."

"You want to get technical or do you want to keep your honor intact?" Sitting Bull said. "What's it going to be, dark glasses or a red face?"

"But Custer's not supposed to be a redskin," interjected Crazy Horse.

Sitting Bull rolled his eyes, then looked at Crazy Horse in utter disbelief. Rain-in-the-Face laughed so hard he should have been Tears-on-the Face.

"Well, all I know is it's a good thing they're not televising it in color," Crazy Horse said, trying to recoup.

"It's going to be on TV?" I moaned. "Everybody in school will be watching."

"Kids from other schools too," Sitting Bull said. "Just don't let the camera catch you with her."

"Look guys, do I have to use sign language? *I do not have a date with Madeline.*"

"You're going to the game with her? Keeping score with her? That's a date in my book," Crazy Horse said.

"Mine too," said General Terry, proudly marching back from the kitchen with another platter of cookies, Gall following her. Gall nodded in agreement.

They had me outnumbered. I could protest all I wanted, but I could see there was no way I was going to win. So I threw my hands up. Which is what Custer should have done at the Little Big Horn.

38

"SCORECARDS! CAN'T TELL the players *without a scorecard!"*

Larry plunked down $1.50 and bought me a scorecard. Larry's girlfriend gave him a stern look, so he bought one for Madeline, too. Not that it mattered. Madeline couldn't tell the players with or without a scorecard. Madeline knew as much about baseball as Elaine Novak knew about math. Maybe less.

Of course baseball scorecards really aren't scorecards. You don't use them to keep track of the score—you have the big scoreboard in left field for that. The scorecard is used to scribble down everything that happens in the inning: that Bauer walked and stole second; that Martin sacrificed him to third; that Mickey hit a home run that landed halfway up the Upper Deck. *Keeping score* gives you a batter-by-batter replay of the game. Usually it's done in modern hieroglyphics. *BB* means a walk...*K* means a strikeout...*DF-7* means a deep fly ball caught by the leftfielder...*ZZ* means the umpire had to have been sleeping.

So there I was, decked out in my brand new *THE MICK* tee shirt, my Rawlings *Mickey Mantle* glove in hand, slouched next to Madeline Schwartz in the sixth row, first base line, baseball cap pulled down over my eyes, my sticky face buried in cotton candy. It didn't take much to imagine the announcement boomed over the Clipper Field P.A:

"GOOD AFTERNOON...AND WELCOME TO CLIPPER FIELD...AND TODAY'S EXHIBITION GAME BETWEEN THE NEW YORK YANKEES AND YOUR COLUMBUS CLIPPERS...AND NOW PLEASE STAND...AS WE RECOGNIZE THE BOY IN THE SIXTH ROW, FIRST BASE LINE SITTING NEXT TO MADELINE SCHWARTZ...."

"NO!" I screamed. But my scream was drowned out by the thunderous roar of fifteen thousand voices. They'd just announced it was the first-ever Foul Ball Day at Clipper Field, which coincided with it being the first-ever annual one at that.

"WELCOME EVERYONE TO FOUL BALL DAY AT CLIPPER FIELD...CATCH A FOUL BALL HIT BY A YANKEE TODAY...COME DOWN TO THE PLAYING FIELD AFTER THE GAME...AND THE YANKEE WHO HIT THE FOUL BALL WILL AUTOGRAPH THE BALL FOR YOU!...PLUS YOU'LL HAVE YOUR PHOTO TAKEN WITH HIM!"

I rubbed my eyes, wiped the cotton candy off my face, and pounded my *Mickey Mantle* glove. I was ready for The Mick. I knew he'd hit a foul ball into the sixth row, first base line, and that I'd catch it.

With one late swing of his bat I knew I was finally going to meet Mickey Mantle.

39

NOTHING HAPPENED IN the first two innings. Oh, there was Skowron's homer in the first, a two-run shot off who else but Mel Fowler, the natural starter for the Clippers on Foul Ball Day. And there was Mortie de Cochrane's round-tripper in the second, which tied things up for the Clippers. There was Mickey's diving, backhanded catch in deep center, robbing Sammy Concierge of a sure triple, and a near unassisted triple play by Fritzie Bickel, which would have put the Clipper second baseman in the record book. There was the busty striptease star, tassels twirling every which way as she swiveled past an usher and two security guards on her dash to the pitcher's mound, where she planted a fat one on a startled Don Larsen. There was the ten-minute brawl when Larsen was hit in the back by a payback fastball thrown with heated envy by Fowler.

But not one Yankee had lined or popped up a foul ball into the box seats along the first base line in the direction of the sixth row. By the third inning there were no more chants of *WE WANT A HIT! WE WANT A HIT!* Like the rest of our section, Madeline and I had joined the growing chant of *FOUL BALL! FOUL BALL! WE WANT A FOUL BALL!*

Not that foul balls weren't flying into the stands, you understand. Some old guy sitting three rows behind the Clippers' dugout got smashed in the mouth trying to catch one hit by Tony Kubek. There was a roar as he managed to stagger to his feet holding up his dentures in one hand and the ball in the other. And some loony fan in the first row in the upper deck almost fell out of the stands reaching for a fastball fouled off by Yogi.

But not one Yankee had lined or popped up a foul ball anywhere near the sixth row, first base line. We were now in the seventh, running out of innings, when Mickey strode up to the plate and stepped into the batter's box again. He'd been up three times already, singling twice and doubling. But he hadn't hit even one foul ball. He was due, and I knew it.

The Mick must have known it too. There was a smile on his face as he swung early and popped a curve ball, which curved high, straight toward the box seats in the sixth row on the first base line. I pounded the pocket of my Rawlings *Mickey Mantle* glove. I was ready.

And that's when it happened.

The roar of the crowd was pierced by Madeline's hysterical scream. Instinctively, I turned my head. And instinctively the ball, the ball that was supposed to introduce me to Mickey Mantle, bounced off my glove into the crowd.

"No!" I screamed.

"NO!" Madeline screamed even louder.

It was in her hair, on her clothes, on her hand-held scorecard. It was all over her. I knew I had to do something and do it fast. There was too much to wipe off with a hot dog wrapper. I couldn't even wipe it off with two or three. I had no choice. I ripped off my tee shirt, my brand new *THE MICK* tee shirt.

"Look at me!" Madeline sobbed. "Look at me!"

"You're going to be okay," I told her.

"Look at me!"

"Forgive me, Mick," I said. Mickey Mantle's face was quickly smeared with bird shit as I wiped off Madeline's.

40

IT WAS HARD NOT TO, but I wasn't about to
ever again question   the constitutionality of oral book
reports—even though they're clearly   a violation of the
cruel and unusual clause of the Eighth Amendment. Mr.
Weinerschein had made it clear if I protested just once
more I'd be sent to the principal's office with no hope of
escaping and finding asylum in the school library.

So there I was, quietly sitting in English as Stanley
Kaplan finished giving his book report on something that
sounded like The Micro-Macro Theory of Crocodile Tears.
You could never be too sure what Stanley was expounding
upon since Stanley was head and shoulders above everyone
else in English class. And it wasn't just because he stood
six-feet and three-and-an-eighth inches in his stocking feet.
Stanley was ranked #1 academically in the entire eighth
grade, ahead of even The Schneid. Stanley was so smart
that not only was he fluent in Latin, but he could speak it
with an ancient Greek accent. Stanley was also class
president, class pet, and ranked #3 in the state among
novice square dance callers, even though he sometimes
called in ancient Pig Latin.

"Okay, who wants to go next?" Mr. Weinerschein
asked.

Mr. Weinerschein was the English department's resident intellectual, having read *Gulliver's Travels* unabridged at the age of nine. When not teaching, he liked to take long nature walks around his block. He could also yodel, which he once did when reading *Swiss Family Robinson* aloud to his class. Mr. Weinerschein was short, maybe five-four, a shy, balding milquetoast, who never used contractions in his sentences when speaking. What he did do, was punctuate his speaking with farts.

"Okay, I will ask again. *Who wants to go next?*"

One hand shot up. "Me! Me!"

It was bouncing Harriet Linzer. If Elaine Novak had the biggest boobs in the entire eighth grade, Harriet Linzer was a close second. Where she beat Elaine was in bounce to the ounce. Harriet's boobs were definitely bouncier. And they'd bounced all over the place in her tryout for the school cheerleading team. Word around school was that Harriet was in the midst of a toe-touch jump when one of those bouncing boobs hit her in the head and she was knocked out cold. That was the end of Harriet's cheerleading career.

Harriet's bouncing boobs certainly had their effect on Mr. Weinerschein. He gave Harriet straight *A*'s, even though she was always a week late in handing in her homework and was so careless with her spelling that sometimes she left out the *n* in Linzer.

"Great job, Harriet," Mr. Weinerschein said, as Harriet finished the ten-minute windup of her book report and, for the moment, her bouncing. "Any questions, class?...No questions?... Jeannette?...Howard?...How about you, Philip?"

157

I shook my head. Mr. Weinerschein nodded his. "Okay then...why don't you go next."

For the first time ever in English class my knees weren't shaking as I rose from my desk. This time I was confident. I'd read the book cover to cover and knew I had the book report that was going to put me on the Book Report Honor Roll. *MY SON IS A BOOK REPORT HONOR STUDENT* would be on the back bumper of Mom's Riviera, maybe the front bumper too.

I was ready, and I knew it.

41

"PHILIP, TELL THE CLASS what your book report is on." Mr. Weinerschein strutted to the blackboard, picked up an eraser, and farted, expelling chalk dust and gas.

"The 1957 Yearbook of the New York Yankees."

Mr. Weinerschein was speechless, but the rest of the class wasn't. There were guffaws and giggles, boos and cheers—your basic eighth-grade cacophony.

"You can't do a book report on a baseball yearbook." Harriet thrust her boobs at Mr. Weinerschein. "Isn't that right, Mr. Weinerschein?"

"Well...I...don't...know," Mr. Weinerschein stammered, obviously taken aback by the thrust of Harriet's position. "No one has ever—"

"A Yankee yearbook isn't a book!" pronounced Stanley in his ancient Greek accent.

"That's right!" Jessica Stern said.

"Yeah!" said crazy Harvey Meshugana.

There was a chorus of guffaws.

"Let him do it, Mr. Weinerschein!" Madeline said. "Give him a chance!"

"He's read it!" David Shmedrik said.

"Yeah!" said crazy Harvey Meshugana.

And back and forth and forth and back it went, with everybody in the class taking sides and shouting until Peter Carella stood up and started singing the alma matter. That stopped the shouting as everybody stood up and sang with him. Those who didn't know the Latin words in the refrain, which was about half the class, faked it. So besides hearing *sursam et suman*, you got *susan and herman* even though they never went out together.

They'd finished the chorus and were starting to go at each other again when somebody cried out "Second verse!" So they stopped belting each other and belted out *susan and herman* again. They'd just about finished the second verse when someone yelled, "Third verse!"

Everybody stopped and looked around, dumbfounded.

"There is no third verse!" Harriet stomped her foot, which got her boobs bouncing again.

What could they do? So back they went, yelling and belting over whether my book report was a book report. But Mr. Weinerschein had had enough.

"I have had enough!" he shouted, throwing an eraser at the gong next to the flag in the front corner.

Everyone stopped at the sound of the gong.

"So what do you say, Mr. Weinerschein?" Harriet asked. Are you going to let him? *Yes* or *No?*"

Poor Mr. Weinerschein didn't know what to do. On the one hand, there was Harriet fluttering her eyelashes at him and thrusting. On the other, there was Madeline saying that according to her big brother Larry, who had just finished his first year of law school, questioning a book report was unconstitutional.

"It's in the Fourth Amendment," Madeline said. "I can recite it with my eyes closed."

And she did.

"The validity of a book report shall not be held in question by this school or any other school."

Mr. Weinerschein said he wasn't up on the Fourth Amendment since he was an only child. "How can anyone expect me to know the Constitution?" His eyes welled with tears. "I never had a big brother who was in law school."

"I have a big brother in pre-law," Howard Kodesh said.

Mr. Weinerschein ignored him. He took two deep breaths to compose himself, slapped his chest, arched his right eyebrow, and farted. He was back in control.

"This is America," Mr. Weinerschein said, and of course he was right. "We will vote on it, class. We will vote on whether the 1957 Yankees Yearbook can be a book report or not. All who say it is, raise your hand."

Madeline, Jeanette, Harvey, Peter Carella, and David Shmedrik raised their hands. So did Howard and me. And Marni Pidler and Frank Gifford—the student council rep, not the football player. So too did Zoe Zanger, Tracy Ferraro, Lisa Kuflink, Boris Shaw, Randi Wasserman, Mark Shapiro…and Marcia Gilbert, who was always late to class.

"Okay," Mr. Weinerschein said, as he finished counting hands. "Who says *No*, that the 1957 New York Yankees Yearbook, cannot be a book report? Raise your hands high."

Harriet and Stanley raised their hands. So did Jessica, Harvey, and Hughie Koncusion, who was captain of the football team despite being a head case. And Annette

Analvitch, Penny Scharlot, Alex Bulgatski, Igor von Martin, Gil Rabin, Tony Boomerelli, Sarah Treitler, Greg Deutsch, Stephanie Barasch, Carolee Wolfram, and Nadeem Curry, who was an exchange student from New Delhi and the first of his family to be mugged in Brooklyn.

Mr. Weinerschein counted the hands. Then counted again. "It is a tie...a tie, 16-16."

"But there's only thirty-one in the class, Mr.Weinerschein," said Stanley, who was a whiz at adding double figures with or without an abacus.

"Stanley is correct," Mr. Weinerschein said. "Okay, who voted twice?"

We all turned around and looked at crazy Harvey Meshugana.

"It is all up to you, Harvey," Mr. Weinerschein said. "What is it going to be? *Yes* or *No*?"

42

"LET US HAVE YOU begin at the beginning," Mr. Weinerschein said. "How does the yearbook start off? What is the first thing we learn?"

"*There's a whole kernel of wheat in every Wheaties flake,*" I answered.

There was a chorus of giggles...maybe two.

"Excuse me?"

I opened up the yearbook and pointed to the ad. "It's right here on the inside cover. *There's a whole kernel of wheat in every Wheaties flake.*"

"Is that it? That is the first thing we learn?"

"Oh no, Mr. Weinerschein," I said. "*Tomorrow, start the day the winners' way—with Wheaties the Breakfast of Champions.*"

The giggles turned to guffaws. I thought Lisa Kuflink was going to have a cow right there on the spot. Just about everyone in the room was giggling and guffawing except Mr. Weinerschein...and maybe crazy Harvey Meshugana.

"Can we move on, Philip? What can you tell us about the characters?"

"Characters?"

"Yes, characters. You do remember characters, do you not? In our book reports we always talk about characters."

I tried to tell Mr. Weinerschein there were lots of characters on the Yankees. Like Billy Martin, who liked to double up on Johnny Walker. And Miller Howell, who didn't see the point of running to the mound when he could waddle.

"I am afraid that is not what we mean by characters," Mr. Weinerschein said. "Characters are what the book is about. Like in *From Here to Eternity*, Maggio is a character."

Well, I wasn't about to contradict Mr. Weinerschein and tell him Joe DiMaggio was not a character. Yogi Berra, maybe yes, but not DiMag. Joltin' Joe may have played his way into Cooperstown, but any baseball fan worth his salt shaker could tell you that when it came to parties Joe DiMaggio was strictly colorless.

"Can you tell us who your favorite character is in the...ahem, *yearbook*?" Mr. Weinerschein asked.

"Easy," I mumbled. "The Mick."

"Who?"

"No, *Who*'s on first," Stanley answered.

"What?"

"He's on second."

"The Mick's in center," Howard Kodesh chipped in.

Mr. Weinerschein ignored him and flatulently strutted his way back over to the blackboard. "And why is he your favorite character? What does he teach us?"

"Humility," I said. "Should I read you what Mickey Mantle says in the yearbook?"

"By all means." Mr. Weinerschein rolled his eyes and this time not at bouncing Harriet Linzer.

So I turned to page 18 and read aloud...

"After I hit a home run I have a habit of running the bases with my head down. I figure the pitcher already feels bad enough without me showing him up rounding the bases."

There was applause from the back row. I couldn't be sure, but I think it was Harvey Meshugana.

Well, that got everybody going again. There was more giggling and guffawing. Poor Peter Carella had long run out of verses to *susan and herman*, but it turned out it didn't matter.

"That is enough, class!" Mr. Weinerschein said. And he arched his eyebrow, threw another eraser, and farted.

43

WITHOUT A DOUBT

THE NUMBERS THAT HAD drawn excitement the next morning were *one-three-nine-two*. That was the winning combination in Esso's weekly Mickey Mantle Tape-Measure Home Run Derby and had everyone in school buzzing. Everyone, that is, except me.

The combination was The Schneid's. Fenny had pulled me away from my gym locker and sat me down on a bench, explaining The Schneid didn't want to tell me because he thought his gloating would upset me.

"Why would I be upset?" I asked, trying to hide my being upset. "The Schneid's always gloating. Remember how he gloated about talking his way out of having to run five laps around the gym for being late? You remember, don't you?"

"Wasn't that the j-j-j-jock-strap one?" Fenny said.

"That's the one all right."

The Schneid had told Mr. Sumersaltz he'd gotten so caught up thinking about riding pummel horses that he was halfway out of the locker room when he realized he'd put his Fruit-of-the-Loin jock strap on backward.

Mr. Summersaltz had been so taken aback by The Schneid's audacity he'd thrown up his hands and said, "Forget it!"

Then there was the time The Schneid had gone around to every table in the lunchroom—even Ziggy Zagsky's—gloating that in a previous life he was Washington's aide in charge of making room reservations. The Schneid said he knew everywhere George Washington slept, on which night, and on which side of the bed, but that he couldn't say *who* Washington slept with since George wasn't a kiss-and-tell general.

And now The Schneid was actually telling everyone at school—everyone, that is, but me—that Esso had called to tell him his *one-three-nine-two* was last week's winner. The Schneid had correctly said Mickey would hit one home run and it would travel 392 feet.

"He didn't tell you b-b-b-because he's afraid if you're upset you won't feel like playing HORSE after school."

"So?"

"He said he n-n-n-needs the money to buy a 1934 Byrd Antarctic Expedition II stamp."

44

ASK ME AGAIN LATER

I KNEW NEXT THURSDAY the flagpole at school would be at half-mast. It's always half-mast on Report Card Day. I used to hope they'd cancel it because of snow until I realized there aren't too many snow days in June, even if you're in Cincinnati.

I've seen kids go nuts on Report Card Day, so crazy some have threatened to kill themselves...or their teacher. So far neither has happened, although one year a boy did hurl himself into the Little Miami River. But since it was June and the river bed had turned into a wadi, no one even bothered to call the life squad. The coroner was disappointed, but everyone knew he'd make up for it during tax season.

Of course, nowadays Report Card Day isn't like it was when I was thirteen and sprouting zits. Back then, Report Card Day used to mean telephoned bomb threats, that is until the school finally got wise and had its phone number unlisted. When I was a kid, Report Card Day meant protest marches with signs like *REPORT CARDS UNFAIR TO UNDERACHIEVERS.* And it meant hunger strikes, at least until the Mister Softee truck came along.

I'd never gotten an *F* on a report card. Heck, I'd never even got an *F* on a test, unless you count Home Economics, which I most certainly didn't. I'd only taken Home Ec as an elective because Mom said it was important for me to know how to cook and sew in case I got married and someday my wife left me for another man. The *F* came when I flunked the final test of the marking period. It was all because I was the only one in the class who was truthful. On the essay question on how to boil water, I'd written *What difference does it make? Whoever heard of boiling TV dinners?*

Like I said, I'd never gotten an *F* on my report card. I'd never gotten a *D* either. But now, thanks to Elaine and her tight sweaters, I was in danger of making history. And I knew if Mom and Dad saw a *D* on my report card they'd do more than incarcerate me. They'd forbid me from entering the Mickey Mantle Tape-Measure Home Run Derby for the rest of the year, and there would go my chance to be the Yankees' batboy and meet The Mick.

"Extra credit," The Schneid was saying. "That's what you need, Felipe. You get Miss Phylum to give you extra credit, and you're saved from a *D*."

The Schneid and I, along with a reluctant Howard Kodesh, were pitching pennies in the Boys' Room. According to nationally established Pitching Penny rules, the penny landing closest to the wall wins.

You're supposed to pitch pennies with pennies, but The Schneid said he'd studied the Presidents and that we'd be better off throwing Franklin Roosevelt against the wall instead of Lincoln.

"Forget dimes, Schneid," I said. "What do I do to get extra credit in Biology?"

"Don't be silly, Felipe. You write a paper for her."

"On what?"

"On what? We are talking about Biology, right?"

"Right," I said. "Biology."

"Look, it's simple. Tell Miss Phylum you're going to write a paper that's biological."

"You mean like on S'mores?" Howard asked.

"That's *spores,*" The Schneid said.

"I don't know, Schneid," I said. "Don't you think I should ask her first?"

"Then ask." The Schneid threw a kiss to Lincoln, then threw him against the wall.

It didn't take The Schneid long to clean Howard and me out of pennies. But it took the rest of the day for me to adjust my backbone enough to walk up to Miss Phylum and ask her if I could write a paper for extra credit.

"Sure," Miss Phylum said. "But it has to be on something we've touched on in class or on field trips. Like frogs and worms and poison ivy."

I asked her if praying mantises would be okay to do even though you wouldn't be able to touch them till they finished mating.

She rubbed her chin. "I guess so."

"Thanks, Miss Phylum. Because I'm thinking of switching careers."

"Oh?" She pushed her glasses up. "From what to what?"

I told her I'd always wanted to someday be a canine psychologist specializing in golden retrievers, but now I wasn't so sure. "I'm thinking maybe I'll practice on praying mantises."

Anyway, I wrote my paper on how female praying mantises need psychological help since they'll sometimes behead their mates before they have sex with them. I titled the paper *Getting the Munchies*. I won't bore you with a recital of all I wrote about praying mantis psychosis. Point is the paper upped me to a *C* in Biology.

It meant Mom and Dad wouldn't make me drop out of the Mickey Mantle Tape-Measure Home Run Derby.

45

CANNOT PREDICT NOW

"FINALLY, I WANT TO THANK Bezalel," I said, with a touch of sarcasm in my voice. "For if Bazalel had been out playing baseball, or whatever they played back then in the Sinai, instead of being stuck at home with nothing to do but build the Ark for his cousin Moses, who couldn't do it himself because he was all thumbs, there wouldn't be a Torah portion about Bezalel...."

There was a murmur from the congregation.

I'd finished my chanting to *shofar* calls and stood there on the *bimah* giving my bar mitzvah thank-you speech. I'd wanted to include a thank-you in advance for all the presents I was going to be bestowed with, but Myron had vetoed that, insisting it was tacky and something bar mitzvah boys just didn't do unless they lived in Shaker Heights.

The preparation for my bar mitzvah had itself been a family extravaganza, which troubled Rabbi Breitzig. He'd been upset upon hearing Mom was going whole hog, believing anything doing with hogs was in strict violation of the dietary laws.

But nothing was about to stop Mom. She was on a mission.

To Mom, it was important I look impeccable when reading the Torah, even if my reading wasn't. The way Mom figured it, none of her friends was going to come up to her afterwards and say "Congratulations, Leah...but shouldn't Skip have chanted *AT-zei* instead of *OH-say,* like you sing in *The Star Spangled Banner?*"

But how I *looked*...well, that was another matter.

There were nights Mom couldn't sleep, worried that if my bar mitzvah suit didn't impress her Canasta group, someone was sure to say "Wasn't it horrible for his bar mitzvah, Leah Kleinmann's son was wearing a suit from Penney's?"

So Mom had looked for a tailor with experience in hand-stitching bar mitzvah suits. Aunt Helen had suggested Chiam Chang, but Mom had ruled him out—unlike Aunt Helen, Mom had trouble understanding Cantonese-accented Yiddish, which was all Chiam spoke. Finally, she settled on Moshe Bader, who'd done circumcisions before moving on to cutting sharkskin instead of foreskin.

Moshe was a jolly, broad-faced, little man, never seen without a plate of rugelach and a bottle of Dr. Brown's Celery Soda—it was why he had to keep pulling his pants up over his paunch. Moshe had a graying beard, bushy eyebrows, and a cherry nose. He probably could have passed for a younger Saint Nicholas if he wasn't always spending Christmas Eve at synagogue...and if he wasn't afraid of falling off rooftops.

"Three buttons," Mom said. "I think the jacket should have three buttons. Don't you?"

"Two is better," Moshe said. "You want three buttons? We make it three buttons. But I think three buttons, you're throwing away money. Three buttons, he'll lose one, and you wind up with two anyway."

Mom said he had a good point. "What about the pants?"

Moshe lowered his head, unloosed the tape measure from around his neck, and lifted his chin. He scratched his neck, then looped the tape measure back around it. He tilted his head, studying me.

"You're not going to measure him with the *tape*?" Mom asked.

Moshe told Mom he didn't need to, that he'd been tailoring long enough to know one inch from two. "Pants, two inches," he said. "Better we should leave two inches for growing room."

"In the length or the waist?" Mom asked.

"Both." Moshe had me turn around. "And maybe two inches in the seat too."

My thank-you speech, which I'd spent almost ten minutes crafting during the seventh-inning stretch of the Reds-Cubs game the day before, was met with deafening silence. Except for when I explained why it wasn't my fault Mickey Mantle wouldn't be coming to the party tomorrow even though the Yankees had the day off. Uncle Harold rose to his feet, shouting "He should've been invited!" before Dad and Uncle Nate wrestled him down. The rest of the family...how should I put it? They reacted in their own way. Grandpa Albert buried his face in his *tallit*. Grandma Bessie sat there paralyzed, and it wasn't from her stroke. Mom cried as the Rottenbergs, the Shmedriks, the Fishbeins, the Sterns, and the Kreplachs all marched to the front door, dragging their upcoming bar mitzvah boys with them. Her face soaked with tears, Mom stared at me, holding up a quickly scribbled note that said, in big, bold capital letters, *INCARCERATION.* Dad looked at Mom and asked if I was too old to be put up for adoption.

Rabbi Breitzig rushed to the pulpit and held up his hands. He probably would have genuflected, but rabbis don't genuflect. Not even in Reform temples.

"Please, please! Everyone sit back down," he pleaded, wiping the sweat off his brow with his *tallit* and glaring at me. "I'm going to have a talk with Philip. He's going to re-do his thank-you speech and deliver it at a special morning service tomorrow…after I've read and approved it."

A hand shot up from near the back.

"Yes?"

"What time will services start?"

"Just as soon as *All My Children* is over."

Everyone sat back down. And with that, Rabbi Breitzig grabbed the *yarmulke* off my head and yanked me off the *bimah.*

46

IT IS CERTAIN

MOM WAS FURIOUS… and this time not at me.

My thank-you speech had been reworked and delivered the next morning, an hour to the dot after *All My Children* went off the air. It went off pretty well too—my speech, that is. Sure, Mom had raised one plucked eyebrow when I thanked her for her timely ovulation, but otherwise she was all smiles. I could read her lips: *See, Lou, I knew he could do it.*

No, what had Mom seething wasn't me. It was Shuller's Wigwam, which she'd booked for my bar mitzvah party.

Despite its name the Wigwam had nothing to do with Indians, though on weekends you did need a reservation since the Wigwam had the best relish tray in the city. "The creamed herring is to die for" was what you'd hear coming from under hair dryers all over Cincinnati. *The relish tray*…that was why the Wigwam was fast becoming the in-place for bar mitzvah parties as well as bingo games.

And that was the problem Mom had run into.

The Wigwam had two party rooms available, Room A and Room C—Room B being used as a stockroom for jars of creamed herring. Mom had booked Room A because of its huge picture window that offered an unobstructed view of the fire house across the street.

"Suppose there's a fire and the alarm doesn't work," she said to Dad. "If we're in Room A we can jump up and down in front of the window to get the attention of the firemen. Then we can wave them over here."

Dad explained that wouldn't be necessary because Shuller's had put overhead sprinklers in each room. "Regulations, Leah," he said. "They're required to."

"Yes, but what happens if they're not working? Or suppose they work, but they keep on sprinkling and won't shut off? The flowers, all our beautiful flowers, will be flooded! And your Aunt Helen can't swim!"

Dad was speechless.

"Better we take Room A, Lou, where the firemen can see us waving for help."

So Room A it was...or so Mom had thought.

She'd gone to the Wigwam early to check that everything in Room A was set up in order before people began arriving. Mom had spent hours working on who would sit with who and where, being careful to make sure Aunt Helen didn't somehow wind up at Aunt Tillie's table. The two weren't on speaking terms since they sat at the same table at the last Hadassah luncheon, blotting the same shade of coral lipstick. Mom also wanted to make sure the centerpieces from the florist were set up in Yankee and not Red Sox caps, which would have been disastrous.

Anyway, when Mom opened the door to Room A, she just about had a cow. The room was already filled with people, and they weren't there for the bar mitzvah party.

They were playing bingo.

Mom went storming upstairs to the Wigwam manager, who told her because of its acoustics, Room A was being used for bingo that night.

"Those aren't spring chickens in there, you know," he said. "Even with a mike, *B-7* can sound like *G-47* when you're that age."

Mom pointed out in the Bronx, where she was from before she went to Oberlin College on a figure skating scholarship, a bar mitzvah party took precedence over a bingo game. The Wigwam manager reminded her she was in Cincinnati, not the Bronx, and that in the Queen City, bingo was king. He said he was willing to give her a choice of Room C or B, the creamed herring room.

So that's why the party was in Room C, even though Mom could have taken B for considerably less money, which no doubt would have made my father happy. Dad had already hit the roof on what the party was going to cost him, particularly when Mom told him she thought she could get Buddy Holly for under five thousand.

47

OUTLOOK GOOD

UNCLE LEONARD WAS PLAYING a brand new accordion. He'd bought it from Wurlitzer after being assured it was water proof—the C-major keys had stuck after his dog peed on his old accordion. Yet even though he was playing *Take Me Out to The Ballgame* as a *hora* number, Uncle Leonard and his new, water-proof accordion weren't attracting much attention at my bar mitzvah party.

What was attracting attention was this kid who looked like he could have been my twin brother if he hadn't had a nose job. Like me, he was dressed in a navy blazer, dark gray pants, and unbuttoned-down blue shirt. Only his striped tie was red and black with a smear of brie with apricot jam. Mine was blue, orange, and chopped liver.

The kid was arguing with Aunt Tillie, who, with her nose job, looked like she could have been his mother.

Aunt Tillie, if I haven't mentioned before, was a thin, gray-haired woman who spent summers in Miami and winters in Maine. She was tall with a wide mouth, buck teeth, and glasses sliding down her nose. She kind of looked like a skinny Eleanor Roosevelt. She was wearing an olive green dress with large pimento polka dots and stained green heels, on which she pronated.

The argument was steadily getting louder, turning heads around the room.

"You okay, Mrs. Bachrach?" Mr. Farkis had decided maybe he should come to Aunt Tillie's rescue. He'd taken a small legal pad from the pocket inside his suit jacket and was ready for action.

"I think alligators have the right idea. They eat their young," Aunt Tillie said. "I think alligators have the right idea. They eat their young." Like I told you, Aunt Tillie was sometimes in the habit of repeating herself.

Mr. Farkis handed Aunt Tillie his card and asked her to call his office should she be assaulted or sassed.

"All this is a lot of bunk!" spat my would-be twin.

Aunt Tillie gave him a look of disgust as she wiped her neck.

"I don't believe in God!" he said, spraying Aunt Tillie with spittle.

Apparently what he *did* believe in were the trays of hors d'oeuvres weaving through the party. He'd cleaned off a tray of *brie en croute* and now had his eyes on the platter of pigs-in-a-blanket—the Blintzkys had assured Mom the pigs had been raised kosher. Before he could be offered one, he smiled at the server and snatched three off the tray.

"You don't believe in God? Then who made the world?" Aunt Tillie was shaking in her girdle as her voice rose. "Mickey Mantle? You probably worship Mickey Mantle."

"Course not," the kid answered. He polished off the second blanketed pig. "Willie Mays is my idol."

I thought Aunt Tillie was going to drop her girdle right there on the spot. Instead, she pulled herself together and waved me over.

180

"Skip," she said, "this is your Cousin Philip from Baltimore."

"*Bell*-more," Cousin Philip corrected her.

"On the south shore of Long Island," I added.

Aunt Tillie looked puzzled, though she'd never admit it. "Well, aren't you two going to say hello? Aren't you two going to say hello?"

"Hi, Philip," I said.

"Whatever," Cousin Philip replied, eying a new tray of hors oeuvres. They looked beyond arm's reach, but he managed to grab one.

"Care for any ma'am?" asked the server.

Aunt Tillie nodded toward Cousin Philip. "What is that he's got?"

"Rocky Mountain oyster," the server said.

"*Rocky Mountain* oyster?"

"Calf testicle. We poach them."

Cousin Philip took the calf testicle out of his mouth and set it back on the tray.

"Your Cousin Philip's disgusting," Aunt Tillie said. "A disgusting atheist....your cousin's a disgusting atheist."

"I am not!" sprayed Cousin Philip.

"You're not an atheist? You said you don't believe in God. That makes you an atheist."

"I am *no*t an atheist!"

"Then what do you believe in?"

"I believe in Willie Mays."

Aunt Tillie shook her head. "He worships Willie Mays. He worships Willie Mays."

"That's ridiculous," I said.

"See!" Aunt Tillie said, looking at Cousin Philip with disdain as she wiped saliva off her chin. "The bar mitzvah boy says Willie Mays is not God. The bar mitzvah boy says Willie Mays is not God."

"I heard you the first time," Cousin Philip said.

"How can you think Willie Mays is God?" I asked.

"I never said Willie Mays is God. I said he's my *idol*."

I shook my head. "If you idolize a baseball player, you idolize Mickey Mantle."

Cousin Philip laughed.

"Laugh all you want," I said. "Mickey Mantle is the best player in baseball."

"No way!" Cousin Philip's face reddened. "WILLIE MAYS IS BETTER THAN MICKEY MANTLE!"

"That's insane," I said.

"Oh yeah? Mickey Mantle wears combat boots."

"That's stupid."

"Mickey Mantle runs like a girl."

"He does not!"

"Does so! And Willie's a better hitter."

"You can't be serious. Mickey's hitting .419 for the month. What's Willie average?" I smiled. I knew I had him.

"So he's in a slump. Watch him break out with a batch of homers."

"Mickey Mantle can out-homer Willie Mays any day of the week."

"NO WAY!"

"YES WAY!"

"I'll bet you at the end of the year Willie has more homers." Cousin Philip jabbed his finger in my chest. "And hits for a higher average too."

"I'll bet you *ten* dollars Mickey does!"

"I'll bet you a *hundred* dollars he doesn't!"

"I'll bet you *five* hundred dollars he does!"

"Where you going to get five hundred dollars?" Cousin Philip demanded.

I had to think fast. "From all the money I'm going to be getting for my bar mitzvah."

48

WITHOUT A DOUBT

I WOUND UP GETTING $479 for my bar mitzvah, not quite enough to cover the bet I had with Cousin Philip. Uncle Harold suggested if I lost I could make up the $21 difference by shoveling snow.

"In the summer?"

"Okay, then how about manure?"

"*Manure?*"

"You shovel horse manure, Skippy, you can pick up $21 before the month's out. I'm telling you, there's money waiting to be had cleaning up stables. That's how Eddie Arcaro got his start." (Eddie Arcaro had grown up in Florence, Kentucky, right across the river from Cincinnati, and gone on from cleaning stables to become the first jockey in racing history to win two Triple Crowns.)

"A good horse averages fifteen or so nuggets a day," Uncle Harold continued. "You gather up all those nuggets, then you sell them to farmers. They're always looking for fresh horse manure. The fiber in it is good for their soul."

"You mean *soil?*"

"That too."

Uncle Harold had arrived at the party in his typical fashion—thirty minutes late and resplendent. He'd gone all out, wearing a shiny, teal blue, double-breasted, sharkskin suit with an orange and white polka-dot bow tie and matching spats. An orange carnation was in his lapel.

"Wow, that is some suit," I said. "Does it light up at night?"

"Got it at Robert Hall," Uncle Harold said proudly. "That way you get two pairs of pants. It was marked down to $39.90... *and* only one size down from what I used to wear." He reached inside his jacket, ripping the pocket in the process, and handed me an envelope with navy blue pinstripes running vertically through a coffee cup stain. I turned it over. On the flap was printed **YANKEE STADIUM.**

"Well, you going to open it?"

"Here?"

"Here." He grinned. "Don't worry, it's not paperclip cufflinks."

Cufflinks. That's what everybody was giving me for my bar mitzvah...cufflinks. From Aunt Tillie, I got a set of silver Ten Commandment cufflinks. From Aunt Helen, I got gold-plated Star of David cufflinks. The Shmedricks gave me Torah cufflinks. The Lowenthals gave me gold knot cufflinks. I got burnished rhinestone cufflinks with musical notes from the Diamonds, elephant cufflinks from the Gottliebs, and Superman-shield cufflinks from somebody who forgot to sign the card. Dr. Hertzman gave me tooth cufflinks, and the Krackauers gave me cufflinks made of subway tokens. From the Planskys, I got Green Bay Packer helmet cufflinks even though my team was the Browns. (The

Bengals weren't even on the drawing board back then.) Myron gave me cufflinks shaped in the Hebrew letter *Beit* so I'd always remember Bezalel.

No one thought to give me a shirt with French cuffs.

Thankfully, Uncle Harold hadn't given me cufflinks. In the envelope, was a wrinkled, scuffed-up ticket.

"Grass stains," Uncle Harold said. "Those are grass stains on it. Maybe they'll come out in the wash."

"*Is this for real?* It's a *Yankee* ticket. It says it's for June 27."

Uncle Harold took the ticket out of my hand and bit into it. "Oh, it's real...Old Timers Day, June 27... they're playing the Tigers at the Stadium."

I turned the ticket over and read the legalese in the bite marks. "Holy bull shark, this *is* a real ticket!"

"What, you think I would give you a ticket that wasn't?"

I thought it best not to answer that.

"Section 214A, Row 17, Seat 11, Yankee Stadium. But don't you worry about sitting in the middle of thousands of strangers, Skippy. I've got the seat right next to you."

"And how am I supposed to get to New York?"

"Fly," Uncle Harold said.

"Fly?"

"Yeah, fly. They have airplanes for that, Skippy."

Uncle Harold explained he'd talked with Mom, and she'd given her approval. "She's letting you come to New York to visit me for a couple of weeks when school's out."

"She is?"

"As long as I have you back in time for Cyma's wedding. I told her not to worry, I'd have you fly back with me, and I'd make sure they sit us together in standby."

"Standby?"

I call *aisle*. You can have the window seat."

I couldn't tell if he was serious. Sometimes with Uncle Harold you never know.

"Window seat's good," he said. "That way you'll see the Statute of Liberty."

"You mean the *Statue* of Liberty, don't you?"

"Isn't that what I said, the Statuette of Liberty?

I wasn't going to tell Uncle Harold he was wrong. Not when he was going to take me to a Yankee game.

"So we're all set, Skippy. It wasn't easy to get the tickets."

Or get them mucked up the way they were, I thought. I just had to ask: "So how did they get the grass stains on them?"

"How? How? Because I used my Polugayevsky."

49

THE WAY UNCLE HAROLD explained, it was one of those days when he wasn't assistant coaching the Hebrew Union College baseball team and was sitting on a bench in Central Park, contemplating his next move. He said he'd shunned his HUC baseball cap to get sun, but due to park regulations banning public indecency he hadn't shunned his HUC sweatpants. Nor had he shunned his mesh HUC tee shirt, even though shunning mesh tee shirts had been legalized by the Democrat-controlled City Council. Suddenly, something hit him, and this time it wasn't from a pigeon. Taking his mesh tee shirt off, he walked over to where these two guys were playing chess. He watched them sweat and squirm and adjust their thinking caps until one of the guys, seeing he had no chance to win, shrugged and resigned the game.

"Think you can beat me, chump?" the winner said, picking his nose at Uncle Harold. "Forget it. No way. I move like a butterfly and mate like a bee."

"*No problemo,*" Uncle Harold said, figuring he'd impress the guy with his mastery of Spanish. "*Usted* want black or white?"

"Doesn't matter," the bee mater said, unpicking his nose. "Either way you're burnt tamale."

"*Yo* don't think so," Uncle Harold said.

"Wanna bet on it?"

"Sure, I'll bet." Uncle Harold had switched to English because he'd exhausted his vocabulary of Spanish.

"Know who I am? I'm the Reigning Chess King of Central Park Uptown from the Reservoir," bragged the bee mater, adding that he'd acquired the title by mating.

Uncle Harold pointed out his sister Bessie used to tease him all the time about mating when he reached puberty. "I hated it," he said.

"The teasing?" said the guy who'd lost.

"No, puberty."

"Listen, joker, I said *I'm* the Reigning Chess King!" the reigning king said.

"Of Central Park Uptown from the Reservoir," his vanquished foe added.

The Reigning Chess King of Central Park Uptown from the Reservoir shot him a look.

"Well, king, it's time to reign it in," Uncle Harold said, pleased with his pun. "I can beat you blind-folded with one arm tied behind my back."

"Two Yankee tickets says you can't."

"Go ahead, I'll let you have the first move."

Uncle Harold blind-folded himself with his mesh tee shirt and put his unlucky pitching arm behind his back. The King smirked and moved Queen's Pawn to Queen's Bishop 4. Uncle Harold eyed it and answered nonchalantly with his standby, the Polugayevsky variation of the Sicilian Defense. Three moves later, Uncle Harold smiled and hummed *Checkmate*. The Former Reigning Chess King of

Central Park Uptown from the Reservoir shook his head in disgust. He pulled the tickets out of his wallet.

"You want the tickets?" he growled. "Here, take your damn tickets!" He balled them up in his hand. With a satisfied smile, he ground them into the grass and stomped on them.

50

THE END OF THE SCHOOL year meant Steven Sklafer would be home from PMI. PMI stood for the Peducah Military Institute, a long-established military prep school in Kentucky. I'm not sure where in Kentucky. It's always been kind of hard to find things in Kentucky, which is how the moonshiners like it.

Anyhow, PMI is no longer around, having closed its door in 1971 due to shrinking enrollment—the year before, there'd been only three new cadets, plus a transfer student from an out-of-state 4-H Club. But back in 1957, the school was flourishing, its Spartan, regimented program having produced some of the country's most disingenuous military leaders. PMI took a special pride in the fact that, to the best of its knowledge, only one of its graduates had ever faced a firing squad and that was some kid named Arnold who'd sold his class secret-code ring to the Russians.

PMI was one school where you weren't encouraged to think outside the box. In fact, you got demerits if you did. You were encouraged rather strongly, however, to take the steep steps, two at a time, up to the dormitory, which was on the fourth floor. It was a way, the commandant of PMI figured, for the school to save money by not having to buy athletic equipment. And to make sure kids like Steven Sklafer didn't take the elevator, the commandant had given strict orders to the janitorial staff to make sure it worked only on Parents' Visitation Day, which so far had been following the monthly postponement schedule for that year.

Food staples like cookies, candy, chips, and Twinkies weren't allowed in the dorm rooms at PMI. Nor was pizza, unless it was anchovied. That was because the nurse's office was staunchly pro-anchovy, maintaining that anchovies helped regulate your urinary tract since eating them made you drink more water.

Steven Sklafer's pop, Bernie Sklafer, who went by the name *Doctor* Sklafer, was an allergist who was allergic to disciplining his son. So he'd left Steven's childhood discipline to Steven's mother, Ginny Milhaus Sklafer, who was simply called Ginny and had no allergies to speak of. Ginny Sklafer never went into her son's bedroom without praying this time there wouldn't be dirty socks left on the floor. And it wasn't just socks that bothered her. One day she caught Steven sniffing Coke up his nose. The next day it was Pepsi.

That did it.

Ginny Sklafer convinced her husband—Doctor Sklafer—they should send Steven off to PMI. Not only would he learn not to leave dirty socks on the floor and be able to tell the difference between good Coke and good Pepsi, but with Steven away she and Doctor Sklafer wouldn't have to fight with him every Thursday night for control of the family TV. Ginny and Doctor Sklafer would be watching re-runs of Coca-Cola commercials on *Ozzie and Harriet* only to have Steven walk in and switch the channel to a commercial for Pepsi.

I wasn't particularly close with Steven Sklafer. Not that I disliked him, you understand. It was just every time I saw him he was always asking me if he could borrow a pair my socks, one sock of which I'd never get back. I learned not to wear argyle around him.

Anyhow, as luck would have it my mother was a second-degree friend of Ginny Sklafer. Which was why when an opening came up, Ginny had called Mom to invite me to Steven's welcome-back party. Ginny had explained to Mom that with Wally Gluck out with the flu and Michael Minson grounded, she needed one more boy to even things out. Mom, of course, had quickly accepted the invitation, thinking this was a good opportunity for me to develop party skills, which she said would be good for me to have if I was someday invited to an inauguration ball in Washington.

"I don't know about party affiliation, but lots of kids are going, honey," Mom was saying. "And you never know who could be running for the White House someday."

I sighed.

"Look at Warren G. Harding," Mom said.

"I did."

"You know about Harding?"

"The Schneid has the postage stamp." I explained commemorative stamps were The Schneid's specialty. "He has the 1948 Centennial of the American Poultry Association and the 25th Anniversary of the Election of Warren G. Harding issued in 1945."

If Mom was impressed, she didn't show it. "Well, Warren G. Harding was playing cornet in high school— pretty good too. Everyone thought he'd be playing with

Sousa someday. But no, he ran for the White House. It was because of him that *G* became a popular middle initial."

I shook my head. "Can't I develop my party skills some other time? The Yankees are on TV that night."

"So?"

"It's *Big Gifts for The Mick Night*. They're going to honor Mickey for winning the Triple Crown last year.

"Triple Crown?"

"Mickey led the league in home runs, batting average, and ribbies. First time anybody's won the Triple Crown since Ted Williams did. And that was nine years ago."

"Ribbies?"

"RBIs...runs batted in. Anyhow, I've made arrangements to watch Mickey get the award."

"You've made *arrangements*? What kind of arrangements, pray tell?"

So I explained to Mom that I'd stocked up on chips, Fritos, and Fig Newtons and that Fenny was coming over with Pepsi and root beer.

"No Eskimo Pies?"

"The Schneid is bringing them."

"Well, you're just going to have to cancel."

"But Mom!"

Mom gave me one of those stern looks of hers. I called it the no-radio-TV-or-telephone look.

"Do I have to point upstairs again?"

I had a choice. I could go to Steven Sklafer's party, where there'd be boys showing off, girls giggling, and Steven Sklafer sniffing Pepsi up his nose. Or I could be incarcerated, with *I Love Lucy* pounded into my head.

Steven Sklafer's sniffing? Or Linnie Junior's incessant *I Love Lucy*?

I didn't have to think twice about it.

51

SHE MOTIONED TO the plastic-covered wing chair next to the plastic-covered sofa in the living room.

"Have a seat. The doctor will be with you shortly," the Sklafers' housekeeper said. "Would you like a magazine to read? There's a *Time* from last October over there on the coffee table. I think most of the pages are still in it. Besides, the news hasn't changed much since then. The *Andrea Doria*'s still sunk."

"Thanks," I said.

"Well, I have to get back to the kitchen. I was draining the oil in the deep fat fryer when you rang the bell."

I'd gone through the cover story on Duffy Daugherty, the Michigan State football coach, and was reading a report about Stevenson cutting into President Eisenhower's farm strength when Doctor Sklafer entered the room. He had a round, double-chinned face with a couple of moles on the left side. He was wearing tan Bermuda shorts, an untucked blue shirt, and popping shelled pistachios into his mouth.

"Ahhh-choo!"

"Could be allergies," Doctor Sklafer said. His accent was New York, maybe Bronx—The Schneid could have told me what street. "Better call and make an appointment. Tell the nurse you saw me on television and she'll take five percent off the bill."

I blinked hard at him.

"No, I'm kidding, Skip. Good to see you again. All the kids are downstairs." He flashed a coffee-stained smile. "What's that you're reading?"

"*Time* from last October. Stevenson's cutting into President Eisenhower's farm strength."

"I wouldn't worry about it," Doctor Sklafer said. "Eisenhower won re-election."

"I know," I said. "So did Rosenfeld. And in a bigger landslide too."

"Rosenfeld? You mean Roosevelt, don't you?"

"Uh-uh. Jeff Rosenfeld. He's our class president again."

Suddenly, there was a loud cheer from the next room. Doctor Sklafer turned. "That's the Yankee game. I've got it on TV."

"Did they make the Gifts Awards already?"

"Just started. Want to watch? I've got a plate of raw carrots and broccoli in the den."

I told him I'd eaten three Three Musketeers on the way over.

"Three Musketeers?" He shook his head. "Bad for your acne."

"Actually, sir, three Three Musketeers."

Doctor Sklafer led me into the den. There on the wall, in a gold frame, was a blown-up check made out to *Doctor Bernard Sklafer*. I couldn't take my eyes off it. It was signed *Mickey Mantle*.

"He came in for some tests. I gave him some shots," Doctor Sklafer explained. "Turned out he's allergic to the Louisville Slugger imprint stamped on the bats. Ever see him run his bat between his legs then scratch his rear end when he's in the on-deck circle? Some fans think it's for good luck. It isn't. He's allergic to the Louisville Slugger imprint."

"*He was in your office! You saw him!* Wait till I tell the guys you know exactly why The Mick scratches his butt!"

"You know, Skip, I really shouldn't have told you this."

"Sorry, sir, I forgot that's privileged information. Uncle Harold told me all about it. He said it's The Hippopotamus Oath."

"It's *Hip-po-crat-ic*. Not hippopotamus."

But I wasn't listening. "You actually touched his—"

"Shhh, not so loud." Doctor Sklafer got up from his chair, went over to the couch, and lifted the cushions up. "This room could be bugged. The State Medical Board could be listening."

"And they'd impeach you?"

"Not exactly. But they could take away my license for violating the Hippopotamus Oath."

"I thought you said it was the *Hippocratic* Oath."

"That was before it got confused with hippopotamuses." He bent down, his knees cracking, and felt underneath the couch. "I think we're okay."

I told him it would be horrible if they took away his license because then he wouldn't be able to drive to the office, probably for a year.

"Maybe you could work out a month-to-month deal with the cab company," I suggested.

Doctor Sklafer lowered his chins and yelled for his wife. On the third *Ginny!* Ginny Sklafer swiveled in. She was carrying a box of Kotex.

Ginny Sklafer was what today you might call a senior hottie. She'd been a twenty-year-old nightclub showgirl when she'd met Doctor Sklafer, who was eighteen years her senior. Ginny still had the sleek long legs of a showgirl, which she loved to show off during Doctor Sklafer's Tuesday night poker game. Doctor Sklafer still had the paunchy wallet of a well-fed medical doctor, which was what had made Ginny overlook his baldness.

"Skip, what are you doing sitting up here watching TV?" the leggy Ginny Sklafer said, batting her eyelashes to keep in practice. "All the kids are downstairs....And how's your mother?"

"Mom's fine."

"Your father?"

"He's fine too."

Uh-oh. I knew this was only the start of her inquisition. I had no choice. I had to head her off.

"Everybody else is fine too," I said. "Except Elaine Novak's grandmother. She still misses her cousin Eddie, but he'll be up for parole in a couple of years."

It worked. Ginny Sklafer stopped batting her eyelashes and looked at me dumbfounded.

"Hey, they're giving gifts to Mantle!" Doctor Sklafer said. "Will you sit down, Gin! You're blocking the picture!"

"I'm not moving one inch, Bernie Sklafer!"

"*Doc*-tor Bernie Sklafer."

Ginny Sklafer set down the box of Kotex. She reached for an ashtray and, without a windup, threw it. It was a curveball that hit the outside corner of the plate, just enough to knock broccoli and carrots to the floor.

"Excuse me, everybody," Doctor Sklafer said. "I'm going to call the police." And he strutted out in a huff.

"Don't worry, Skip," Ginny Sklafer said. "He always says that. He'll strut into the bedroom, put on his scrubs and gloves, and stand in front of the mirror for twenty minutes admiring himself."

And with that, she turned off the TV just as Mickey was given a custom-built Batmobile complete with automatic transmission, 44-inch super swamper tires with custom rims, and smoke bombs.

"Skip honey, will you be a dear and take this box downstairs?" She handed the box of Kotex to me. "Just put it in the bathroom. But open it first, okay?"

"You want me to open it and put it in the bathroom?"

"Of course. When it's open it saves time if one of the girls needs it in a hurry."

So with the box of Kotex tucked under my arm, I started down the steps to the party. Before I hit the last step, there was a sudden squeal coming from my right.

52

I DROPPED THE UNOPENED box of Kotex on the floor and turned toward the squealing. Elaine Novak was kissing Steven Sklafer right on the lips, and she was doing it smack in the middle of a circle of whooping eighth graders, which included *girls.* Some of them I knew…Jeanette, Diane, Randi Wasserman, and, of course, Elaine. And while I never liked to admit it, I knew Madeline too.

Steven Sklafer unpuckered his lips from Elaine's and winked at me.

"Hey, you made it, Skipper! Everyone's spun. You can spin next." He picked the empty Pepsi bottle up off the floor and handed it to me. "You do know how to play, don't you?"

I didn't want to admit that I didn't, particularly in front of a circle of eighth graders already whooping it up. Fortunately, I didn't have to.

"Of course he knows how to play!" Madeline said. "And he's a good kisser too!"

The circle stopped whooping and looked at me. I knew it was useless to explain the kiss between Madeline and me was strictly accidental, caused by a kick to Tommy Salamo's nuts. So I put the Pepsi bottle back on the floor and, with a look on my lips that said I knew what I was doing, spun it.

The bottle stopped in front of Greg Deutsch. As Jeanette squealed, Greg puckered his lips and blew me a kiss.

"I am *not* kissing Greg Deutsch!"

That brought on more squeals from Jeannette, with Randi and Diane joining her.

"You don't have to *kiss* Greg," Steven Sklafer said. "Just shake his hand and spin again."

"Maybe if you spun the bottle the other way," Randi said. "To your right instead of to your left."

I shook Greg Deutsch's hand, then gave the Pepsi bottle a good spin to my right instead of to my left. It stopped in front of Randi.

"Fix!" Diane yelled.

"Spin again, Skipper," Steven Sklafer directed.

"Which direction?"

"Doesn't matter. Just spin it already."

So I spun the bottle a third time. The bottle stopped between Elaine and Madeline. I walked up to Elaine, a smile on my face, a bounce in my step.

"Whoa there, fella, not so fast!" Steven Sklafer said. "It's pointing at Madeline."

Diane nodded in agreement.

I looked around the circle for help, but everyone was nodding in agreement...except for Madeline, who was now puckering. I didn't have much of a choice. I had to kiss Madeline, she with the...well, you know. And so, with an entire circle of eighth graders cheering encouragement, I closed my eyes, held my nose, and kissed Madeline, praying my upper lip wouldn't get caught on her braces.

To my surprise, Madeline's mouth didn't taste like broccoli. Nor did it taste like Brussels Sprouts, cauliflower or asparagus. What it tasted like was pistachios.

I sneezed.

53

IT IS CERTAIN

"I NEED SOME THINGS at Bilkers," Mom said, no longer talking to herself about Warren G. Harding. She handed me a laundry list, though it wasn't a list of things for the laundry room.

"Broccoli? You want me to pick up broccoli?"

"You heard me. And a pound of corned beef. Better make that a half-pound with fat and a half-pound lean with no fat."

I wanted to ask her if Jack Spratt and his wife were coming for dinner, but thought better of it.

"And a loaf of rye bread at Overmyers."

"Why can't I get the bread at Bilkers? I'll be there."

"Overmyers," she said. "Their rye has smaller seeds. Oh, and while you're at Bilkers, get a nice big tomato. Make sure it's firm, full, and with good color."

I wasn't sure how you were supposed to do that, and to be frank I didn't really care. A tomato was a tomato...unless we're talking about Elaine's.

"And make sure you smell the tomato."

"Is that it?"

"No. You've got to feel the tomato. Squeeze it. But don't squeeze it so hard that you bruise it...."

Most mothers would have stopped right there. But not mine. The only stopping Mom did was to catch her breath.

"You don't want a tomato that's too soft...."

"Too soft, Mom, got it."

"And stay away from tomatoes with cracks, blemishes, or signs of worms."

I was about to ask her about signs of caterpillars, but thought if I did she'd make me pick up cauliflower too. Best I not bring up caterpillars...or centipedes either, for that matter.

"I'm on my way."

"You wait just a minute, fella...I haven't finished. I need a dozen eggs, oatmeal, and celery....And you'd better get a couple of rolls of ultra-thick toilet paper too. Your father's running low."

"Ah-Aahh-Choo!"

I didn't know it then, but I was allergic to the perfume they put in ultra-thick toilet paper. Even the mention of it was enough to start me sneezing.

"Gezundheit...Make sure it's ultra-thick and not semi. Last time he had to use semi...well, never you mind. You got it, *ultra-thick?* "

I sneezed again.

"Gezundheit! How many times do I have to tell you, Skip? When you sneeze, turn away from other people!"

"Okay," I said, wiping my nose with the back of my hand.

"And I better not catch you sneezing into your hands again! You'll spread germs!"

"Okay, okay."

My sneezing must have triggered maternal instincts Mom had besides nagging. Since I'd outgrown coloring books, she said I could buy a couple packs of baseball cards too.

"How about three packs?"

"Don't push it!"

Negotiations over, I hopped on my bike and rode down to Bilkers….oh, and Overmyers too.

I had a brand new Schwinn Phantom back then. It was black and stainless-silver chrome, trimmed in red, and had red-white-and-blue streamers streaming off the handlebars. Not to brag, but I had the snazziest-looking bike in Cincinnati...well, at least in the neighborhood. Dad had fastened a big basket on the handlebars and one on each side of the rear tire. He said the baskets would be useful for carrying things like his overdue library books back to the library. Dad was going to put a basket on the back of the bike too, but Mom said it was overdoing it since he never had that any books more than a week late.

On the tire spokes, I'd clipped on baseball cards with clothes pins from the laundry room. Once you started pedaling, the baseball cards would flap against the spokes, making the Phantom sound like a motor bike.

It was Fenny who said a cool-looking bike like mine ought to have a name befitting it.

"How can you have a b-b-b-bike like that without a name befitting it?" he asked.

"I don't know," I said. "Does your bike have a name?"

"Sure. Its name is Nellie."

"That's a girl's name."

"You think I don't know that?" Fenny said, reminding me that he had a girl's bike. "Your b-b-b-bike needs a boy's name. You know, something like M-M-M-Malcolm."

"I don't think so."

"Howard?"

"Nope."

"Sam?"

"Uh-uh."

"Irving?"

"Uh-uh."

"How b-b-b-bout Maurice? You know, like Maurice Chevrolet."

"The bike's a Phantom, not a Chevrolet."

"So what if it's a Phantom? M-M-M-Maurice sounds classy."

"Yeah, and Diarrhea sounds fast."

"I suppose Fido's out too," Fenny said, scratching his head.

"It's a bike, Fenny. Not a dog sled."

Now I have to say this about Fenny Farkis...he tried. He rattled off a list of names for a boy's bike—from Aaron to Zorro—most of which I've long since forgot. What I haven't forgot is that I ruled them all out and that I was getting pretty exasperated. I could tell Fenny was too.

Finally, we selected the name for my bike. Well, actually it wasn't Fenny and I who selected the name. It was a specialist on bike-naming who did.

54

UNCLE HAROLD HAD WANTED to go with *Philippe*, which he said was Peloponnesian and meant *lover of sea horses*. I tried to explain to him as gently as I could that a bike was pedaled by foot power, not seahorse power.

We were sitting in a row boat in Burnet Woods, throwing bread crumbs at the ducks. I'd brought along some stale Wonder Bread. Uncle Harold had brought seeded rye.

"I dunno, that's Greek to me," Uncle Harold said. "Well, if that's what they teach you in school these days, then I guess we'll go with something else." He sighed. "I don't want you to flunk marine scientology."

I knew it was useless to try to tell Uncle Harold I wasn't taking marine scientology, or any other scientology for that matter. So I just explained while I wasn't in danger of flunking, I was worried about getting a *D* on my report card in Biology all because I wasn't paying close attention in class, at least not to Miss Phylum. I thought it best I not mention Elaine's boobs since it was liable to get him all worked up remembering his experience in the lingerie department at Penney's.

"Well, if a bike does run like you say, then we should go with a name based on that," Uncle Harold said. "Let me think a minute." He broke off a piece of his seeded rye and threw it between a couple of ducks. They quacked and swam away.

"Guess they don't like aged seeded rye," Uncle Harold said.

"Uh, think maybe it's because they just don't like mold?"

"Aged, mold...what's the difference?"

I just looked at him. "So what about the name?"

"Name?"

"For my bike."

"Here, take the oars," Uncle Harold said. "How do you expect me to think when I have to keep us from going in circles?"

He started humming *Row, row , row your boat*....He was on *merrily, merrily, merrily, merrily* when he suddenly stopped, smiled, and announced he had the perfect name.

"Dalaigh!" he said.

"*Dale-ee*?"

"Not *dale-ee...dawl-ee*. D-A-L-A-I-G-H...Dalaigh. It's Garlic for *fleet of foot*. Isn't that beautiful, Skippy? What makes your bike fleet is your pedaling. *It's all in the foot powder*."

"And it's *Garlic*?"

"Oh, definitely. Garlic is Irish."

"Huh?"

"Irish. You know, like Notre Dame and Florida State."

I was going to tell him Florida State was the Seminoles, not the Irish, but I thought if I did, I might get him started on a rain dance. No, best not to say anything about college mascots.

Uncle Harold must have realized I was confused. "Actually, Dalaigh is *Northern* Garlic. Northern Garlic is the formal name for the Northern Irish dialect."

I shook my head in disbelief. I knew a thing or two about dialects. After all, Miss Tsuris The Agony had us study dialectical materialism in Social Studies. But I was afraid if I told Uncle Harold about Marxism, I was liable to get him started on the Marx Brothers.

So it was Dalaigh, baskets crammed with corned beef, broccoli, milk, eggs, tomato juice, celery, instant oatmeal, two packs of baseball cards, and a tomato from Bilkers, on which I was foot pedaling hard to Overmyers when I saw Elaine. She was standing inside the Clean Clothes coin-operated laundromat. She was wearing a halter top, and she was waving at me. I should have simply waved back, but I didn't.

Instead, I had to show off.

55

MAYBE IF THE CINCINNATI Police Department had put up a sign that said *NO WHEELIES PERMITTED ON SIDEWALK, Sunday, 2 P.M.-3 P.M.* the whole outcome would have been different. But there was no bicycle sign of any kind, and so I was doing a look-at-me, no-hands, front-wheel wheelie when *bam!* I was no longer doing any kind of wheelie. I was crumpled on the sidewalk, nose dripping juice from a bruised tomato and spitting out pieces of broccoli between my teeth.

My bike had rammed into two trashcans double-parked outside the laundromat.

Elaine came running. "Are you okay?" And then she saw the tomato juice trickling from my nose. "Oh my God, you're *bleeding!*"

I tried to tell her it was just a bruised tomato, but she wasn't buying.

"You think I can't recognize a bruised tomato?" She had me tilt my head back to stop the trickling.

What could I say? And why would I say anything when she was cradling my head in her cleavage and brushing oatmeal out of my hair?

"Let's go inside and get you cleaned up," she said. It seemed like a good idea since we were right outside the laundromat, which, though it had a soiled reputation, did do cleaning.

I must have lost a lot more tomato juice than I thought, because when I stood up I felt weak and stumbled. Elaine quickly grabbed me. I stumbled again, and she put her arm tightly around my waist to hold me up.

I made sure I kept stumbling.

56

"DON"T WORRY ABOUT the flat tire," Elaine said, mentioning nothing about my bike chain being broken. Instead, she said her parents belonged to Triple A, which she explained meant she could use their membership number any time since she was a minor.

"I called them once when I got stuck mowing the lawn. The lawnmower just sputtered and stopped. They came within half an hour with a tow truck and towed it away."

"Triple A came and towed your *lawnmower*?"

"Uh-huh. To a mechanic. He said there was nothing wrong with it. It just needed more gasoline."

I lowered my chin and looked at her.

She motioned for me to keep my head titled back. "I'll call Triple A. They'll send someone out here to tow your bike to the nearest bicycle shop."

Before I could say I didn't think there were any service stations in the Free World that towed bikes, unless they were maybe tandems, Elaine was leaning over the counter and ringing the bell to get the attention of the attendant on duty.

"I need to make a call," she said.

"You haven't used the phone already, have you, honey?" The attendant explained customers were only permitted to make one call a day from the laundromat's phone. "And please don't lean on the counter that way," she added. "It's not a resting place for boobs. You're liable to break it."

"Sorry," Elaine said. She explained she hadn't made her one entitled call and asked if the laundromat had the number for Triple A.

"No, honey, we sure don't. But I know the number for AA."

Elaine politely shook her head, saying no, she needed Triple A.

"Well, I guess I could let you call Information and make it a freebie," the attendant said.

So Elaine called Information, then got Triple A on the line. She said something to them, then something else. Smiling, she turned from the counter and looked at me. "See, I told you they would."

I stopped picking pieces of broccoli off my legs. "You're kidding me. You're going to tell me Triple A is going to tow my bike to a bicycle repair shop?"

"I just did," she said, walking back to me. "They weren't going to do it until I told them my cousin Howard Hughes is on their board of directors."

"*Howard Hughes* is your cousin?"

She shot me a look that said *What, are you nuts?*

"What are you doing at the laundromat anyway?" I asked. Not that I was sorry she was, you understand.

"Our washing machine's not working." Elaine checked the time on the dryer and sighed. "Mom sent me over here to do the laundry."

I saw this was the perfect opportunity to impress her with my knowledge of starting washing machines, which

I'd learned in shop during the lesson we had on electrocution. So I asked if they'd checked to see if the washing machine was plugged in.

"We couldn't find the cord. And we don't know where the outlet disappeared to."

Normally, I wouldn't have believed somebody could be that whacky—other than Uncle Harold, of course—but I knew with Elaine it was more than possible.

"Anyway, Triple A said somebody will be here within forty-five minutes. What time is it now, and why are you still wearing a Mickey Mouse Club watch?"

I knew Elaine always had to be the girl getting all the attention, and she could get jealous at the mere mention of another girl's name. Best not to tell her I wore the watch as a tribute to Annette Funicello.

"It's my mother's," I lied, and I told her the time.

"Oh no! I was supposed to mail it for Mom and I forgot! If it doesn't go out today—"

"If *what* doesn't go out today?"

"Her entry in the Publishers Clearing House Sweepstakes. It has to be postmarked by *today.* That's the deadline. You miss that, and you don't win seven thousand dollars a week for life. My mom is going to kill me!"

"Elaine, you know what the odds are of winning a Publishers Clearing House Sweepstakes?"

"No, what?"

"One billion, three hundred million to one," I said.

"That's pretty good, isn't it?"

I told her that her mom would have a better chance of getting struck by lightning.

215

She wrinkled her nose. "That's silly. Why would she want to get hit by lightning?"

I had no answer for that.

"Mom is going to kill me! If her entry doesn't go out in the mail today, I'll be grounded! *What am I going to do, Skip? What am I going to do?"* Elaine's beautiful almond-shaped, golden-brown eyes started to well.

"Take a deep breath," I said. And she did.

"Take another one," I said, my eyes glued to her heaving chest. And she did.

"Good...another one."

"Another one? Why?"

I didn't want to tell Elaine the reason I wanted her to take deep breaths was so I could enjoy the rise and fall of her boobs. Instead, I told her there was a mailbox next to Overmyer's. I looked at my watch. "Last pickup is in ten minutes. You can still make it!"

"I can?"

I nodded. "If you hurry."

"Thanks," she said, tears unwelling. "Can I get you anything from Overmyers when I'm done?"

"No, I'm okay," I said, though all the lint in the laundromat was starting to get to me.

"Sure?"

"*Ah-Aaah-Choo!*"

"That is *so* gross! You're not supposed to sneeze into your hand and then wipe your nose with it! Next time use a tissue or something."

What could I say? I nodded.

"Sure you don't want anything from Overmyers? Maybe tissue?"

"Well, as long as it's not ultra-thick. I'm allergic to the perfume they put in ultra-thick."

"No ultra-thick then."

"And maybe you could pick up a loaf of rye bread. But it has to be one with the small seeds."

She gave me one of those blank expressions of hers.

"My mother likes theirs better than Bilkers."

"Okay," she said, and I could tell she really didn't get it. Not that I did myself, you understand.

So Elaine was on her way down the street to mail her mother's sweepstakes entry to Publishers Clearing House ...and to pick up a loaf of rye for mine. She was almost out the door when she stopped and turned around.

"Almost forgot, do me a favor, will you, Skip? Keep an eye on the dryer."

"Sure, Elaine. Be glad to."

"It should stop in about twelve minutes or so. Could you check and see if the clothes are dry then? If they're still a little wet, could you put another nickel in?"

"Sure."

"You won't forget?"

I promised her I wouldn't.

"I'll pay you back when I get back."

And she was out the door, leaving me holding Mom's bruised tomato and waiting twelve minutes or so for the dryer to stop.

Except I didn't wait twelve minutes.

57

THE SCHNEID AND I were sitting on the floor in his family's new bomb shelter. His father had ordered one from the Nieman-Marcus catalog. It came with air blowers, filters, flashlights, six Nieman-Marcus private label fallout protection suits, and a first-aid kit. You were expected to provide your own food and water.

"My dad says bomb shelters could be a twenty billion dollar business in the coming years," I said.

"*If* there are coming years," The Schneid said.

The Schneid had a yellow marble in one hand and an egg roll in the other. We were playing Chinese Checkers…or at least The Schneid's version of it. He liked to eat Chinese food when playing Chinese Checkers.

"That way you get the real favor of the game," he explained. "It's the way they play it in Shanghai."

"What about Hong Kong and Groton?"

He looked at me like I was crazy. "Groton's not in China. It's in Connecticut."

"That's New England," I said. And I proceeded to recite to him the names of all six New England states in reverse alphabetical order.

So there we were, playing Chinese Checkers in the Schneider bomb shelter. We'd picked up some lo mein, spare ribs, and egg rolls at Forbidden Dragon. The Schneid paid for it with money he'd won playing *HORSE* with Howard Kodesh.

"Watch this, Felipe." The Schneid chomped half his egg roll and, using his chopsticks to pick up a marble, jumped over two of my greens. He handed his chopsticks to me and smiled. "Your turn."

"With chopsticks?"

He nodded. "You can do it."

"No thanks," I said. "I'll stick to the Connecticut way." I hopped one of my marbles over another and into the adjacent hole.

The Schneid polished off his egg roll, all the while studying the board. Suddenly, his eyes lit up.

I shook my head. The Schneid had triple-jumped and landed in his opposite pagoda.

"You win again, Schneid."

He nodded. "So why did some old lady at the laundromat call you a *roquefort*? That's a blue cheese. Did she say sharp or salty?"

"She meant *pervert*."

"Why would she call you either one? What did she catch you doing?"

So I told The Schneid the whole story behind *roquefort* and how I was trying to impress Elaine by doing a no-look, no-hands wheelie and how Mom's tomato became a bruised tomato when two double-parked trashcans collided with my bike even though I clearly had the right of way and how Elaine called Triple A and got them to come by telling them her cousin was Howard Hughes and how she made me promise to keep an eye on her clothes tumbling in the dryer while she rushed to the post office before it closed to mail in the entry to the Publishers Clearing House Sweepstakes for her mother and pick up a loaf of rye bread from Overmyers for mine.

I was ready to go into how I reached my hand into the dryer to snatch Elaine's bra and how before I could close the dryer door, shorts, tee shirts, socks, pajamas, panties, and bras came tumbling out into a big pile on the floor. Suddenly, I felt one coming on again.

"Uh-oh, I'm going to sneeze. You got a tissue?"

"Don't have any, Felipe. Just use your hand."

"That's exactly what I *should* have done, Schneid, but I didn't!"

And with that, I sneezed.

"You're not making...*gezundheit*...sense, Felipe."

I explained to him that Mom said when I sneezed I was supposed to use a tissue, but because I didn't have a tissue handy at the laundromat I'd done the only thing I could do when I snatched Elaine's bra tumbling out of the dryer. I'd sneezed into it, then wiped my nose with it, and stuffed it under my shirt just before she walked back in.

"That's when the woman called me a *roquefort*!"

"Who did?"

"The woman who saw me stuff Elaine's bra under my shirt. She called me a *roquefort*."

The Schneid cracked upon a Fortune cookie, read the message inside, then handed it to me. *Ignore previous fortune,* it said.

"Sure you don't want one?" he asked.

I shook my head. "She said *roquefort*. I knew she meant to say *pervert*, but her English wasn't too good."

"Why, where was she from?"

"I dunno. Some place in Europe, I think."

"You *think*? You don't know which country?"

"How am I supposed to know which country? All I know is she sounded like Bela Lugosi."

"That would make her Transylvanian," The Schneid explained Transylvania was once a part of Hungary and that the Hungarian language belonged to the Ugrian group of the Finno-Ugrian family.

I told him I didn't know his family was Finno-Ugrian. After all, he'd never mentioned it before.

"We're not Finno-Ugrian." The Schneid said he was, however, related to Sitting Bull on his mother's side. "We still have Sioux relatives on the Rosebud Reservation, but we don't have any in Europe."

He added that there weren't too many Indian reservations in Europe. "On the other side of the Berlin Wall, you'll find Pawnee and Shoshone. Maybe a few Cannoli too. But that's it."

"I thought Cannoli was Italian pastry."

"They copied it from the Indians," The Schneid said, looking perturbed. "It was a tribal delicacy."

Anyhow, I wasted no time. The next morning I got up early, took Elaine's bra out from beneath my *Playboys,* and stuffed it in my school bag, right under my newly annotated issue of *The Sporting News*

At lunchtime, Elaine's bra was in Ziggy's hands, and Mickey's '51 rookie card was finally in mine.

58

I DON'T KNOW who started it, and I suppose it doesn't really matter. Today, they'd call it trash talking, but back then it was your basic *Oh yeah? Sez who?* All I know is one moment Fenny, Schwabbie—who was known as Millard Schwab by Mr. Weinerschein—and I were out in Schwabbie's backyard hitting fungos, and the next moment we were the Aracoma Sweat Sox, gearing up for a bragging-rights game against the boys in Brookcrest.

It had been decided since Schwabbie had the biggest backyard around—it was about two hundred feet to the sassafras trees ending the Schwabs' property—that's where the game would be played. Which was why the Brookcrest boys were calling their team the Viz, short for Visitors.

"Good thing we've got the home-field advantage," Schwabbie said. He cocked the bat back, swung, and hit a slow roller that stopped before it reached the woods.

"Advantage? How's that an advantage?" Fenny asked.

"We've played in my backyard before."

"S-S-S-So?"

"We're near the top of the food chain."

"Food chain?"

"I meant *top of the hill.* We're near the top of the hill, right?"

"Right."

"So we're more used to playing in thin air."

It was my turn. I cocked the bat, swung, and missed. "They're still going to be tough to beat," I said. "The Viz are loaded."

Schwabbie agreed with me. "I batted against Jimmy Blintz in Knothole. He's got a pretty wet spitball."

"Yeah," Fenny said, "b-b-b-but we've got The Schneid." Fenny grabbed the bat from me and hit a scorching line drive through the legs of the Meltzens' Great Dane.

"The Schneid bats fourth, cleanup, and he plays third," Schwabbie said. "I'm at first, Fenny's at second, and, Skip, you're at short—"

"Center field, Schwabbie. That's where I belong. I've even got the glove." I told him it was the same model Mickey played with and that his signature was etched right on the pocket. "I'm a natural center fielder...just like The Mick."

"You forgetting Mantle had to be *taught* to play center field, that he started out as a shortstop? Besides we need a shortstop, and since there's no one else, who better than you?"

Schwabbie took the bat from Fenny and swung away. This time, the Great Dane staggered away yelping.

"Guess they won't be breeding him any time soon," Fenny said.

Okay, the Aracoma Sweat Sox had an infield. But we still needed an outfield and, of course, a pitcher and catcher. Which is what I told Schwabbie and Fenny.

"You two, The Schneid, and me. That's four," Schwabbie said, rubbing a mosquito bite on his ankle. "We need five more guys to have a team. Who else do we have in our neighborhood that can play baseball?"

"Stingman will play," Fenny said. He smacked the mosquito chomping on the back of his neck. "We'll put him in left. And we can probably g-g-g-get Jelly to pitch."

Jelly Roll Olsen was called that not because he was Danish, but because he played stride piano like Jelly Roll Morton did. Jelly said he'd learned to play that way by listening to a recording of *Jelly Roll Blues* on the radio and could now play basic ragtime rhythms with either hand.

Okay, we had Jelly pitching and Stingman in left field. But we still needed two more outfielders. And a catcher, too. This wasn't going to be easy.

"Do we really need two more outfielders?" Schwabbie asked. "Couldn't we get by with just one more? I mean, we've got Jelly pitching. How many balls are they going to hit out of the infield?"

Fenny looked at me.

"He's right," I said. "*One* more outfielder. And we still need a catcher."

"My little brother," Fenny suggested.

"No!" Schwabbie and I shouted.

"Why not? We make T.T. our c-c-c-catcher. He stands fifteen feet b-b-b-behind the plate and catches b-b-b-balls on a b-b-b-bounce."

I couldn't believe him. "You really want T.T. giving signals to the pitcher? What if Jelly shakes the sign off? You really want a catcher who's going to run off to tell his mother?"

Fenny admitted I had a good point, but reminded us we still needed somebody behind the plate.

"Judy Groesbeck's uncle and aunt usually visit during the weekend," Schwabbie said. "Judy lives across the street from me, and I can always tell when the Capelmans are there by their bright pink Caddy in the driveway."

"The Capelmans have a b-b-b-bright pink Cadillac?" Fenny asked.

"Well, not always. Sometimes it's dirty."

It was my turn with the bat again. Fenny cringed.

"Uh, excuse me guys," I said, swinging and hitting a soft pop-up right in front of me, which Schwabbie caught with his bare hand. "What does this have to do with getting a catcher?"

"Well, the Capelmans' son comes with them," Schwabbie said. "Ferdy's our age. I've played badminton with him, and he's hit it back a few times. That's not too bad."

"Not too bad? That's horrible," I said. "Forget Ferdy Capelman."

"Hey, wait a m-m-m-minute!" Fenny said. "You say *Ferdy C-C-C-Capelman*?"

"Yeah," Schwabbie said. "So?"

"If he's the Ferdy C-C-C-Capelman I'm thinking of, d-d-d-do you know who he's related to, Skip?"

"You're going to tell me he's related to Mickey Mantle?"

"Well, not exactly."

"So who is he related to?"

"Glen S-S-S-Sudek."

"Who's Glen Sudek?" Schwabbie asked.

225

"He's Ferdy C-C-C-Capelman's g-g-g-godfather," Fenny said. "*And* he's M-M-M-Mickey Mantle's cousin.

"Wow! Is Mickey Mantle in the Mafia too?"

"Sudek's not *that* kind of g-g-g-godfather," Fenny said. "I'll b-b-b-bet he comes to the game if Ferdy plays."

"Ferdy plays," I said.

59

"I THOUGHT OUR friendship meant something to you."

"It d-d-d-does," Fenny said. "Come on, Skip, you know it d-d-d-does."

"Then don't even *think* about putting my sister in the outfield."

First T.T. and now Linnie. I don't know where Fenny's brain was when he came up with the idea of asking Turkey Lips to be on our team. I knew it was unlikely to be the onset of dementia since back in the Fifties people typically didn't show signs of dementia until they were thirty.

"Okay, No Linnie—"

"No girls, period. I'm not playing if there's a girl on the team."

"Me neither," Schwabbie said.

"Okay, okay! No g-g-g-girls, *period.*"

Fenny and I had sat down on the grass, trying to come up with another outfielder. Schwabbie had thrown his glove down next to us and was lying on his back, using the glove as a head rest. A dandelion was hanging out of his mouth.

We'd ruled out Mugsy Kegel because of his uncontrollable temper. When Mugsy got mad it was lights out. We were afraid he'd whack the pitcher with his bat if he got hit by a pitch. And we'd ruled out girls—even if they could hit the ball like Bari Baum, who played fastpitch t-ball and would become a man when she grew up. But the fact of the matter was we still needed one more outfielder, and there was no one left in the neighborhood. This required some thinking.

"Maybe I can get M-M-M-Matty," Fenny said.

Schwabbie sat up. "Matty who?"

"M-M-M-Matty...Schwartzman."

"Who's this Marty Schwartzman?" I asked.

"Not M-M-M-Marty, *Matty* Schwartzman. M-M-M-Matty Schwartzman is...Matty is my foster cousin."

This was news to me. I told Fenny he'd never mentioned he had a foster cousin Matty. Or Marty either for that matter.

"That's 'cause I d-d-d-didn't know M-M-M-Matty was my foster cousin until...until I found out."

"And when did you find out?"

"When d-d-d-did I find out?...This m-m-m-morning."

Schwabbie spat the dandelion from his mouth. "A *foster* cousin? I don't get it."

Neither did I. Still, I knew in the Farkis family anything was possible. Fenny had some relatives who were pretty strange. His Aunt Lillie in Florida, for example. Aunt Lillie was determined to teach tricks to the iguanas she was raising. The way Aunt Lillie looked at it, if seals could do tricks so could iguanas, even though according to *National Geographic* your average iguana has one-tenth the brains of a seal. Fenny said last he'd heard Aunt Lillie was trying to get her iguanas to clap their claws while balancing beach balls on their noses. To keep the iguanas, who she'd named

Lewis and Clark, from clawing themselves as they clapped, she'd taken them in for pedicures.

Then there was his grandfather's half-brother Walter in Wilkes-Barre, who claimed he had evidence John Wilkes Booth was the victim of a smear campaign. Walter said Booth hadn't assassinated Lincoln and that Abe had shot himself in the head rather than listen to more of the incessant jabbering from his wife Mary on who was likely to wear what to the Tony awards that year.

Nevertheless, a foster cousin seemed a little farfetched.

"You expect Schwabbie and me to believe you just now discovered you have a foster cousin?" I said.

"Yep," said Fenny, who started singing. *"Way d-d-d-down upon the Swanee River…* you know who wrote that?"

"Old Folks at Home? Sure, Stephen F. Foster," Schwabbie said. "What does that have to do with anything?"

"Well, M-M-M-Matty's an indirect d-d-d-descendant of Stephen F. Foster," Fenny said. "And so is my m-m-m-mother."

"Which, of course, makes you a distant indirect descendant," Schwabbie said.

While all this was enlightening, I told Fenny he was forgetting Matty didn't live on or off Aracoma. "What are we going to do about that? What do we tell Jimmy Blintz?"

"We just tell him M-M-M-Matty has been living down by the Swanee River, b-b-b-but is staying at m-m-m-my house for the summer."

Just like Fenny predicted, Jimmy Blintz had no objection when we told him Fenny's family had taken on a Foster child.

"And M-M-M-Matty solves our pre-game problem," Fenny was saying.

"We have a pre-game problem, Farkis? What's that?"

"You can't start a g-g-g-game until you do the National Anthem. It's right in the rulebook, Jimmy. M-M-M-Matty knows practically all the words. And we won't need a b-b-b-band. M-M-M-Matty Schwartzman can sing *a campanella* before the g-g-g-game."

"He sings like Roy Campanella? Couldn't he sing like Willie Mays?"

"It's not *a campanella*," I said. "He means *a-capella*—singing without accompaniment. No band, just Matty."

"I don't know about this," Jimmy said. He ran his hand through his hair. Dandruff flew out. "Why couldn't we just play *The Star Spangled Banner* on a record player and be done with it?"

So I explained to Jimmy that sure, you could play a record, but you'd run the risk of it sounding scratchy, maybe even skipping. "Look, people are going to be paying fifty cents to watch the game. You think they're going to want to listen to a scratchy *Star Spangled Banner* that skips right over *what so proudly we hailed*? No, they're going to want their money back."

"Plus not only will M-M-M-Matty sing *The Spangled B-B-B-Banner,* but he'll s-s-s-sing it falsetto," Fenny said. "The crowd will love it."

"He sings with falsies on?"

"Not *falsies,* Jimmy, *falsetto*," I said. "It's singing like…well, it sounds like you're singing like a little girl."

"Why would you want to sing so you sound like a little girl?"

I told Jimmy I didn't know. "You know why, Fenny?"

Fenny looked at me and shrugged. "All I know is the crowd will love it. Trust me on this, g-g-g-guys."

Okay, we had the National Anthem taken care of. And with Uncle Harold calling balls and strikes—which he promised he'd do when he wasn't signing his autograph for ten dollars a pop—we had an umpire.

Everything was in place. We were ready to play the Brookcrest Viz.

60

WE PLAYED THE GAME before an overflow crowd of twenty-seven-and-a-half, which included a man in a lime-colored polo shirt who Fenny said was none other than Glen Sudek—the Glenn Sudek who was Mickey Mantle's cousin and who could introduce me to The Mick. We would have had a crowd of twenty-eight watching the game, but little Deron Myerson, who was five months old at the time, got tired of sucking his thumb and fell asleep.

We were down 2-0…and we hadn't even reached the second inning yet. Jelly must have had the jitters pitching in front of a crowd of twenty-seven-and-a-half people, because he walked the first batter up for the Viz on four straight pitches. That was followed by walks to the second and third batters.

I'd just about had it with Jelly's pitching, and it must have shown.

"Cotton candy!" he yelled over to me at short.

I called time and walked to the mound. "*Cotton candy*? Holy bull shark, you've walked the bases loaded, and you want cotton candy?"

"That's the problem," Jelly said. "Adele Sommers and I were eating cotton candy before the game started." He showed me the cotton candy stuck to his fingers. "It's hard to grip the ball."

Jelly clearly had a big problem on his hands, and that spelled trouble for our team. I did the only thing I could think of....

"HERE, BOY!"

Yogi had polished off Mrs. Guttman's two-day-old fudge brownies and was humping her leg when I called him. I pointed to Jelly's pitching hand.

"YOGI…LICK!"

Yogi was...oh, maybe three-years-old back then, part cocker spaniel, part poodle—what they call a cock-a-poodle. Which is probably why he'd wake us up every morning at the crack of dawn with his howling.

Yogi Kleinmann was my dog...well, the family's dog...okay, truth is he was anybody's dog who would feed him Chef Boy-Ar-Dee. Yogi got so he could smell an open can as far as Deer Park, which was five miles away as the scent of meatballs blows.

We'd gotten Yogi when he was eight weeks old. He was the collicky runt of the litter, but he was cute and could out-lick his bigger brothers and sisters. Dad said I could name him, which of course I did. Everyone assumed I'd name him *Mickey,* even Uncle Harold, who you'd assume would be a specialist at assuming. But this time Uncle Harold assumed wrong. Naming the little licker after my idol would've been blasphemy. So instead of *Mickey,* I named him *Yogi.*

As Yogi grew up most people who knew him thought his name should be *Tes*, short for *Testosterone*. Yogi had a proclivity to hump everything in sight. Animal, mineral, or vegetable, it didn't matter to Yogi. Most dogs will pee on a fire hydrant. Yogi would hump it. Then he'd go looking for more. In his heyday, Yogi was humping half the hydrants in our neighborhood, though not necessarily in the same afternoon.

It got so bad that Mom wanted to write to Ann Landers for advice. Dad said forget Ann Landers, maybe if we put something in Yogi's food he'd calm down enough so he wouldn't get stiff when he wasn't supposed to—like when Mom was hosting her Canasta group.

It happened the afternoon Yogi followed his humping of Mrs. Levenson's left leg by humping her right. Mom had seen enough. She'd gone to Dad, begging him to come up with something, anything, to unbend Yogi's joint.

That's when Dad had come up with the idea of saltpeter.

Dad, being Dad, thought it was a pretty good idea. But Mom, being Mom, had reservations. She told Dad she was worried the saltpeter might put hair on Yogi's chin. Poor Dad. All he could do was look at Mom and suggest maybe she talk with her therapist next time about electrolysis.

As it turned out, putting saltpeter in Yogi's food had no effect on him. In addition to being part cocker spaniel and part poodle, Yogi must have been part bloodhound, because he could smell the saltpeter when Mom put out his Chef Boy-Ar-Dee. He'd sniff the meatballs and leave his dish untouched. Then he'd go off to hump another fire hydrant.

Say what you will about his testosterone disorder, Yogi was a natural-born athlete. We'd give him a Pee-Wee football, and he'd zig-zag all over the field, tail between his legs, not once zigging into his yesterday's shit. No one could tackle Yogi. We'd try tripping him up by diving at his paws, but he'd never break stride. He was the best broken-field runner I ever saw, and that includes Gale Sayers.

Yogi could jump pretty high too, particularly if you were carrying a platter of hamburgers right off the grill. He probably could have been a good basketball player were it not for the problem he had dribbling. You'd never see Yogi dribble. He'd slobber. Which is why we never encouraged him to play basketball, even though he could drool behind his back.

But it was baseball that Yogi truly loved to play. Never mind he couldn't hit a lick, Yogi would tear around the bases, waging his tail in heated frenzy as he crossed home plate. All it took was a yell of *HOME!* Yogi would lick his chops, kick up his paws, and streak to the Promised Land. No one, not even Mickey himself, could run the bases like Yogi could.

A couple of quick licks and the cotton candy was gone from Jelly's fingers. But the bases were still loaded with Viz with the always dangerous "Farts" Blatz up. Farts was called that because...well, you had to be downwind of Farts just once to know.

I motioned Ferdy Capelman to the mound.

"Take off your catcher's mask, Ferdy, and give it to me."

Ferdy gave me his mask, and I jogged off the field with it, jogging back with a replacement.

"Here, put this on." And I handed Ferdy the gas mask.

Turned out Ferdy didn't need it, because on Jelly's first pitch Farts hit a towering pop-up to center field where

Matty stood, his oversized cap pulled down over his oversized, dark red sunglasses, which practically covered all his face.

"Mine!" Stingman yelled, crossing over in front of Matty.

"No, mine!" Matty yelled, waving Stingman off.

"It's mine! I called it first!" Stingman yelled.

"I got it! I got it!" Matty screamed, pushing his oversized, dark red sunglasses, which were sliding down his nose, back up with one hand and pounding his glove with the other.

As the two stood there in the outfield, yelling at each other about whose ball it was, the ball dropped in between them. The three Brookcrest runners had circled the bases when Matty picked up the ball. After kicking Stingman in the shin, he threw a rocket to Schwabbie that nailed the hustling Farts sliding into third.

Jelly managed to get out of the inning without further damage, but we couldn't do any damage to Jimmy Blintz in our half of the first...or the second, or the third, for that matter. The Viz were up 5-0 going into the fifth, and I was praying for rain.

61

ACCORDING TO THE SCHNEID, baseball rules are clear about rain even when the skies aren't. The Schneid was explaining it was right there in Rule 4.10(c): *"If the game is ended by rain before the bottom of the fifth, all runs are erased and the game has to be replayed from the beginning."*

I looked skyward, called time again, and asked Uncle Harold if he'd do a rain dance.

"Sure, Skippy," Uncle Harold said, adding that when he was younger he'd danced up a storm at open-air Moonlight Gardens, though never in the rain. "What tribe do you want me to do?"

"Tribe?"

"Tribe. You know, like the Comanche, Pawnee, and Mahogany. They all have their own rain dance."

"There are *Mahogany* Indians?"

These days there aren't many left," Uncle Harold said. "They went the way of cigar stores."

Anyone who's ever played baseball knows you don't get anywhere arguing with the umpire. So I bit my lip, not pointing out to Uncle Harold if he was right about the Mahoganys they had to be the only Indians who smoked Perfectos and Panatelas at peace treaties. No, you never tell the umpire he's wrong, particularly if the umpire's Uncle

Harold. Arguing anything with Uncle Harold, on or off a baseball field, was usually futile. So instead of bringing up cigars, I simply told him I didn't care which tribe's rain dance he did as long as it worked.

"In that case I'll do a Chappaqua," Uncle Harold said, explaining he considered himself a specialist in Chappaqua rain dancing despite being censured by the tribe's dance committee for chanting the war dance instead of the rain dance at an invitational powwow.

But the likelihood of Uncle Harold misstepping wasn't my only concern.

I knew enough about Indians to know they still had dress codes for their rain dances. Generally, dancing in galoshes is not permitted, nor is dancing with an umbrella. Most tribes consider it unseemly...unless you happen to dance like Gene Kelly. Then there are tribes in Southern California that insist you wear mid-thigh fake deer moccasins, a designer label headdress, and not much else, not even an umpire mask.

Of course, Schwabbie's backyard was not in Southern California. It was a break for Uncle Harold since it meant he didn't have to worry about violating the rain dance dress code. Not only that, the mask he had on would've caused problems had he been umpiring in Southern California. You just don't rain dance wearing a hand-me-down umpire mask in Southern California...unless you're at Venice Beach.

Uncle Harold must have taken three or four Chappaqua rain dance steps before he stopped with a whoop.

"Whoops!" he yelled through his hand-me-down umpire mask. "You talk about close calls, I could have lost my temporary umpire's license! Baseball rules, Skippy, are specific. Umpires are not permitted to rain dance, not even when dancing with an umbrella. Sorry, no rain dance."

And with that, he put his umpire mask back on and resumed his arms-crossed stance behind home plate, leaving us down 5-0 going into the fifth and not a cloud in the sky.

62

IT WASN'T THAT suddenly we started banging out hits all over Schwabbie's backyard. It was more like the Brookcrest defense coming apart, sort of like Grandma Bessie's knitting. Still, the Viz hung on, even as Ferdy's routine grounder up the middle went through Jimmy Blintz's legs, the shortstop's legs, and the center fielder's legs—three errors altogether. It was a 5-4 game as I came to the plate.

The crowd wasn't exactly on its feet cheering, but they were cheering none the less. And it wasn't for Uncle Harold's autograph, which he'd already reduced from ten dollars to ten cents in a desperate attempt to drum up business. No, the crowd was cheering for me to break my streak. Three times I'd been up, and three times I'd popped out. I clenched my teeth. No way was I going to pop out again. I was due to hit one to the second baseman, and I knew it.

But this time I had it wrong.

I hit a slow roller—not to the second baseman but to the first baseman. He charged in, fielded the ball with his bare hand, and threw hurriedly to Jimmy Blintz covering first. Except Jimmy wasn't covering first. He just stood there on the mound looking totally perplexed... thirteen-years-old and in the midst of a senior moment. The throw ended up in the neighbor's yard, and by the time the ball was retrieved I was standing on third.

I was still standing there as Ferdy went down on strikes, and The Schneid lined to the shortstop for the second out. Then Matty Schwartzman came through with a clean single to left. I danced home with the tying run, but no one was cheering. Matty lay crumpled over the first base bag holding his leg, screaming in pain. He'd pulled his hamstring.

"Now what do we do?" Ferdy said, as Fenny and The Schneid helped Matty off the field.

"Somebody has to run for Matty," Schwabbie said.

"Yeah, but who?" Stingman asked. "There's no one you can put in to pitch run."

"Oh yes there is," I said. "YOGI...HERE, BOY!"

Yogi was napping by a plate of crumbs from Mrs. Fatuzzi's upside-down cake, no doubt dreaming of fire hydrants, but his ears perked up.

"YOGI...FIRST BASE!"

With a whine, Yogi walked to *third* base.

"YOGI...NO! *FIRST* BASE!"

Yogi looked at me, lifted his back leg, and peed on the third base bag. Satisfied, he trotted over to first. We had our pinch runner.

Yogi was sniffing the first base bag for more upside-down cake as Jelly ambled up to the plate. Jelly took Jimmy Blintz's first two pitches for strikes, belched, and then, with a mighty over-swing, bounced a grounder down the left field line, past the outstretched glove of the Viz third baseman. The ball rolled into left field, past the outstretched glove of the left fielder, as Yogi sat at first base, licking his balls.

"YOGI...HOME!"

Yogi perked up his ears, then raced straight to home plate.

"YOGI...NO! SECOND...THIRD... *THEN* HOME!"

Yogi yelped and skidding, made a U-turn to second. He rounded second and was halfway to third by the time the Viz left fielder finally got to the ball and fired it to the shortstop. But Yogi wasn't about to stop. With his mouth drooling, he rounded third and headed for home as the Viz shortstop caught the ball, whirled, and threw a bullet to the catcher guarding the plate.

"YOGI...SLIDE!"

Yogi slid headfirst into home plate as the catcher tagged him on his rabies tag. There was a howl and a yelp that I knew wasn't Yogi's. Yogi had nipped the Viz catcher.

"OUT!" Uncle Harold yelled.

Yogi growled at Uncle Harold.

"SAFE!" Uncle Harold yelled.

Yogi licked Uncle Harold and, with his head held high, stood on home plate wagging his tail. He'd scored the winning run.

The Aracoma crowd went wild. We mobbed Yogi as he peed on home plate. I petted his head as The Schneid plucked a tick off his ear—Yogi's, that is.

"Wow, head first! Now that's a slide!" yelled out a kid from the first row of the crowd, which also happened to be the only row in the crowd. "I'm sliding that way from now on."

"He's my cousin," Schwabbie explained, turning to Ferdy and me. "Thinks he's some kind of jock. But my Uncle Harry says he's not that bad a ballplayer. His name's Petey, Petey Rose. C'mon, I'll introduce you."

"I'd rather meet Glen Sudek," I said.

"He's my godfather," Ferdy piped up.

"I know," I said. "Can you introduce me?"

"Sure," Ferdy said. And he walked away.

"Hey, wait a minute!" I yelled at him. "I thought you were going to introduce me."

Ferdy stopped and turned around. "Huh?"

"To Glen Sudek." I pointed to the man in the lime-colored polo shirt.

"Him?"

I nodded.

"Huh? He's not Glen Sudek."

"But—"

"That's Mr. Poindexter, my clarinet teacher. Can I go now?"

63

I WAS STILL SEETHING at Fenny, and I don't think anyone would blame me. Matty Schwartzman—the Matty Schwartzman who'd hobbled off the field in the ninth after singling me home with the tying run, the Matty Schwartzman with the oversized, dark red sunglasses that made him look like a cicada, the Matty Schwartzman who'd sung *The Star Spangled Banner*, stunning the crowd by ad libbing it—was *not* Fenny's foster cousin. The soothing falsetto voice was not falsetto, but the voice of a *girl*. Matty Schwartzman, in fact, wasn't Matty Schwartzman.

Matty Schwartzman was *Madeline Schwartz*.

"Why did you do it, Fenny? Why did you do it?"

"Why? Look, we needed another outfielder, d-d-d-didn't we?"

"Yeah, but you had to go and pull one over on me. *Madeline?* You had to use *Madeline*? A girl?"

"B-B-B-But she has no trouble passing for a b-b-b-boy, does she?" Fenny reminded me that Madeline had the flattest chest of all the girls in the eighth grade. "And she can hit a b-b-b-ball too. Hey, did she s-s-s-single you in with the tying run, or didn't she?"

"You had me believing Madeline was your cousin!"

"*Foster* c-c-c-cousin."

"And Glen Sudek? You said that man was Glen Sudek."

"So I was wrong. You've never b-b-b-been wrong about Sudeks?"

I had to admit Fenny had a point. Not only that, but more important he had plunked down thirty-five cents for my milkshake. The way Fenny probably figured it, buying me a milkshake would make up for deceiving me.

He was right.

We were standing outside this new little hamburger place which Jelly said had great chocolate shakes. That we were standing was because they didn't have any seats, not even stools at the counter. They also didn't have any carhops.

What they did have were these two stupid-looking giant golden arches out in front with a huge sign that read *OVER 60,000 SOLD.* Underneath, in small letters and in parenthesis, were the words *in Southern California.*

"Jelly s-s-s-says it's their first franchise in Cincinnati," Fenny explained. "He s-s-s-says they only sell hamburgers, fries, Cokes, and shakes."

"That's all?

Fenny nodded.

"That's it, Fenny? No pizza? What, they couldn't even do a simple cheese slice?"

"No pizza."

I shook my head. This was no way to run a place that was kid-friendly. "You can't sit down...no carhops...you can't get pizza."

"B-B-B-But they do have napkins. And they're folded fresh daily."

I looked at Fenny and shrugged. Maybe it was the kind of place that was popular in Southern California, but I knew there was no way McDonald's was going to make it in Cincinnati...unless maybe it was west of Vine Street.

64

I COULD HAVE KILLED Uncle Harold, and I wanted to. But I knew if I did, when I got back to Cincinnati Grandma Bessie would never speak to me again.

"I'm sorry about this, Skippy, I really am," Uncle Harold was saying. "I can't figure it out. I should have had enough gas to make it. It's exactly .75 miles to Yankee Stadium, and with half a gallon in my tank you'd think we would've made it with almost a pint to spare."

"It's not .75 miles!" I snapped at him. "How can it be? It's a quarter-mile from your house to the next block! It's got to be more like 7.5 miles to the Stadium."

"Is that what it is…you sure?" Uncle Harold said. "I was never good with decibels when I was in school. I always put 'em in the wrong place."

Old-Timers Day was scheduled to start at two o'clock, and it was already past one. We'd already missed the festivities and now it looked like the time we got to Yankee Stadium and parked the car, the Old-Timers Game—the game with DiMaggio, Lefty Gomez, and Charlie Gehringer—would be long over.

I'd flown to LaGuardia the day before, and Uncle Harold had picked me up and driven to his place without any problem. That was yesterday. Today, Uncle Harold had run out of gas before we even hit Pelham Parkway.

Luckily, there was a pay phone on the corner. Uncle Harold borrowed a dime from me and called Tony's Shell station two blocks down the street. In less than an hour, someone came over with the half pint of low octane Uncle Harold asked for.

Old-Timers Day has been a tradition at Yankee Stadium for I don't know how many years. Some say it started with Lou Gehrig Appreciation Day in 1939, when the dying Iron Horse gave his *I'm the luckiest man in the world* speech. Others, like Marty Appel, who for years was the Yankees PR man, say it goes back to the final game of the 1947 season. Take your pick. Me, I'd go with Marty.

Anyhow, every year since whenever the Yankees have invited about fifty former players to take part in Old-Timers Day. One-by-one they take a bow as their name, position, and feats are read to the cheering crowd that's packed the Stadium. Until he died, DiMaggio was always introduced last—always to a standing ovation—as *baseball's greatest living player.* You introduced him that way or he wouldn't show up, and what kind of Yankee Old-Timers Day would it be without Joe DiMaggio?

The game itself is played two innings...maybe three at most. That's about all some of the old-timers can last. Besides, the game isn't for true competition as much as nostalgia for the fans, more than thrilled to see their favorite players from yesteryear make it to the plate even once.

On the car radio, Mel Allen was announcing the starting lineups for the Old-Timers Game....

"And at second base...from the Detroit Tigers...he finished his career batting over .300 thirteen times, leading the American League with a .371 average in 1937...a cornerstone of three Tiger pennant winners...called The Mechanical Man for his remarkable consistency...Hall-of-Famer Charlie Gehringer...."

I looked at Uncle Harold and sighed.

65

"HEY, MISTER! THREE BUCKS TO WATCH YOUR CAR!"

The kids from the tenements near Yankee Stadium may not have known about Al Capone and Frank Nitti, but they sure knew extortion and had mastered it by the age of nine. If you didn't give them the three dollars they asked for, odds were better than excellent when you came back to get your car after the game you'd find your tires slashed and not a kid in sight.

Uncle Harold gave the juvenile godfather three dollars, and we joined the other latecomers hurrying along to the ballpark.

"There it is, The House that Ruth Built," Uncle Harold said. "Really something, isn't it?"

"Yeah, it sure is."

"You know, Skippy, if I hadn't had my arm broken, I could have pitched there."

I rolled my eyes.

"What, you don't think so? Never question your Uncle Harold, Skippy. Wait till you see the surprise I have for you after the game."

"What's that?"

"Didn't I just tell you never to question me?"

Uncle Harold and I walked through the turnstiles into the mobbed concourse. There were vendors selling scorecards, vendors selling Yankee yearbooks, vendors selling hot dogs and Crackerjacks and beer and peanuts and Eskimo Pies and cotton candy. Vendors selling Rolaids.

"C'mon, Skippy," Uncle Harold said. "This way. Stick with me."

We joined the mass of fans funneling straight ahead until we were at Checkpoint Charlie at Gate 3. There stood Charlie. He had, of course, been vetted and was snappily dressed in a perfectly ironed and starched usher uniform with a Yankee baseball cap on his head.

"Tickets."

Uncle Harold showed him our tickets.

"Upper Deck," Charlie said. *"Follow the ramp."*

We did a one-eighty and were heading toward "follow-the-ramp" when Uncle Harold announced he had to go to the john.

"Wait here. I've got to take a leak."

Five minutes later, Uncle Harold was still in the men's room. Either he was streaming like a horse or he'd struck up a friendship. I was getting more and more anxious, and then a voice came over the PA.

"GOOD AFTERNOON AND WELCOME TO YANKEE STADIUM...HERE ARE TODAY'S STARTING LINEUPS...FOR THE TIGERS, LEADING OFF AND PLAYING SHORTSTOP, HARVEY KUENN...KUENN...."

There was a chorus of boos but no Uncle Harold.

"BATTING SECOND, IN CENTER FIELD, BILL TUTTLE...TUTTLE...."

More boos and still no Uncle Harold.

251

"BATTING THIRD, IN RIGHT FIELD, AL KALINE...KALINE...."

Finally he came out, zipping his fly up with a look of relief on his face.

"Look, I had to go. Let's go!"

Up the ramp we went to Checkpoint Steven on the second level. This time we were halfway through the gate before we were stopped.

"Tickets."

His face flushed, Uncle Harold smiled and showed Steven our tickets.

"Upper-Upper Deck," Steven said. *"Follow the ramp."*

Back on the follow-the-ramp we went, with Uncle Harold now panting and grimacing.

"BATTING FOURTH, IN LEFT FIELD, DAVE PHILLEY...PHILLEY...."

"You okay?" I asked him.

"Prostate. Got to piss."

"NO!" I screamed.

"Yes," Uncle Harold said, and in a flash he was gone. But he didn't get very far before a security guard stopped him for going the wrong way on a one-way ramp.

Two piss stops later, we reached the end of "follow-the-ramp." We'd passed the restroom line and gone as high as we could go, past a sign that read *Highest Elevation in American League Urinals.* We'd reached the Upper-Upper Deck.

They'd announced the official paid attendance at 50,338 and the 338 must have been high up in WW, jam-packed into the 52nd row. Nose bleeds were everywhere. We stumbled our way through wave after wave of elbows and knees and spilled beer and slippery peanut shells till we got to our seats.

That's when we saw it.

Uncle Harold took a handkerchief from his pocket and, grumbling to himself, wiped off the mess on the seat. Now I have to tell you despite my familiarity with pigeons, I was no expert on bird shit. But as high up as we were, I knew it had to be the work of a loose-boweled Peregrine falcon.

"Must have been a Peregrine falcon," I told Uncle Harold.

"Must have been a herd of them," Uncle Harold said.

I knew it was useless to try to tell him birds didn't fly in herds. So I just explained a herd was unlikely because Peregrines were an endangered species.

"He's gonna be endangered all right if comes back here and messes with me!" Uncle Harold looked up to the sky, flipping the bird to an unseen bird. "I don't take crap from no bird."

Suddenly, he closed his eyes and, just as quickly, came that all-too familiar grimace.

"I know, I know," I said. "Prostate."

And with that he was gone, scrambling back through the waves. Someone must have kneed him where it hurts, because I heard him howl as he ran down the aisle with his legs crossed.

66

I DIDN'T SEE much of the game. Oh, I heard it all right, heard the overflow crowd cheer each time the Yankees got a hit. But I didn't get to see too many of them.

And it was all because of the Winnebago brothers.

The two of them must have weighed half a ton dripping wet, which they were most of the game since they kept spilling beer all over themselves. The Winnebagos had parked their wide-load bodies right smack in front of us. I couldn't see over them, and I sure as heck couldn't see around them. Inning after inning, it was more of the same. The only time I could catch even a glimpse of the action on the field was when one of the Winnebagos would lean forward and hand signal a vendor. They hand signaled vendors selling hot dogs and pop, vendors selling beer, the vendors selling cotton candy, Eskimo Pies, peanuts, and Cracker Jacks. Vendors selling Rolaids.

When his prostate wasn't acting up, Uncle Harold was busy ogling the busty redhead to our left, that is when he wasn't ogling the busty blonde five rows down. Uncle Harold would later swear the blonde was a reincarnation of Marilyn Monroe—which now that I think of it was kind of silly because Marilyn Monroe hadn't died yet.

Like I said, I didn't see much of the game. But I didn't have to see much to know Don Larsen just didn't have it that day. Even with the Winnebagos parked in front of me, I could see the big scoreboard in left-center, and it said Larsen was behind on the hitters.

By the bottom of the third, the Tigers had taken a 5-2 lead, and Larsen was showering in the Yankee clubhouse.

By the bottom of the seventh, the Winnebagos had long left, the vendors had long run out of Rolaids, and the Yankees were trailing 6-3.

"Don't you worry, Skippy," Uncle Harold said. "They'll come back. Just you wait and see."

Wait and see must have been the magic words, because suddenly the Yankee bats came alive. Richardson lined a one-out base hit and scored on Kubek's triple. Lumpe's grounder back to Foytack should have been the second out, but the Tiger pitcher picked up the ball and threw wildly to first, allowing Kubek to score. With Foytack tiring, the Tigers brought in Sleater to face Yogi. Yogi was known as a bad-ball hitter, so Sleater threw him one right down the middle. Yogi swung late and popped out to Harvey Kuenn at short for the third out.

Going into the eighth, the Yankees were down just one run. There were two out when Mickey took his stance in the batter's box. I knew, I just knew, with one swing The Mick was going to tie the game, that at long last I was going to see him hit one of his tape-measure home runs.

Sleater's first pitch to Mickey was right over the plate. He didn't swing: *Strike one*. Sleater missed with the next two pitches: *Two balls, one strike.*

"Curveball," Uncle Harold said. "Watch, he'll curve Mickey at the knees."

Sleater threw a fastball high in tight. Mickey fouled it into the seats behind first: *Two balls, two strikes.*

Sleater missed again with a fastball low and outside: *Full count, three-two.*

"Fastball," Uncle Harold said. "Three-two count, he's got to come in with his fastball."

But with a three-two count, Sleater threw a wicked curve that just missed the outside corner of the plate.

Mickey dropped his bat and started toward first base. But he didn't get very far....

"STEE-RIKE!" yelled the umpire. *"YER OUT!"*

A thunder of boos rained down on the umpire. They came from left field, from right, from the box seats behind home, and high in the upper deck. They came from the men's room, which had a TV above the urinals. They came and came and came.

The Mick stood there dumbfounded at the call. But Casey Stengel wasn't. He stormed out of the Yankee dugout, and he didn't look happy. Smoke was coming out of his ears. Casey stood there at home plate, jaw to jaw with the ump, screaming up a storm and kicking up dust. From where we sat I couldn't be sure, but I think Casey was rabidly foaming at his mouth too.

It all got him nowhere. Casey was tossed out of the game for trying to drown the umpire in bodily fluid, and the Yankees were out of the inning.

"Don't you worry," Skippy," Uncle Harold said. "They'll get to Sleater next inning. You wait and see."

But the Tiger reliever fanned both Simpson and Slaughter to start the ninth. There were two outs, with Lumpe due up, when Yankee coach Frankie Crosetti, who'd taken over the managerial reins from Casey, called Lump back to the dugout. The Crow was sending in a pinch hitter.

Elston Howard was now in his third season with the Yankees, but even with all the talent he had it'd been hard for Casey to find room for him in the starting lineup. So Casey was mostly using Ellie to give Yogi an occasional rest and to sometimes play the outfield. That Ellie couldn't run fast didn't mean beans to Casey. Or to the writers who covered the Yankees. Elston Howard, they told their readers, was one of the nicest guys you'd find around the league even if he was a Negro—which is what they called African Americans back then.

Ellie took Sleater's first pitch for a strike. The second pitch was a fastball, knee-high and right over the plate, just like Ellie liked them. He swung hard and drove it deep, deep to right field...but not quite deep enough. Al Kaline stood at the wall, pounding his glove.

And that, as they say, was the ballgame.

I looked around. Everyone was feeling kind of down. Everyone that is but Uncle Harold. He was looking at me and smiling that stupid smile of his.

"I've got a surprise for you, Skippy," he said. "Didn't want to tell you till after the game. We're going down to the Yankee clubhouse. You're going to meet Mickey Mantle."

67

"HUBIE OWES ME. He owes me big time," Uncle Harold said. "Don't you worry, Hubie will get us into the clubhouse. Heck, he'll probably insist on introducing us to The Mick."

Hubie Suvpansky was the Yankees' third-string catcher. The reason he was backup to the backup had nothing to do with his bat, though he was a .225 lifetime hitter. It had to do with his play behind the plate, which was often an adventure. In 1958, Hubie would be gone from the Yankees, traded to Kansas City, where he would lead all American League catchers in errors.

Anyway, Uncle Harold said he had an in with Hubie Suvpansky. The way Uncle Harold explained, it went all the way back to when he was pitching for the Poughkeepsie Scalpers. That was before it was politically incorrect for athletic teams to nickname themselves after people who bought tickets for later sale at higher than regular prices. Once the pendulum swung, the Poughkeepsie Scalpers would succumb to mounting public pressure and become simply the Poughkeepsie Humidity, and no one could quarrel with that, particularly in the summer.

But I digress.

There was Uncle Harold playing in Poughkeepsie, where he quickly became known as both a pitching and hitting threat—pitching for the then Scalpers and hitting on just about every female, attached or unattached, between sixteen and sixty.

During one of his hitting sprees, he happened to hit on this gal from New Haven, who was in town staying with her best friend's second cousin for the first time…or something like that. He met her at the pawnshop, and within hours the two were an item. That night they were necking on her best friend's second cousin's couch when they were hit with, what they call in Latin, *necking interruptis*. Out from behind the couch came the ten-year-old kid brother of the gal's best friend's second cousin. He stood there, in front of the couch, grinning at the happily entwined couple.

"Uh, kid, don't you have something to do now?" Uncle Harold cued.

"Nope," the kid answered. "I'll just stay here and watch you guys. Can you tell yet if they're real or if she's wearing falsies?"

"What will it take for you to leave the room?"

"Twenty-five cents."

Uncle Harold didn't have any change on him, so he gave the kid a buck. But the kid didn't have any money to make change.

"You owe me. You owe me big," Uncle Harold said. "What's your name?"

The kid told Uncle Harold his name, and Uncle Harold never forgot that Hubie Suvpansky owed him big time.

68

SITTING ON A STOOL outside the Yankee clubhouse was a Summo-sized security guard dressed in an official New York Yankee security kimono. Pinned on it was what looked like a tarnished Phi Beta Kappa key, along with a nametag that read *Security Guard, Isoroku Knish, Ph.D.*

Knish had a GI Joe walkie-talkie on his right hip and a half bottle of Mogen David on his left. He was inhaling what Uncle Harold said smelled like a pickled herring and wasabi pizza with extra horseradish. Uncle Harold insisted the raw slices of meat on the pizza were *dasoku.*

"*Dasoku?*"

"Snake legs. Jewish people eat them in Japan. Sometimes with raw gefilte fish."

"*Nu?* Youlookingforsumpin'?" Knish garbled, munching a slice of pizza, which, because of its fumes, he held upside down. He didn't seem to notice the trail of horseradish dripping all the way down to the sawed-off Samurai sword on his lap. Not knowing how sharp the blade was, I thought it best not to say anything.

Uncle Harold told him we'd come all the way down from the Upper-Upper Deck to see Hubie, but Knish's mouth was full so he couldn't swallow what Uncle Harold was saying.

"Youareherefor*who?*"

"Hubie," I said. "Hubie Suvpansky."

Knish wiped a herring off his pickled chin. "Yankees got Mickey. Yankees got Yogi. Yankees got Whitey and Moose. And you want *Hubie Suvpansky?* Nobody asks for Suvpansky. Not even his mother."

"We go back a long way," Uncle Harold said, explaining he was Hal Green and that he used to pitch for the Chillicothe Scalpers before they became the Chillicothe Humidity. If Knish was impressed he didn't show it.

"And this little *nebbish?*" he asked, apparently referring to me. "Looks little like Ricky Nelson with zits."

"Nope, he's my nephew with zits," Uncle Harold said. "And other than my cousin Harry, there are no nebbishes in the family."

"You sure about that?"

"Pretty sure," Uncle Harold said. "Well, there's my nephew Philip in Baltimore."

I was about to tell Knish that Philip lived not in Baltimore, but in Bellmore and that Bellmore was on the south shore of Long Island. But I thought why embarrass Uncle Harold when he could do a good job all by himself. Best I not say anything about postal codes. Or the first book of the *American Zip Codes* trilogy for that matter.

"Anyway," Uncle Harold was saying, "this boy here is my nephew Philip."

"Thought you said nephew Philip was in Baltimore."

"Bellmore," I said, unable to hold back. "On the south shore of Long Island."

Knish looked lost. So did Uncle Harold, who had a history of getting lost in Bellmore while looking for the racetrack, which, of course, has always been in Belmont and not Bellmore.

"Actually, he's called *Skippy*," Uncle Harold said.

"Who?"

"My nephew here. We call him *Skippy* so nobody will confuse him with Philip in Baltimore."

"Bellmore," I said.

Knish scratched his head.

"Are you really a Ph.D?" I asked him.

Knish nodded. "Wrote dissertation on Loman history."

"You mean *Roman* history," Uncle Harold said.

Knish scowled at him. "What, you think I can't pronounce *R*?" He took a deep breath. "Grimy grumpy gremlins greedily grabbing greasy griddlecakes gruesomely."

"Wow, you did that in one breath!" I said.

Knish smiled. "If I say *Loman*, I mean Loman. L-O-M-A-N...Loman. Willie, Biff, and the rest of the family."

Uncle Harold looked puzzled.

"Death of a Salesman," I said.

"Oh, that," Uncle Harold said. "We had to read it in mortuary science. I got an *Incomplete."* He looked at me with sadness in his eyes. "That's why I couldn't go out for football. The coach really wanted me out there too. Said he thought I'd make a good tackling dummy."

"Feh...football, schmootball," Knish said. "You and Skip-ala wait on dotted line." He pointed at the white dots in front of his feet. "Going inside and see if Suvpansky can come out. And no funny business from you two. Got eyes peeled in back of my *keppe*."

In minutes he was back, peeled eyes in the back of his *keppe* and all.

"*Bubkes*," he said. "You've got *bubkes*. Moose said Suvpansky just left with some *zaftig* blonde with...." And he stuck out both hands, palms up, from his chest. "Moose said she wanted him right away to surprise her cousin taking the train in from New Haven. Something like that. Not sure. Anyway, no Hubie Suvpansky. You happy now?"

"No Hubie Suvpansky?" Uncle Harold whined.

"ISN'T THAT WHAT I SAID?" Knish screamed, waving his sword, which looked like it was stained with blood—either that or red horseradish.

"Well, I guess that's...that," Uncle Harold said, fixated on the sword, his lip quivering and shaking in his penny loafers. "Sorry, Skippy...no...Hubie."

I was ready to cry, but Uncle Harold, whose eyebrows never left the sword being waved, beat me to the punch.

"Stop crying already!" Knish said, putting down his sword. "Maybe I can get Yogi."

I shook my head. Uncle Harold sighed.

"How about Woodling? Think I can get Gene Woodling."

"Actually, we want Mickey Mantle," I said.

"Oh, *Mantle!* Why didn't you say so?" And Knish grunted again. "*Oy*, now I have to go back inside." With that, he turned and started back inside the Yankee clubhouse. "Be right back," he said. "Do nothing funny."

"I know, I know," I said. "Your eyes are peeled in the back of your *keppe*."

Knish shot Uncle Harold a look that could wipe the smile off the Mona Lisa. Uncle Harold shrugged his shoulders.

So Uncle Harold and I stood on the dotted line while Knish went back inside the clubhouse. Within minutes he returned, a pickled smile on his herring-ed face. He handed a photo of Mickey to me.

"You don't understand," I said. "We want to *meet* Mickey."

He laughed. "You want to *meet* Mickey? *Mickey Mantle?* A million *pishers* like you want to meet Mickey Mantle. Anyway, Skip-ala, he's not in clubhouse. Just left. See that blue, pin-striped T-Bird pulling out of lot? That's Mickey Mantle."

He looked at us and guffawed. "HE WANTS TO MEET MANTLE! LITTLE PISHER WANTS TO MEET MICKEY MANTLE!*"*

He was making such an infernal racket I knew there'd be dozens of calls to the police complaining about loud guffawing going on in a public neighborhood. And I was, of course, right. In minutes there were police sirens wailing.

"I think we should get to D'Aglamino's," Uncle Harold said.

"I think we should get there *now*," I stressed.

So Uncle Harold said *Sayonara*, I said *Shalom*, and we hurried off to D'Aglamino's, leaving Isoroku Knish standing there guffawing.

69

SOME PEOPLE SAY it doesn't matter whether you win or lose, it's where you went after the game. Uncle Harold and I went to D'Aglamino's.

D'Aglamino's is on Arthur Avenue in the Bronx and has been an institution in New York for generations, probably going back to when your great-grandparents were in diapers, and makes the absolute best ice cream you'll ever taste anywhere. And I'm not the only one who says that. Aunt Tillie does too.

D'Aglamino's is the kind of a place where fathers and mothers take their sons and daughters…and where uncles take their favorite nephews.

Unbelievably long lines are the norm at D'Aglamino's, and the line Uncle Harold and I were in was no exception. We were, in fact, so far from the soda fountain we had to be near the Bronx Zoo. Uncle Harold was grumbling something about the game and the Yankees' cruddy base running, but I paid no attention. The running I was worried about had nothing to do with the Yankees. Running out of chocolate syrup before we got to the soda fountain, that was my worry.

Sundaes, banana-boat splits, and top-heavy double-dip cones were being dripped left and right from the flurry of hands behind the fountain. The smell of hot fudge was everywhere. We were close enough to hear distinct human voices above the whirling of milkshake blenders. All sorts of customers were asking scurrying D'Aglamino's kids all sorts of things.

"What kind of flavors do you have?" asked some man who obviously had never been to D'Aglamino's before.

"What *flavors* do we have?" whined a frenzied D'Aglamino's girl from behind the fountain. She'd slipped on a banana peel, and a boat of ice cream, syrups, and whipped cream was smeared all over her ample chest.

"You want to know all the flavors? Take a look. They're all over my arms, they're all over my apron and shirt. See something you like, sir?"

"How about the left breast?"

I couldn't see if he got what he wanted, and to tell you the truth, I really didn't care. Like Grandpa Albert used to say, *First things, first.* And right then the first thing on my mind was an ice cream soda to end all ice cream sodas. We kept inching forward, and then it happened. We were *"Next!"*

"Double chocolate-chip ice cream soda with three scoops, please," I said to the girl with the multi-flavored left breast. "And could you put two cherries on top of the whipped cream?"

"One double chocolate-chip ice cream soda with three scoops," she repeated. "Two cherries on top of the whipped cream. And you?" she said, looking straight at Uncle Harold.

"The usual."

"A second straw and a second spoon," the girl with the multi-flavored left breast said. "Would you like that to go or stay?"

"Both," Uncle Harold answered.

"That'll be twenty-five cents," she snorted.

"Here's a quarter," Uncle Harold said. "Keep the change."

Now the fun began. We'd bought the ice cream soda to end all ice cream sodas and had the receipt to prove we paid for it. Uncle Harold waved the receipt at the manager then carefully pocketed it, saying he needed it for his tax return. Now all we needed was a place to sit down and slurp away. I was feeling kind of drowsy from sitting out in the sun all day, so I knew an empty table wasn't going to be easy to find. But I managed to spot one across from the restrooms. I grabbed the double chocolate-chip soda with three scoops, whipped cream, and two cherries, Uncle Harold grabbed the second straw and spoon, and we quickly grabbed two of the seats at the table.

That's when we noticed it.

It was all over the wobbly chairs. Uncle Harold took a couple of napkins and, grumbling to himself, wiped off the puddles of vanilla ice cream.

"Must have been a little kid," I told him.

"Must have been a herd of them!" It was a woman's voice.

I turned to my left.

She was sitting at the next two tables. In front of her were three fully-loaded banana boats and a gigantic plastic cup with Harry Bellafonte's picture on it—that's the cup

D'Aglamino's always gave you when you asked for a giant-sized banana milkshake.

You couldn't forget girth like hers, and I didn't. Despite her oversized pink-rimmed sun glasses, which covered most of her face, I had no trouble recognizing her from last summer. I'd seen her at the Cincinnati Garden when Ringling Brothers was in town.

She was The Fat Lady.

There was a belch, and the first boat was history. Then she winked at Uncle Harold and gave him a seductive triple-chinned smile.

Uncle Harold looked at her and blanched. "Prostate," he announced, making a mad, panicked dash to the men's room.

If The Fat Lady was disappointed she didn't show it. Instead, she shoveled the second banana boat into her mouth, washing it down with a gulp of the Belafonte. She belched, smiled at me, and belched again. She probably would have cut one too, but everyone knows women don't fart in public, not even fat ladies.

"Would you like to split this banana split with me?" she asked, motioning to the third boat. "I really shouldn't eat all of it, but they want me to. I'm on a new high-fat diet because I need to gain fifty pounds. My outfits are getting too loose on me."

"No thanks," I said.

"You're all decked out in a Yankee shirt and Yankee cap. Were you two at the game?"

"Yes ma'am."

"I heard the Yankees lost...and in front of people too! How did Mantle do?"

"A single in the first. But I missed seeing it."

I was going to tell her the reason I missed seeing it was because the Winnebago boys were blocking my view, but I didn't want to upset her by making disparaging remarks about wide-bodied baseball fans. Best I not say anything about the Winnebago brothers...or Ringling Brothers for that matter. Instead, I told her I'd also missed Mickey after the game.

"Knish said he'd already left the clubhouse."

"Kah-nish?"

"Well, I'm not sure it's *Kah*-nish. It could be *Kay*-nish. Or maybe the *K*'s silent."

She looked confused, and frankly I couldn't blame her.

"He's the security guard. And he made fun of us."

"That's horrible." She wiped a tear from her eye."You poor, poor child. You must be suffering emotionally," she added therapeutically. "It's a pity you didn't get to meet Mantle. He's really a nice guy."

And she belched again.

"You know Mickey Mantle?"

"Not exactly. His wife belongs to our church sisterhood. Sometimes Mickey comes to early mass with her when he's in town. When he does, he likes to put tickets in the basket they pass around."

"Yankee tickets?"

"Box seats. The Mantles are pretty devout, you know."

"Church! He goes to church! I hit my forehead. "Why didn't I think of that?"

"Well, don't worry about it. Life goes on. Enjoy your ice cream. Tomorrow's a new day of sundaes."

Philip Schlaeger

70

THE MICK WASN'T AT CHURCH on Sunday. He must have been tipped off the church was going to being taken over by Corinthians...precisely *14:11.*

That was the passage in *1 Corinthians* Father Thomas Dolan was talking about. Not that the congregation of Saint George and the Dragon was listening, you understand. By the time Father Dolan got to his interpretation of...*I thought as a child,* the choir was snoring in three-part harmony.

In truth, half the balcony had already tuned out, some muttering *Amen* as they nodded off. Others in the congregation weren't as restful. Like the worshipper in the second row, who'd started kicking the pew in his sleep. It was loud enough to draw the attention of Father Dolan. He stopped in mid *Amen* and quickly called upon Saint Apnea, the patron saint of sleep disorders, to intervene. While Father Dolan was waiting for St. Apnea—at the moment no doubt busy intervening elsewhere—he lost the other half of the congregation.

But *14:11* wasn't lost on Ira. To him, it was clearly a message from above.

Ira Luwis lived two doors down from Uncle Harold in the Bronx apartment towers they called Co-Op City. Though he was only fourteen, Ira had a lot in common with

Uncle Harold as they were both school dropouts. Every afternoon at three-thirty, the two of them would swing together in the playground between buildings 23 and 42. But not today. With Uncle Harold home nursing a cold, he'd asked me to go to the playground in his place.

Ira had on a red, white, and green striped tee-shirt, which he'd untucked from his grass-stained Levis. On his feet were high-top Converses, triple-knotted so he wouldn't trip over the laces.

"You move the dots in *14:11*," he said, "and know what you get?"

"No, Ira. What do you get?"

"You get *1:411*. Gee whiz, isn't it clear?"

"What's clear?"

"That's going to be the winning combination in the contest this week...*1:411*. It's a sign. Those are the numbers the Bible wants you to go with. Mickey's going to hit one home run, and it's going to travel four hundred and eleven feet."

"That's what the *Bible* says?"

"New Testament. Corinthians is New Testament."

"Ridiculous," I said. "You're going to sit there playing Jacks and tell me that's why *1 Corinthians 14:11* was the topic for the sermon?"

Ira scooped up four jacks before the ball bounced. "The sermon could've been on something like the spread of violence in kindergarten classrooms, or why the Gospels never said anything about cheating on Easter egg hunts. But that wasn't the sermon, was it? It was about *Corinthians*."

"Ira, nothing personal, but you don't know what you're talking about."

"You questioning *Corinthians*? You know what *1 Corinthians 14:11* tells us?"

"No, but—"

"What *1 Corinthians 14:11* says is we should put away childish reasoning."

"So?"

"So, don't you see it? That means your entry shouldn't be based on the ERAs of the pitchers Mickey will be facing this week. That's childhood reasoning."

"You've got to be kidding! *Corinthians*?"

"Yeah. They're superheroes. You know, like the Fantastic Four."

"Hey, maybe the Corinthians should do a movie serial!" I said. "Think they could get Errol Flynn?"

Ira suddenly beamed. *"Fivsies!"*

He'd tossed his ball into the air and scooped up all five jacks before the ball bounced.

71

"AND I'M TELLING YOU I have so been to Mickey Mantle's house!"

You couldn't miss recognizing Ira's voice when he got agitated, and Ira Luwis was agitated.

"Right, you were at The Mick's house, and I'm the Dolly Lemon," Ryan said.

"That's *Dali Lama*," said Aaron, who knew all the provinces of Tibet like the thumb of his hand, but nevertheless wasn't a licensed Buddhist.

"You writing a book?" Porky said, eying the double chocolate cake sitting on Ryan's plate. "Say, Ryan, if you're not gonna eat that cake, okay if I have it?"

"Sure, Pork."

Porky snatched the cake, shoving it into his mouth.

We were in the pavilion at Glen Head Park in New Rochelle. It was Ira's sister's Sweet Sixteen party, and while Maureen and her friends were out on the floor doing the Hokey Pokey, Ira and I were standing next to the punch table, talking baseball with Ryan Rappaport, Porky Babirusa, Gordon Hymandinger, some kid I didn't know, and Aaron Levy, who everybody knew.

"You've really been to The Mick's house?" I asked Ira. "You've actually been inside?"

"Well, I haven't actually been inside. But I've seen his house. My brother Jerry took me there."

"Jerry is *your brother*?" said the kid I didn't know. "*Jerry Lewis?*

"Jerry's his half-brother," I said. "And it's Luwis with a *u,* not Lewis with an *e.* "

"*Half* brother?" Gordon asked. "What happened to the other half?"

"What's the difference?" Ryan said. "What are you a half-wit?"

That got Porky guffawing. Which isn't a smart thing to do when your mouth is stuffed with double chocolate cake. I now had a half-eaten helping of double chocolate cake on my plate, and it wasn't half eaten by me.

Ira wasn't nonplussed. Fact is he was pretty plussed. But he pulled himself together enough to explain Jerry had a newspaper route in Mount Vernon and was delivering papers after school when he saw a mailbox with *Mantle* on it.

"Can't be," Ryan said. "The Mick doesn't live in Mount Vernon. He lives in Bronxville. Right, Pork?"

"You writing a book?" Porky said.

Ryan ignored him. "Ira, why would he live in Mount Vernon when he can afford Bronxville?"

"Nope, it's Mount Vernon," Ira insisted. "He lives at the end of his…you know, college sex."

"*Cul-de-sac*," Aaron said. "It comes from the Latin *cûlus saccus*. It means dead-end street."

"You writing a *Latin* book," Porky said, reaching across the table for some punch. "Ah, Skip, if you're not going to eat that cake can I have it back?"

"You're not serious, are you?" said the kid I didn't know. I'm not sure, but from where I stood it looked like he was going to throw up.

"Oh, Porky's serious all right," Ryan said. "Wait till you hear him oink."

Oink or not, I wanted to steer the talk back to Jerry Luwis and Mickey's mailbox. "How do you know Jerry's not pulling your leg?" I asked Ira.

We all looked at him—except for Porky, who'd grabbed the cake back off my plate and was already swallowing it, and the kid I didn't know, who'd rushed to the bathroom, holding his hand over his mouth.

"Yeah," Ryan said. "How do you know Jerry's not putting you on?"

"Because," Ira said, "he took me there."

72

SHE WASN'T THE PRETTIEST girl at the party, but she had to be the smartest. She must have been because she'd ignored Ira, Ryan, Gordon, the kid I didn't know, Aaron, and Porky, and walked right up to me, her teeth glowing.

She was green-eyed and freckle-faced, her strawberry-blonde hair in a ponytail. She was wearing a yellow party dress with spaghetti straps and had kicked off her heels.

"Hi, I'm Alice," she said, glowing at me. "You're cute."

I didn't know what to say, so I didn't.

"His name's *Skip*," Ira said, pointing at me. "S-K-I-P."

"I know how to spell *Skip*!" Alice snapped.

"So do I!" Gordon said.

But Alice's attention was elsewhere. "Wow, listen! It's Maureen's Sweet Sixteenth, and they're playing *Daddy's Little Girl*. Isn't that neat?"

"I guess so," I said.

"So, Skip, would you like to dance?"

"To *Daddy's Little Girl*?"

"No, silly. I'm going to ask them to play something we can *really* dance to. You *do* jitterbug, don't you?"

Me? What could I say? So I didn't...I just nodded. Alice grabbed my hand and led me to the middle of the dance floor.

"Can't we start in a corner?" I asked.

"Uh-uh. You're cute. I want the rest of the girls to see us together."

Now you have to remember I was only thirteen then, meaning cute or not I didn't have much experience dancing with girls. But if you recall, I was a genius at math. So I counted *1-2-3...4-5-6,* shuffling my feet as I tried to keep time to the music.

"Stop counting *1-2-3... 4-5-6* out loud!" Alice said. "And why are you looking at your feet? You think you're gonna lose them?"

I raised my eyes from the floor and looked into Alice's, counting silently to myself as I danced in place, trying to avoid collisions. Finally, *Sh-Boom* mercifully ended, and she smiled at me.

"I knew you could jitterbug."

But she wasn't finished. The music had started up again and the band was playing that new mambo song Rosemary Clooney was singing all over the radio.

"C'mon, Skip, let's see if you can do a mambo." And Alice started singing, "*Hey mambo! Mambo Italiano....*" She gave me her hand and shook her hips. I stepped on her toes.

She grimaced. "Gee, you're good. Can you dip?"

I didn't know why she was calling me a *dip.* I mean just because I stepped on her toes. But she was kinda cute, so I decided to let it pass.

"*Dip.* Everyone knows what *dip* is."

This required quick thinking on my part. "Oh sure *that*," I said. "Anybody can do that. But I never do it. It looks dumb."

"*I* like it," Alice said. "Let's dip."

She pointed to a couple near us. The girl was leaning backward on one leg and bending her knee, while the boy was leaning forward and bending his. It looked like some kind of mating ritual.

"See, Ricky and Gail just did it!

"Well, let 'em. I'm not."

"That's 'cause you know you can't. *Hey, mambo. No more mozzarella!"*

"Oh yeah?"

I dipped her. But I leaned her back much too far. In panic, Alice grabbed my shoulders, and I fell on top of her. I could tell she didn't have the flattest chest in her school.

"I told you I don't like to dip."

Alice pushed me off and picked herself up off the floor. Shaking her head, she led me to a couple of chairs over by the wall, and we sat down and talked. We talked about Buddy Holly, and we talked about movies. Alice said she'd just seen *Love in the Afternoon* and that Gary Cooper was her favorite actor. I told her Coop was better in *Pride of the Yankees.* We'd just started talking about baseball and the Yankees' sudden trade of Billy Martin over that Copacabana thing when she said, "Oops, it's time for me to go home. He's here."

She grabbed my hand. "C'mon, I'll introduce you."

And that's how I met Mickey.

73

HE WAS WEARING a blue, pinstriped golf shirt and yellow slacks. Perched on his head was a Yankee baseball cap, the brim bent in that trademark Mantle roll. He had the broad shoulders, the bull neck, the lopsided toothy grin…and a very Mantle-unlike paunch hanging over his belt.

"Mickey Rabinowitz," he said, offering me his hand. "I'm sorry, son, I didn't catch your name."

"It's Skip," Alice said, as I stood there dumbfounded. "Skip Kleinmann."

Mickey Rabinowitz nodded. "*Skip*…nice nickname. Reminds me of the dog I had when I was a kid." He turned to Alice. "Honey, did I ever tell you about the time me and Skippy—"

"Not now, Uncle Mickey!"

Uncle Mickey shrugged and reached into his pants pocket. "Here, Skip, let me give you my card."

"Uncle Mickey!"

"What? What?"

"He's not interested in your card, Uncle Mickey."

"It's okay," I said.

"Mickey's Sports Mania," Uncle Mickey said, handing me his card. "That's my business. We're the largest sports memorabilia store in Midtown. And what we sell is

authentic. You walk into the store, you're walking into a sports Hall of Fame. Babe Ruth, Bob Feller, Johnny Unitas, Rocky Marciano…you name 'em, we got 'em."

"Mantle?"

"Matter of fact, Skip, Mickey was in last week to sign autographs."

"Holy bull shark! The Mick was in your store?"

Uncle Mickey looked at Alice. "Bull shark?"

Alice shrugged.

"We try to schedule him whenever we can," Uncle Mickey explained. "Having Mickey sitting in the window signing autographs brings a lot of people into the store."

"Skip's a big, big Mickey Mantle fan," Alice pointed out.

"That right, Skip? Then you oughta come to Mickey's next autograph signing. I'll introduce you."

"Holy bull shark!"

Uncle Mickey smiled. "Mark down August 17. That's when he'll be in."

My head slumped to my chest.

"What's wrong?" Alice asked.

"Cyma," I said. "August 17, I have to be back in Cincinnati. It's my cousin Cyma's wedding."

74

WE WERE ALL STANDING by the Mantle mailbox. Except for the kid I didn't know, who turned out to be Denny McKrowsky, whom you've no doubt heard about. After leading his junior high's basketball team to a 5-17 record, Denny skipped high school, was drafted by the Royals—before they became the Kings—and went on to become a fourth-team NBA all-star until he got caught selling cigarettes to a minor. That they were candy cigarettes meant no difference to the NBA, which suspended him for a year and took away his driver's license.

Anyway, there we all were (except Denny, of course), looking at Mickey's mailbox, trying to decide what we were going to do next. I suggested we walk up and ring the bell.

"We can't just walk up and ring the bell," Gordon said. "What if no one's home?"

After Gordon told us he didn't like being called *Idiot*, we argued over what to say if The Mick answered the door. I knew we couldn't simply say *Mr. Mantle, we were just in the neighborhood, saw your mailbox, and thought we'd say 'hello'* even if it was more or less the truth. After all, what if he was in the bathroom when the bell rang? Opening the door to four star-struck, tongued-tied kids. unable to say anything while he zipped up his fly, wouldn't go over too big. We needed to figure out some kind of plan.

"Anybody got an idea?" I asked.

Porky had been stuffing his mouth with a concoction of Hostess cupcakes and Twinkies. He stopped and scratched his belly. "My idea? A few chocolate chip cookies would be nice." And he went back to his two o'clock feeding.

Ira had been walking the dog—just one of the tricks he was practicing with his yo-yo. "Census," he said. "We could say we're taking a census."

Ira must have hit on something because Gordon started jumping up and down. Either he'd gotten all excited with the thought of taking a census or he had to pee.

"That's it, we're doing a *senseless*!" Gordon said, his jumping up and down screeching to a stop. "And we want to know who's the toughest lefthander for him to hit."

"That's not what census takers ask, you nincompoop," Ryan said.

"And it's *census*, not *senseless*," Aaron said, speaking slowly to emphasize the words.

"Well, what do they ask?" Gordon asked.

Aaron explained census takers were required by law to go around knocking on people's doors to ask personal questions about things like income, education, and bowel movement habits of each individual in the household.

"What if nobody's home when they knock?" Gordon started jumping up and down again.

"Then they ring the bell," Ryan said.

"You writing a book?" Porky said.

With that, the discussion on what we should do ended. Aaron nodded at me.

I rang the doorbell as Gordon stopped jumping up and down and peed.

75

MERLYN MANTLE OPENED the door. She was dressed in a New York Yankees bathrobe with New York Yankees slippers on her feet, half-frame reading glasses on her nose. She looked like Liberace…Liberace with platinum hair in rollers.

Merlyn was chewing a wad of Bazooka. She smiled at us and blew a bubble.

I looked at Ira. Ira looked back at me. Aaron nodded, giving me a push.

"Yes, boys?"

"Uh, Mrs. Mantle?"

"Oh, I'm not Mrs. Mantle. I'm the live-in housekeeper."

"Is Mr. Mantle in?" I sputtered.

"No, he isn't. He's away." She popped her bubble.

"Do you expect him back soon?" Ryan asked.

That must have required some thought, because she took off her reading glasses and wiped them on her New York Yankees bathrobe. She started to put them on, hesitated, and squinted at her New York Yankees watch.

"He's in Bellmore." She popped another bubble. "He should be back Sunday night."

"Bellmore?" I said.

"I mean Baltimore," she said. "I always get confused."

"Thank you, ma'am," said Aaron, who always knew exactly what to say at times like this.

We were halfway up the street when Gordon stopped us, bewildered as only Gordon could be bewildered. "What's he doing in Baltimore? Don't the Yanks have a game to play?"

"Yeah, and they're playing it in Baltimore," Aaron said, no doubt thinking, *Gordon, you dimwit, how can you be that stupid?* Of course Aaron, a proponent of political correctness since the age of three, would never have called Gordon a dimwit. Instead, he merely blurted, "Gordon, how can you be so stupid? And your fly's down."

Gordon zipped up his fly and sniffled. "You don't like me, do you?" His eyes were now wet. So were his pants. It was obvious he was pretty upset.

"Of course he likes you," I said. "Tell him, Aaron."

"Of course I like you, Gordon," Aaron said, trying not to grimace. "Tell you what, why don't you come over tomorrow and play some ping-pong?" He looked at Gordon and smiled. "Fifty cents a point?"

"Fifty cents a point? A whole fifty cents? What do I do if I lose again?" Gordon whined. "That'll leave me with nothing in my piggy bank."

"You have nothing in your piggy bank now," Ira said. He stopped walking the dog. "Here, you try, Gordon."

He handed the yo-yo to the yo yo.

Gordon beamed. He carefully stuck his finger in the loop. "Like that?"

Ira nodded. "Go ahead."

Holding his finger in the loop, Gordon smiled. His finger was turning blue.

Suddenly, he threw the yo-yo-down. The yo-yo unwound, bounced back up, and smacked him in the forehead. Gordon rubbed his head. "Like that?"

"Not quite," Ira said. "And you still have nothing in your piggy bank."

Piggy bank momentarily drew Porky's attention away from the last of his two-thirty snack of Hostess cupcakes and Twinkies. He looked around, shrugged, and licked his fingers.

"You wouldn't have to pay the whole thing right away, Gordon," Ryan said. "You could do fifty-cent installments."

"I dunno," Gordon said, scratching his head. "I lose, it could be a dozen installments. That's almost twelve!"

"Uh, Gordon, twelve *is* a dozen," Aaron said.

"Really?" Gordon was counting his fingers. "Is that right, Porky?"

"You writing a book?" Porky looked at Gordon and oinked.

Gordon had finished counting his fingers. "Ten," he said. "There's ten."

"Maybe you should count your toes, too," Ryan said.

I stopped Gordon before he could take his shoe off. "He's kidding," I said.

"I knew that," Gordon said. "Didn't I?"

Aaron rolled his eyes.

Gordon smiled. "Anyway, Aaron, my mother says I shouldn't play ping-pong with you anymore. Besides, tomorrow I have an appointment at my optimist."

"You have an appointment at the optimist?" I asked.

"Mom says I need to have my eyes checked."

"You dimwit!" Aaron said, forgetting political correctness for the moment. "That's *optometrist*, not optimist."

"What's the difference?" Porky said. "You writing a book?"

76

THE MICK WAS BACK in town. The night before he'd gone hitless in a game in Kansas City, a game in which Yankee pitchers threw away a 6-1 lead.

But now the team was home in Yankee Stadium, and Mickey was home in Mount Vernon, in the white Cape Cod house at the end of his college sex, no doubt resting up before the 8 P.M. opener of a big three-game series against the Cleveland Indians.

I was excited. There wasn't any doubt about it, I knew today was going to be the day I would finally meet Mickey Mantle.

So there we were standing outside the Mantle house, and I was staring at the front door, my mouth dry, my palms sweaty, my knees shaking. Today, they'd call it symptoms of stage fright or maybe erectile dysfunction. But back then I didn't know what either was. I just knew in my condition this was no time for me to ring any doorbell, much less Mickey's. Which is why I told Aaron since Ira was the one who first brought us to the house, this time he should be the one to ring the doorbell. No one was about to object. Not even Gordon.

Ira rang the bell, and once again it was Mickey's housekeeper who came to the door. She looked pretty much the same as last time—New York Yankees bathrobe, slippers, and all. But this time her hair rollers were white instead of gray. It was obvious, Aaron would later say, she wore white hair rollers when the Yankees were home and gray when they were away.

"Yes, boys?"

Ira didn't know what to say, so Ryan jumped in. "Is Mr. Mantle available?"

"I'm afraid he just started his piano lesson."

"I didn't know he played piano," I said.

"He just started. This is his second lesson. The first lesson was canceled."

I was going to explain to her if the first lesson was canceled then this would be the first and not the second lesson. But I knew if I did, she'd call the Board of Education to complain I was being smart with her, and the Board of Education would see to it I lost whatever chance I may have had to someday maybe be a state-licensed praying mantis psychologist.

Best not to say anything about the second lesson being the first. Instead, I asked her how long today's lesson, which I knew would combine the first and the second, would be.

She squinted at her New York Yankees watch. "Hmmm, should be about an hour. They just started."

"Thank you, ma'am. We'll come back later," said Aaron, who you could tell always knew what to say in situations like this.

"We've got an hour," I said. So what are we going to do?"

Ira said he was going to rock the baby with his yo-yo. "Maybe hop the fence too."

"I don't know about you guys," Ryan said. "But I've got to pee." With that, he hopped on his bike and tore off down the street looking for a suitable tree. At Sequoia Circle, he turned right and was quickly out of sight.

"Now what do we do?" I repeated.

"I don't know," Aaron said. "Anybody else have to pee?"

77

"I THINK MICKEY'S LESSON must be up by now," I said. My mouth dry, my palms sweaty, my knees shaking, I walked up to The Mick's door and rang the bell.

"I see you're back," the housekeeper said, wiping her reading glasses on her New York Yankees bathrobe. She'd changed to a sleeveless one, which did nothing for her armpits. "I think Mr. Mantle's done with his lesson. Let me see if I can get him for you."

With that, she closed the door.

I couldn't tell you how long we stood there waiting. I do remember Gordon gave us a sheepish look and started jumping up and down.

"Hang in there, Gordon," I said. "You can do it."

"Just don't do it." Ira said.

Finally, the door re-opened.

He must have stood about five-four, built like a bloated fireplug. There was no buffed body, just a bulging belly which hung out from under his undershirt. Tattooed just above his navel were the words *Semper Pie.* Two crushed cans of Bud were in one hand and a half-smoked cigarette in the other. On his head was a baseball cap with a big red *P*, which I knew didn't stand for Poughkeepsie despite the humidity.

"Hi fellas," he said. "Mrs. Simpleton said you wanted to see me."

"You're not him!" I said.

"No, I'm me."

"Can you prove it?" The challenge came from who else but Gordon.

"He's kidding...isn't he?"

"We wish," Ira said. He'd split the atom and was now throwing his yo-yo behind his head to Gordon's applause.

"Your friend's got a big bump on his head," the Semper Pie man said. "Looks like it's turning blue. What happened?"

"Gordon? Oh, he hit himself in the head with a yo-yo," I said.

The Pie Man squeezed Gordon's shoulder. "You know, Gordon, I used to be pretty good with a yo-yo back when I was your age. Got yo-yo in my blood."

"Really, Mr. Mantle? Gosh!" Gordon goshed.

"Actually, yo-yo wasn't in my blood. I was never any good with a yo-yo. So don't worry about it, Gordon. Look at me. I still grew up to drink beer." He laughed and *Semper Pie* jiggled.

"I don't get it," I said. "Your mailbox says *Mantle*."

"Of course. That's my name."

And then it must have hit him. "Oh, you want *Mickey* Mantle. I'm *Mikey* Mantle...*M-I-K-E-Y*. No *C* before the *K*."

I looked at Aaron. "No *C*," I said.

"Happens all the time," Mikey Mantle said. "Sometimes I think I ought to change my name."

"Why don't you just drop the *Y*?" I said. "That way you're *Mike* Mantle, and people won't confuse you with Mickey."

"Tried. But people still get hung up on my last name."

"Then why don't you change it?"

"I don't know what I'd change it to," Mikey said, scratching his head.

"How about your mother's maiden name?" Ira suggested.

"Oh, I couldn't do that."

"Sure you could," Aaron said. "It's legal."

"Maybe so. But I still couldn't."

Aaron persisted. "Why not?"

"Her maiden name was DiMaggio."

78

"SHE *CANCELED*? What do you mean she *canceled*?"

"Cyma canceled her wedding again. I'm telling you, Leah, it's off."

"Why does she keep doing this?" Mom asked. "This has to be the third time."

"Fourth," Aunt Tillie said.

I guess I should explain. My cousin Cyma had this thing about weddings, so she'd elope…without the groom. "What if I've made a mistake," she'd say. "I can't afford a divorce lawyer."

And indeed she had a point. Even with a college degree from Purdue in agricultural marketing, Cyma couldn't have been making that much money going door-to-door selling eggs, even if they were extra-large.

Uncle Harold and I had flown back to Cincinnati for Cyma's wedding two days before, with me in the window seat. Uncle Harold had called *aisle*, saying being on the aisle allowed him better views of stewardess legs

"It's not fair." He slowly sighed, then sighed again. "They always put the better legs in first class."

The plane, a DC8-30 prop jet, had arrived two hours late at the Cincinnati airport, which wasn't located in

Cincinnati but Kentucky—no doubt because leases on runways were cheaper there. That the plane arrived at the gate behind schedule wasn't because of a strong reverse tailwind, but because Uncle Harold had been trying to impress the stewardess. He kept telling her, now that the plane had touched down on the runway, to ask the pilot when he could take a turn at the wheel.

"But I *do* have a license," he said. What he didn't tell her was he had trouble parallel parking at gates.

Anyhow, we did get to Number 6 before Cincinnati closed for the night, and now Uncle Harold was telling anyone who'd listen that he was glad he hadn't brought a wedding present with him.

79

ASK ME AGAIN LATER

"A *PYTHON? NO, you are* not *getting a python!"*

"But Mom—"

"That's all I need in the house…a python." And grabbing a handful of tissue, she went back to watching Edie explain to Pa Hughes about how she felt about Penny's reaction to the   affair with Jim.

"But, Mom, Fenny's mother is letting him have a gerbil."

As the World Turns broke for a commercial in the middle of Pa Hughes's coughing spasm. "A gerbil is *not* a python!" Mom said.

"So, I can have a gerbil then?"

My strategy worked. I got the gerbil. I named him George…George Gerbil.

"He looks like a rat," Linnie said. Her front teeth had finally come in. She now looked like Bugs Bunny.

"He's not a rat," I said. "He's a gerbil, and his name is George."

Linnie had waltzed into my bedroom, Linnie Junior in tow, to see the new addition to the family. She'd brought a leaf of bib lettuce with her as a present. The lettuce was wilted, but I figured George wouldn't care.

"Well, he looks like a rat to me," Linnie said. "What if he bites Linnie Junior when she's sleeping? Rats do that you know."

"He's *not* a rat! He's a gerbil!"

Linnie looked at George, who took a sniff of the lettuce and peed on it. "Why couldn't you get something that *doesn't* bite?"

"Like a python? They don't bite."

"A pylon doesn't bite?" From the way Linnie glared at George it was obvious she wasn't happy he'd peed on her present.

I shook my head slowly. "It's not a py-*lon*. A *pylon* is what you put in the road. A py-*thon* is a snake."

"Well, couldn't a snake be lying in the middle of road?"

"Sure, it could," I said. "Until a car runs over it."

She shuddered. "You know I don't like roadkill!"

At the mention of *roadkill,* Linnie Junior started to cry. Linnie stuck a pacifier in her mouth. The pacifier popped out and fell to the floor. Linnie Junior began crying again.

"Now look what you did!" Linnie didn't look too happy. "I can't give her a pacifier that's been on the floor. She could get germs."

"Maybe she's crying cause she needs her diaper changed. Maybe you gave her too much Milk of Magnesia."

Linnie brushed a strand of hair out of Linnie Junior's eyes. "There, there...is that what you need, a new diaper?"

"I Love Lucy."

"Look, Linnie I tried, I really did. But Mom wouldn't let me have a python. And I wasn't about to ask her if I could have a piranha."

"Why not?"

"You kidding? Supposing it gets sick? You know how Mom's liable to get, she'll feel sorry for it and hand-feed it. Besides, when they're not in a feeding frenzy piranhas are …well, they're boring. So we're stuck with a gerbil."

I picked up a dirty sock from the floor and wiped George's pee off the lettuce. "Here, Turkey Lips, maybe you can take it back and exchange it for arugula."

Linnie shook her head. "I still think he looks like a rat. And he better not bite Linnie Junior. He bites her, and I'm calling the exterminator."

"He isn't going to bite her," I said. "Gerbils are smart. They can tell if wood's been treated with Milk of Magnesia."

80

YOU MAY RELY ON IT

"AND AFTER THE GAME they've invited us to the clubhouse to meet all the American League All-Stars," Dad was saying. "Ted Williams...Nellie Fox...Jim Bunning...Al Kaline...Early Wynn...Yogi Berra..."

"And Mickey Mantle!" I said. "Don't forget The Mick!"

Dad smiled at me. "I haven't. He'll be there."

Dad had come through with two box seat tickets to the All-Star game. Hudepohl Beer was televising the game on Channel 9, and the distributor had given Dad the tickets as a reward for being his Number 1 customer...at least east of Vine Street.

Being the major local sponsor, Hudepohl had access to both team clubhouses after the game, and they'd invited Dad and me to be their guests. Dad had told them we'd like to spend our time with the American League All-Stars since Cincinnati was in the National League, and we never got to see American League stars play at Crosley Field.

Finally, finally I was going to meet Mickey Mantle!

I was halfway out the door when Mom called me back in.

"You better take a sweater. They tell me it can get cold by the fifth inning, and Uncle Harold says the restrooms at Crosley Field aren't heated."

"Aw, Mom, do I have to?"

"Yes, you *have to*, and I don't want to hear another word about it." She folded her arms across her apron.

"All right, all right, I'll take my orange sweater."

"Take your blue one. It goes better with your acne."

"But—"

"No 'buts.'" She untied the apron. It fell to the floor. "Don't you touch it! Not without washing your hands!"

Mom's neurosis was flaring up again.

"Suppose one of my friends sees you wearing an orange sweater? What am I going to say at the next Canasta game, that your acne's made you color blind?"

"But Mom, nothing looks good with zits."

"Blue! Do I have to spell it out for you?"

I was going to tell her it wasn't necessary since every kid I knew in school, with the possible exception of Howard Kodesh, could spell blue…yellow and purple too. But I knew if I mentioned that, Mom would see red. Best not to say anything colorful.

Instead, I grabbed my blue sweater and ran out the door before Mom could tell me to change socks—no matter to her the dermatologist had declared my ankles acne-free. Dad was waiting in his Olds with the engine running. He had on the orange sweater Mom had given him for his birthday—no doubt telling him, as he unwrapped it and held it up, he could wear it out of the house since he didn't have zits.

"Let's get going," Dad said. "Got your glove?"

"Yep, it's right here. I wrapped the stupid sweater around it so it won't get cold on the way to the ballpark."

"So the stupid sweater won't get cold?"

"No, Dad, my glove."

"Huh?"

I explained to him that you could get a pretty cool breeze in the car when the driver's window was rolled down.

"Yeah, so?"

"You never know, it could crack the leather. Maybe even damage a vowel in Mickey's signature. The sweater will prevent it from breaking out in cracks, and it won't matter if the sweater gets cold since it's already blue."

Dad gave me a puzzled look. "C'mon, we're running late!" And with that, he shifted from Reverse into Second and stripped the gears.

Philip Schlaeger

81

THE TAXICAB WAS STUCK in traffic, along with what must have been half the population of Cincinnati. We were bumpering along the parkway, and I knew cars had to be backed up halfway to Dayton. I looked at my watch. Dad looked at the meter. We both looked at each other and sighed.

"You don't think we'll make it? Hey, relax," the cab driver said. "You're with Maxie. I know a taxi shortcut." And with that, he suddenly cut the Dodge over to the exit lane.

"Ramp Speed 15 MPH," he said, hitting the brakes. "That's what the sign says. Gotta be more careful. I was going twenty-five." Maxie shifted to Neutral, and we coasted off the ramp, right onto his taxi shortcut.

"Can't you go any faster?" I asked.

"Twenty-five. See that sign there? That's what it says the speed limit is."

I eyed the speedometer. "You're going twenty-*two*! That's *under* the speed limit. What kind of taxi driver are you?"

"Polish," Maxie said.

Suddenly, we came to a complete stop. The car ahead of us had stopped. And so had the car in front of that one and the car in front of that one and the car in front of that one. Buicks, Fords, Pontiacs, Plymouths, Chevies, Lincolns, a Nash Rambler, and Maxie's Dodge taxi...we all had our engines idling as the longest and slowest train in world history chugged by.

I sat there biting my nails, wondering how much longer it would be before we ran out of gas, if the nearest station was within walking distance and if it gave out Top Value stamps. "Dynamite," I mumbled to myself.

"Sorry, what did you say?" Maxie asked, his attention on the meter, which had just hit $9.00.

"Wish I had dynamite right now. Give me two sticks of it, and I'll blow that train clear off the tracks."

"Check the trunk," Maxie said, his nostrils flaring to a crescendo of blasted horns.

"That does it! I've had it with the honking going on behind us!" Maxie rolled down his window, hung his arm out, and extended a finger, signaling the car behind to go ahead and pass.

"Stay in the car," Dad said, momentarily taking his eyes off the meter. "He's kidding about the dynamite in the trunk. Tell him, Maxie."

Maxie rolled up his window, turned, and smiled. "Hope you guys brought an umbrella for the game."

It had started to drizzle.

82

HE WAS ACTUALLY USING a blow dryer. Not on his hair, but on our box seats. Satisfied both were now dry, he sprayed them with Mr. Clean. Then he reached into his official usher's jacket, took out an embroidered Cincinnati Reds handkerchief, and wiped the seats with Pledge until they gleamed.

Dad handed him a dollar.

On the field the mike was handed to Mel Allen.

"AND NOW THE STARTING LINEUP FOR THE AMERICAN LEAGUE ALL-STARS....LEADING OFF AND PLAYING SHORTSTOP...HE WAS THE AMERICAN LEAGUE'S ROOKIE OF THE YEAR IN 1953 AND BATTED .332 LAST YEAR...THIS IS HIS FIFTH ALL-STAR GAME...FROM THE DETROIT TIGERS...HARVEY KUENN...."

The usher sprayed the seats with Glade Air Freshener.

To me it smelled something like acacia wood, though I can't be sure. I do know it definitely wasn't linoleum.

Dad handed him another dollar.

"BATTING SECOND...AT SECOND BASE...A SEVEN-TIME ALL-STAR...HE'S LED THE AMERICAN LEAGUE IN BASE HITS FOR THREE STRAIGHT YEARS...ONE OF THE TOUGHEST BATTERS TO

STRIKE OUT...FROM THE CHICAGO WHITE SOX...NELLIE FOX...."

"Anything else, sir?" the usher asked.

"Well, I have a couple of fives," Dad said. "But I was going to use them for bratwurst, pop, Crackerjacks, ice cream, and cotton candy."

"And chili dogs, Dad," I said. "Don't forget chili dogs. You promised!"

Dad nodded. "And chili dogs...oh, and Rolaids."

"BATTING THIRD...IN RIGHT FIELD...IN 1955 HE BECAME THE YOUNGEST PLAYER TO EVER WIN AN AMERICAN LEAGUE BATTING TITLE...HE'S ALSO THE YOUNGEST PLAYER EVER TO HIT THREE HOME RUNS IN A SINGLE GAME...THE MAN THEY CALL 'SIX'...FROM THE DETROIT TIGERS...AL KALINE...."

"Well, beep me, sir, if there's anything else I can do for you," the usher said. He smiled and handed Dad an official Cincinnati Reds beeper. "If it starts raining again, you'll probably want to beep me for an umbrella."

"BATTING FOURTH...IN LEFT FIELD...HE'S A FOUR-TIME AMERICAN LEAGUE BATTING CHAMPION AND THE LAST PLAYER TO BAT OVER .400 IN A SINGLE SEASON... THIS IS HIS THIRTEENTH ALL-STAR GAME...FROM THE BOSTON RED SOX...THE MAN THEY CALL 'THE SPENDID SPLINTER'...TED WILLIAMS...."

Something was wrong and I knew it. "Dad, Casey's got The Mick. What's he doing having Ted Williams bat cleanup?"

"Don't know. Guess he wants Mickey batting fifth against a left-handed pitcher."

"But Mickey's a *switch hitter*! He can bat right-handed against Simmons."

"Good point," Dad said.

"BATTING FIFTH...AT FIRST BASE...HIS THIRTY-TWO HOMERS LAST YEAR WERE SECOND BEST IN THE AMERICAN LEAGUE...THIS IS HIS THIRD TIME AS AN ALL-STAR...FROM THE CLEVELAND INDIANS...VIC WERTZ...."

First, Ted Williams batting cleanup, and now he had Wertz batting fifth. Whatever Casey Stengel was doing, it made absolutely no sense.

"BATTING SIXTH...IN CENTER FIELD...HE'S LED THE AMERICAN LEAGUE IN STOLEN BASES THREE TIMES AND IN TRIPLES TWICE...IN HIS FIFTH ALL-STAR GAME...ONE OF THE BEST DEFENSIVE OUTFIELDERS IN THE GAME...FROM THE CHICAGO WHITE SOX...'MR. WHITE SOX'...MINNIE MINOSO...."

"DAD! WHAT HAPPENED TO MICKEY?"

People were turning around and looking at me.

"Don't know, Skip."

There was a tap on my shoulder. It came from a fat guy sitting behind me. He was wearing a *1957 All-Star Game* tee shirt and a Cincinnati Reds cap. He'd tapped me with his scorecard. "Guess you didn't read the *Enquirer* this morning. Stengel told Mickey he wants him to stay home and rest."

"Rest?"

"So Mickey didn't make the trip."

I grabbed Dad's arm. *"Dad, he's not even here! The Mick's not here!"*

Had Casey finally lost it? How could you play an All-Star game without the top star in the game?

But that's what Casey Stengel was going to do.

83

IT TURNED OUT THE MICK had twisted a knee the day before. It was the latest in a streak of leg injuries that began in the 1951 World Series—ironically, on a fly ball hit by Willie Mays.

Grandpa Albert said he was sitting a couple of rows up from the wall in right-center and saw it all.

It happened in in the fifth inning of Game 2, with the Yankees ahead, 2-0. The Giants had two out when Willie hit a high fly to right-center, between the aging thirty-six-year-old DiMaggio and the nineteen-year-old Mantle. Mickey came racing across the outfield as only he could. Suddenly, he put on the brakes. There was DiMaggio camped out under the ball. At the last moment, the Great Man had yelled "I got it!"

As he tried to get out of DiMaggio's way, Mickey's right shoe caught the rubber cover of a sprinkler head in the outfield—a groundskeeper had forgot to cover the drain that day. Mickey's right knee collapsed.

"There was a sound like a tire blowing out." Grandpa Albert winced.

Mickey lay on the ground, failing to move. Grandpa Albert said he thought Mickey was unconscious.

They carried him off the field on a stretcher. There was no team doctor, no wheel chair, no ambulance—Mickey had to take a cab to the hospital. No one realized it, but his anterior cruciate ligament had been torn.

That was the start of it.

Two years later, in 1953, The Mick sprained his left knee while trying to get a quick jump on a line drive hit nearly over his head. Fluid accumulated in the kneecap.

In 1955, it was his right thigh. He tore the back of it, racing down the first-base line to beat out a bunt.

Then in '56—the year he won the Triple Crown—he'd torn ligaments in his right knee, the one he'd already had surgery on. Casey wanted him out of the lineup, but The Mick wouldn't listen. He put on a leg brace and kept playing.

This time Casey wasn't taking no for an answer.

"Doesn't matter if Mickey plays or not," the guy sitting behind me was saying.

"How can you say that?"

"Because with him or without him, the American League loses." He signaled the beer vendor. *"Hudepohl!"* he called out. "Want one, kid? On me."

"I don't think so," Dad said.

"The American League is not gonna lose," I said. "They've got better pitching."

"Look kid, the American League has lost six of the last seven All-Star games. Last year it was 7-3…not even close."

"That means they're due."

"They've been due since Abner Doubleday." He took his first swallow, a big one, and promptly belched. "How about a *root* beer?"

I shook my head. "Well, they're gonna win this time!"

"I wouldn't bet on it."

"Well, I would." I looked at Dad, who was beeping the usher. "Can I?

"Okay with you, Pop?" the guy said to Dad.

"Well….I guess it depends on what the bet is."

It was 6-2 American League going into the bottom of the ninth, and I could taste the king-size chili dog.

The fat guy behind me signaled for his third beer…maybe it was his fourth—I wasn't really counting. "It's not over till it's over," he announced.

Dad looked at me. "Didn't Yogi say that?"

I smiled. "It's over." And indeed it looked like I wasn't the only one in the ballpark thinking that. Fans were heading up the aisles—no doubt to beat the rush to Skyline. But as Uncle Harold liked to say, the chickens hadn't crossed the street yet to hatch the eggs. It wasn't over. Not yet.

Musial led the National League's rally off with a walk and scored on Willie's triple down the right field line. A wild pitch by Billy Pierce brought Willie home. Suddenly, it was 6-4 AL.

The next two batters got on base. Eddie Mathews went down on strikes, but Ernie Banks singled, driving in a run.

With two out, the NL was down just one with the typing run batting in the person of big Gil Hodges.

Casey signaled to the bullpen for Bob Grim. The Yankees' hard-throwing right-hander came through, getting the Dodger first baseman to line to left for the third out.

The American League had ended the losing streak, holding on to win, 6-5.

"C'mon, Skip," Dad said. "Let's go to the clubhouse."

Reporters and photographers were already there. All the AL players were whooping and hugging and pouring bottles over each other like a bunch of seventh graders. I got to talk with Nellie Fox, Whitey Ford, Early Wynn, and Al Kaline. Yogi showed me how he signaled for a curveball, Ted Williams showed me how to swing a bat, and Bob Lemon sprayed me with something that sure wasn't lemonade. I met every AL All-Star that day…well, all except one. I didn't get to meet Mickey Mantle.

I was beginning to wonder if I ever would.

84

SIGNS POINT TO YES

MOM WAS MAKING a surprise party for Uncle Harold's fifty-fifth, which was why she was telling me not to touch the surprise cake under penalty of incarceration. I told Mom that I thought Uncle Harold's birthday wouldn't be until January.

"January fifth," she said. "Peculiar People Day."

"Then—"

"It's not his birthday we're celebrating, honey. Today marks the fifty-fifth straight day Uncle Harold's worked the same job."

Mom said since fifty-five was a new unofficial record, a celebration was in order. She thought a surprise party would be a nice surprise.

"Who's coming?" I asked.

"Just the family. Your father, Linnie, you, and me. Oh, and of course Grandpa Albert and Grandma Bessie. And I told your sister she's *not* to bring Linnie Junior."

"No stupid doll?" My sigh of relief must have been pretty loud because Mom quickly shushed me.

"Shush, he thinks I just invited him over for a nice family dinner."

"But Mom, he's not even here yet."

"He will be...in about fifteen minutes." She looked out the window. "If it doesn't start to rain. Then you know what happens. He does his Gene Kelly thing. Starts dancing down the street, singing *Singin' in the Rain*."

"Without an umbrella," I added.

If I followed Mom's thinking—which, as you've seen, can sometimes be hard to do—since she wanted to start dinner around six thirty, she'd told Uncle Harold to be here at five forty-five so he'd be here at six thirty. (Where did I lose you?)

"I told him that so he won't be late."

"What are we having?"

"Don't be silly, Skip. Today's Tuesday, isn't it? What do I make on Tuesdays?"

"Hot dogs. We're going to celebrate an important day in his life with *hot dogs*?"

"It's a surprise. Grandma Bessie is going to make them on the grill. Your job will be to stand by with a back-up fire extinguisher."

It was now six forty-five, and Uncle Harold still hadn't arrived. What Mom didn't know, couldn't have known, was Uncle Harold had figured Mom would pull some ploy and wasn't going to be tricked. He decided he'd be late anyway.

It was just before seven when he showed up. By then, everyone was tired of practicing *SURPRISE!* So when Uncle Harold opened the door....

"surprise."

"Sorry I'm late," Uncle Harold apologized, a knowing grin on his face. He explained to everybody—everybody except for Linnie, who was moping because she couldn't bring Linnie Junior to the party—that he'd been rear-ended at a *NO OUTLET* sign on his way over. "But I got her telephone number. I'm going to call and ask her out."

"And who's the lady we are talking about this time?" Mom asked. It was pretty obvious she was disappointed with *"SURPRISE!"* sinking to *"surprise"* after all that practicing.

"Her name's Elaine...or Eileen...maybe Ellen."

"You sure it couldn't have been Elsinore?" Grandma Bessie asked, telling us Elsinore was the grade school she went to in New York before the name was changed to honor Jules Verne. "It was such a shame too. Elsinore was such a pretty name."

"No, I don't think it was," Uncle Harold said, now stroking his chin and humming *Singin' in the Rain.*

"You don't think Elsinore was a pretty name, Harold?" Grandma Bessie said, clearly hurt. "What, you think Jules Verne's better?"

"No, it began with a *C*," Uncle Harold said. He lathered up a potato chip with Cheese Whiz and popped it into his mouth. "Charlene, that's it!...Or maybe it was Charmaine."

"You sure it wasn't Champagne?" Mom said.

"No, I know champagne," Uncle Harold said. "I'm a specialist. Some people think *'27*'s good, but *'28* is actually better."

"Forget champagne," Mom said. "Tell us how you got her number."

"Whose number?"

"Charlene, or Charmaine, or whoever. Just not Champagne."

Uncle Harold licked Cheese Whiz off his fingers, then, with a smack of his lips, reached into the bowl for another chip. Mom pretended not to notice, but I wasn't fooled. I knew Mom had lost her appetite for potato chips.

"And where does this woman live?" Mom asked.

"Charlene or Charmaine?"

"I don't know. Take your pick."

"Oh, she lives someplace that's on the way to her job...or maybe it's on her way home," Uncle Harold said. "Hmmm...." Uh-oh, I could tell from his *Hmmm*, he'd come up with another of his improbable ideas. "I think I'll take her dancing outdoors next time it rains."

That would have stopped most inquisitions, but Mom, as you know from the car ride she gave Elaine, can be pretty persistent. "And where does she work?"

"Who?"

"Charlene, Charmaine, or whatever her name is."

"Downtown. She's got a pretty good job, Leah. She's a financial advisor."

Uncle Harold reached back into the bowl. "Sorry, anybody want some more?"

We all stared at him. Uncle Harold shrugged and grabbed the last few chips.

"Has she ever been married?" Mom asked him.

"This time she's divorcing Glen Sudek."

"Glenn Sudek?" The name got my attention.

Uncle Harold nodded, his mouth full of potato chips. "Tell youth motherth, Skithy."

"You mean tell her that Sudek is Ferdy Capelman's godfather?"

Uncle Harold swallowed the chips. "I mean that he's Mickey Mantle's cousin."

"Second cousin, I think," Grandma Bessie said. "Glen and Mickey are supposed to be pretty close."

Uncle Harold nodded. "Mickey came all the way in from New York for Sudek's last divorce. He should be in for this one too."

85

IT WAS A HOT DOG dinner to be remembered. Mom had gone all out and bought Kahn's Signature Select Prime, which while low in fat was also low in prime. What Signature Select Prime was high in was flatulence. Which was why Uncle Harold and I were banished to the garage right after we'd cut more than the cake.

So there we were, Uncle Harold and I, cutting up in the garage. I'd picked up a fly swatter and was swatting away. Uncle Harold was filing his nails and humming a syncopated rendition of *Singin' in the Rain* while the flies buzzed in chorus. He'd stop humming only long enough to yell out *"Bogie at six o'clock!...Bogie at three-thirty!"*

"So how did you do it?" I asked him.

"Do what?"

"Grandpa Albert told me you met your sports idol when you were my age. How did you do it…and who was he?"

"Clarence Tubbs," Uncle Harold said. "I was setting pins in the bowling alley."

"Holy bull shark, he walked in? You were lucky, Uncle Harold."

Uncle Harold smiled that stupid smile of his.

"But I never heard of Clarence Tubbs. He didn't play for the Giants, did he?"

Uncle Harold shook his head. "Don't be silly, Skippy. Clarence was a professional bowler." He sighed. "You should have seen him make the seven-ten split. He'd roll the ball down the gutter and it'd bounce out, knock the seven pin right across into the ten."

As long as Uncle Harold and I were banished together, I figured I might as well take advantage of it. Uncle Harold had never talked about his ability to calculate the number of home runs a baseball team's top slugger would hit throughout the week, so I didn't know if he was a specialist at it. But I knew there was one way to find out.

"Well, you got me on that one, Skippy." Uncle Harold smiled a calculated smile, then shook his head. "No, I'm not a specialist in calluses. As you know, I never went beyond decibels in school. Didn't see the point. But I think I maybe can help you. I've got an apostle I think would fly."

I didn't want to tell Uncle Harold that he meant *postulate* not *apostle,* and that the Apostles were a rock-'n-roll band. So I merely said, "Let's see if your apostle flies."

"Okay, Skippy, here we go. Now pay close attention."

And off he went, with me paying close attention. To be honest, I didn't know if I'd be able to follow him, but I figured there was a chance I could since I had plenty of exasperating experience in trying to follow Mom.

The way Uncle Harold explained it, his "apostle" was based on averages—at least I think so. As you know, with Uncle Harold you can never be quite sure. Anyhow, Uncle Harold said the key to his apostle was to see what the pitcher had been surrendering in home runs for each day of the week.

"So if on three Mondays he went *5-5-3*, what would his average be, Skippy?"

"Something like 4.2," I said.

"Sounds close to being about right. But then it could be 42. I'm not sure about the decibel."

"Forget the *decimal*, Uncle Harold. Then what happens?"

"You look at the strikeouts per game of each starting pitcher Mickey will face during the week. Then you look at how many home runs he's given up on, say, Mondays."

"Mondays?"

"Mondays. They follow Saturdays and Tuesdays. Depends which way you look at it."

I didn't want to tell Uncle Harold that Tuesday came before Saturday—at least on the calendar Julius Caesar just finished standardizing in time for his luncheon date with Claudius and Brutus at the Forum and that not even the Ides of March affected the order of the days. I knew if I said that, I'd have to hear him retell the story of when he saw Caesar at the Carnegie Deli... Sid, not Julius. So I didn't bother to set him straight.

Instead, I asked him what happens after you look at the home runs a pitcher gives up on Monday.

"I'm not sure yet, Skippy. But I'll think of something." With that, Uncle Harold switched from humming the second verse of *Singin' in the Rain* to singing it.

Suddenly, his eyes lit up, and he stopped singing. I checked all around me. There were no bogies coming in, which meant he'd stopped because he'd come up with another one of his ideas. Either that or it was his prostate.

"*Sudek,*" he said.

"Sudek?"

"Glen Sudek. Don't you get it? She'll do it for me."

"Do what for you?"

"I'll have her tell Sudek unless he wants the alimony check to come late, he'd better see that you meet Mickey Mantle."

It sounded good, but I reminded Uncle Harold that Charlene, or Charmaine, or whoever hadn't even gone out with him yet.

"She will when I call her," Uncle Harold said. He winked at me and started humming. But it wasn't the same old tune.

"That's not *Singin' in the Rain*," I said.

"*From This Moment On.*" He smiled. "Cold Porter. I'm a specialist in humming Cold Porter."

"*Cold* Porter?"

"Yeah, you know. Cold Porter. Gets them crying to go out with me. Never fails. You want to meet Mickey Mantle? Leave everything to your Uncle Harold. I'll have her humming."

"I thought you'd had her crying."

"Who?"

"Charlene or Charmaine," I said. "Or whoever."

"But now she'll be humming."

"And what's humming going to do? How's that going to help me meet The Mick?"

"Are you kidding? When a girl hums at you, Skippy boy, it means she's happy. Once I have her humming, she's

320

going to be happy to have Sudek arrange for you to meet Mickey Mantle."

86

SHE WASN'T HUMMING Cold Porter. She was stomping…and she was stomping mad.

Uncle Harold had arranged to meet her at the Skyline at 11079 East Galbraith, and that's where Charlene, Charmaine, or whoever was… right on time at seven thirty. Problem was there'd been a problem. It wasn't that Uncle Harold was his usual late self—he was actually early and for a change had the day right too. No, the problem was Uncle Harold, being dyslexic, was not at the Skyline Chili at 11079, but at the Skyline at *97011*. Not only that, he was at 97011 *West* Galbraith, which is about as far away from 11079 *East* Galbraith as you can go within Cincinnati city limits and still be in the 25 mph speed zone.

"Hey, Toots, at least I wasn't at *Gold Star* Chili," Uncle Harold had said, trying to explain the mix-up right before she hung up on him.

That had been a week or so ago, and Uncle Harold still hadn't been able to hook up with her, getting busy signals every time he tried to call. Finally, he got a recorded message from the telephone company: *The number you have finally reached has been changed to an unlisted number available only to telemarketers. If this is an emergency, please hang up and try again later.*

Undaunted, Uncle Harold went for broke. He emptied his pockets of change and sent roses, which he was assured were made from the finest unlined paper. He had them sorted, arranged with a pretty pink paper clip, and specially delivered by bike. Lonnie, his newspaper boy, had assured him for twenty-five cents the roses would be thrown on the front porch. What Lonnie didn't tell Uncle Harold was his accuracy had been tested by the *Enquirer*, and he'd almost passed on his second try.

Problem was this time there was no second try.

With just one chance to hit the target, Lonnie threw and missed—though he did come close, the roses landing only a front yard away from the porch where they were supposed to, scattering every which way as the paper clip came off. Uncle Harold's would-be girlfriend, whose name he'd yet to remember, never got the roses, and her homophobic next-door neighbor never called Uncle Harold to thank him.

"Well, that's that," I told Uncle Harold, after hearing all sides of his story the next day. "Guess I can forget all about meeting Glenn Sudek."

We were in the basement playing ping-pong. I had him 5-2, and it was my serve.

"I wouldn't say that," Uncle Harold said.

"You forget? You told me she was going to set it up with Sudek to have me meet The Mick."

"Charmaine," Uncle Harold said. "I wasn't sure before, but I remember now. Her name's Charmaine. Guess I shouldn't have called her *Toots*."

"Doesn't matter." I slammed the ball at him with my backhand… 6-2. "You blew it with Charmaine, and you blew my chance to meet Mickey Mantle. You blew it big time, Uncle Harold."

"I'm really sorry," Skippy," Uncle Harold said, and I could tell he was. "But I'm going to make it up to you…..C'mon serve it."

"Okay, you asked for it." I hit a hard, top-spin serve that handcuffed him. He hit the ball into the net. It was 7-2. I decided to be merciless and switch back to my right hand. "When, Uncle Harold? When are you going to make it up to me?"

"*When*? Before I die."

This time he flailed at my serve—I'd aced him again. "How are you going to make it up?"

"Well, I haven't worked it out yet, but I'm going to give you the winning numbers."

I shook my head. "Come on, Uncle Harold, you're going to make me a weekly winner in the Mickey Mantle Tape-Measure Home Run Derby?

Uncle Harold smiled that stupid smile of his.

"Skippy, you can bank on it."

87

"I KNEW IT WAS GOING to happen! I knew it!"

"What?" The Schneid said. It sounded like he was on a party line.

"That I'd wake up one morning and never see my zits again," I said. "Dad was right!"

"Hey, that's great!"

"No, it isn't. *I'm blind!*"

"What are you talking about?"

"Dad warned me. He said I'd go blind if I didn't stop doing it. And it's happened. I was looking in the bathroom mirror and suddenly everything went black."

And I explained when he'd called I couldn't get to the phone without stumbling.

"You're not blind," The Schneid said. "The lights went out in the neighborhood. CG&E says they'll have it fixed within an hour. C'mon, Felipe, let's go bird watching."

It had a big water slide, which was awaiting an official inspection by MAWS—Mothers Against Waterslide Splashing—and an acre of chlorine water, the shallow end of which was used by little kids to pee in. The deep end had three diving boards and was roped-off for Olympic figure-dunking. But what made Sunlite Pool truly outstanding was that it was the best place in Cincinnati to go bird watching.

Which was the reason we were there.

Bird watching, of course, has nothing to do with the Audubon Society. Bird watching is a sport practiced by red-blooded males around the globe, its popularity unaffected by exclusion from the Olympic Games. Always covert, bird watching takes a healthy supply of male hormones, patience, and a trained eye that can spot and carefully track beautiful birds of the species *homo sapien* without their taking flight.

"Humming bird," The Schneid was saying.

"Where?"

"Over there, three blankets to your left. The one in the itsy-bitsy, teeny-weeny, cream-colored, polka-dot bikini."

"Looks yellow to me," I said.

"Her humming's not bad, but off key," The Schneid said. "Donizetti wrote the *Il Dolce Suono* aria to be hummed in F-*sharp*."

"You don't think she's a little skinny, Schneid?"

"Maybe a little. But those are nice opera sunglasses. Puccini's, I think."

"I think her name's Marcia…yeah, Marcia."

"Puccini, Marcia…it doesn't matter," The Schneid said. "She used to be in the school choir until Mr. McPawling found she was humming the words."

Suddenly, The Schneid hooted then whistled. He'd spotted another bird. "Quiet." He held a finger to his lips. "Don't make a move….Over there."

"Where?"

"To your right. Just past three o'clock. The dark blue bikini with the glittering white numbers on the demi cups. That has to be that girl from New York."

I looked, not believing my eyes. She had to be a perfect ten in the ranking of any boy worth his hormones…maybe even an eleven.

"She's in town visiting her cousin," The Schneid said. "Can you believe she's just fifteen?"

"Fifteen? She's got a better figure than any girl in our senior class…probably at UC too."

"Robin…that's her name, Robin," The Schneid said. "She lays out like that in the sun too much longer, she's gonna be Robin Red Breast."

Robin had a New York Yankees sunbonnet pulled down on her head, a New York Yankees dog collar around her neck, and was sprawled, boobs up, on what looked like a New York Yankees beach towel. She'd slipped off the straps of her top, Coppertoning more of her chest and arousing the attention of bird watchers like us.

"Come on, Felipe," The Schneid said. "Let's get a closer look."

He tightened the cord on his trunks, I tightened mine and, with our towels draped over our shoulders, we strutted around the deep end of the pool till we were within a couple of empty lounges from Robin.

"Holy bull shark! Will you look at that, Schneid?"

"I am," he said. "I can't be sure from here, but I'd say they're C's."

"Really? You think so?"

"Yep, 36 C's," said The Schneid, who had a reputation of being usually right on the money in guessing weights and bust sizes.

He took a deep breath and, sucking his stomach in, re-tied his cord. I re-tied mine. Robin sighed and sat up, holding the demi-cups of her bikini top to her glistening boobs as she slipped a strap over each shoulder.

"You two staring at something?"

I wanted to say what we were staring at was her boobs, which were something to be stared at! But I knew if I said that she'd snap her towel at us and yell for the lifeguard, who would kick us out of the pool before we'd had a chance to splash Maureen Levenson and Maxine Kabakoff, who were sitting at the edge of the shallow end, dangling their toes into the peed-in water. No, best I not say anything to Robin about our staring at her boobs.

Instead, I told her we were admiring the Yankee dog collar around her neck.

"It's Rookie's," she said.

"Rookie?"

"You know, The Mick's boxer," The Schneid said.

"He gave it to me for giving him his suppositories," Robin said.

"You gave Mickey Mantle *suppositories*?"

"No, silly boy, Rookie."

While I kept my eyes on her boobs, Robin explained she worked part-time for a vet in Bronxville. "Mickey brings Rookie in every time he has a problem."

"That's nice," said The Schneid, who always knew just the thing to say at a time like this.

Me, I didn't know what to say. Not that I could, you understand. Seeing Robin's boobs up close was definitely making me speechless.

"Mickey helped hold him down when I gave him his suppositories. He was so happy Rookie didn't bite him that he gave me Rookie's collar. 'Robin, you deserve it,' he said. Mickey wanted to give me Rookie's leash too, but I told him it wasn't necessary."

"You *know* Mickey Mantle?"

"Of course, silly. And Rookie, too. He's my favorite dog...well, maybe next to Error."

"Error?"

"Hubie Suvpansky's schnauzer," The Schneid said.

"Mickey...Yogi...Moose...Whitey...a lot of Yankees bring their pets in," Robin said. "They give Doctor Sudek tickets, but he doesn't go much."

"*Sudek*...where have I heard that name before?" The Schneid asked.

"Probably his son," Robin said. "He lives in Cincinnati. You'd like him. Glen's the real baseball fan."

88

I HATED TO GO to the dentist, almost as much as I hated broccoli. But Mom said I had to go, that it was time for my checkup.

"All the junk food you've been eating, I wouldn't be surprised if you have a couple of cavities."

"Not my fault, Mom," I said. "You think I *want* to eat all that broccoli and Brussels Sprouts?"

"I beg your pardon?"

"Junk food. You said it yourself...I've been eating too much junk food. Maybe you should cut down on broccoli to once a month."

"Brocoli once a month isn't funny."

"I know," I said.

I was going to tell Mom that forcing a minor to eat broccoli also was no laughing matter. But I knew if I did she'd probably start dishing out double portions, and I'd have to clean my plate or face incarceration. Best I say nothing funny about broccoli...or Brussels Sprouts either, for that matter.

"Mom, do I *have* to go?" I pleaded. "After all, I went last time."

"You want to spend the rest of the day in your room? That's about enough out of you!"

And it was.

Doctor Hertzman was our family dentist. We'd been going to him ever since Mom had read about the Marquis de Sade and came away impressed. She was convinced when the Marquis wrote *The only way to a woman's heart is along the path of torment*, he was speaking about her marriage. Once she found out Dr. Hertzman was not only a disciple of de Sade but a practicing sadist in good standing in the community, she decided to make Dad go to him for his root canals.

Actually, Dr. Hertzman was what today they call a *sadomasokiss*. Which explains why he had twice strapped his last dental assistant in his chair, kissed her, and then, without giving her any novacaine, made her watch his attempts to commit suicide by jumping out the window— never mind that he had a ground-floor office.

Dr. Hertzman's obsession with suicide all stemmed from his introductory subscription to *MAD* magazine. He'd gotten all worked up after reading that dentists had the highest rate of suicide of any of the medical professions, including veterinarians. Dr. Hertzman didn't think *MAD* was joking about a thing like that. And he was right. According to The Schneid, a study in Washington State of twenty-two occupations revealed dentists had a suicide rate second only to sheepherders.

But it wasn't being second to sheepherders that upset Dr. Hertzman. It was the American Dental Association. The way he figured it, he'd best jump out the window before he fell behind his colleagues. Dr. Hertzman's compunction for missing out on his suicide was why Beverly and Nicki, his new tag-team dental assistants, made sure he never was left in his office alone…other than when there was a lingerie sale at Penney's.

Benjamin Randall Hertzman had gone to one of the top dental schools in the country…or so he said. I'd never heard of Molar State, but Dr. Hertzman said they ranked right up there with Ohio State and Michigan, that the only difference in the schools was the caliber of football played.

"Ohio State and Michigan? They were the big boys even then," Dr. Hertzman would say. "They played Division I. We played two-hand tag."

Doctor Hertzman had gone to dental school because his parents had insisted. They'd explained to Benjie—as they called him—if he ever expected to marry a proper Jewish girl someday, he'd best be a dentist. Either that or be a Rothchild. When shown a battery of albumin, cholesterol, and acne tests had proven conclusively the Hertzmans were in no way, shape, or form related to the Rothchilds, the decision had been made for them. If they wanted a proper Jewish girl for a daughter-in-law—which they most assuredly did—their Benjie best become a dentist. When Benjie passed the entry exam to Molar State—after failing those of Ohio State and Michigan—and was offered a partitioned room with board, the Hertzmans bit.

Benjie had done well enough at Molar State to not only retain his partition, but to be trusted with his own window. The school felt Benjamin Randall Hertzman had earned the window when he'd displayed no suicidal tendencies after receiving a *D* in Dental Anesthesiology.

They were, of course, proven wrong years later.

89

"LOOKS LIKE YOU HAVE *2-4-1-1*." Dr. Hertzman licked his choppers. "Drill, baby, drill!"

Unfortunately for me, the numbers I had weren't the winning entry in the weekly Mickey Mantle Tape-Measure Home Run Derby. Even more unfortunate, they were where Dr. Hertzman had found cavities. The two *1*s meant I had two cavities in the Number *1* tooth—one of the upper right molars.

Every tooth in your mouth, from the small lower molars to your upper incisors, has its own number to distinguish it from all other teeth—it doesn't matter whether or not they have broccoli stains. That way the dentist can look at your chart next time you come in and know immediately which molars, bicuspids, or whatever do not need deep drilling or extraction. However, even with 20-20 vision, the dentist can misread your chart and take out the wrong tooth. Yet once the mistake's brought to his attention, he'll generally put the tooth on a special amalgam chain for you and let you keep it as a necklace…usually not even billing you for it.

So there I was, tilted back in Dr. Hertzman's dental chair, the Goodwill tag still on it. I kept telling myself it was going to be okay and reassuring myself it wasn't. In times like this, The Schneid would always say, it helps to think positive thoughts. "That way it won't hurt as much," he'd tell me.

I'd decided to do my thinking about Annette Funicello.

But thinking about Annette Funicello and drooling into the little cup next to the chair wasn't helping any. Neither was thinking about Miss February or Miss March. I went through month after month of Playmates, thinking positively about each one, all the way to the newly revealed Miss August and nothing was helping.

"Hold still!" Dr. Hertzman said. "Do you want me to prick your sciatica with the needle?"

I wanted to tell Dr. Hertzman I didn't want him to prick *any* nerve with his needle, which looked big enough to shoot up the Budweiser horses. But with his hand in my mouth, I couldn't say anything.

"Okay, let's rock and roll!" Dr. Hertzman said, excitement in his voice. He pulled his hand out of my mouth. "Ladies, if you please."

Beverly, who in high school had been state heavyweight wrestling champ, and Nicki, who'd been light-heavy runner-up, held me down. Next to them, Tommy Salamo was a rank amateur. Not that I'd ever tell him that, of course.

Dr. Hertzman nodded to Beverly and Nicki and pirouetted, blowing a kiss to the ceiling. *"This is for you, Momma!"* He paused, a sadistic smile on his face.

"Ready...aim...."

"NOOOOOO!!!!" I screamed. And I clamped my mouth shut.

"Open up or I'm jumping out the window!"

I shook my head.

"Open up!"

"Should I do it for him, Dr. Hertzman?" Beverly asked.

"No, let me!" Nicki cried. "She always gets to."

"Look Philip, it's easy," the sadomasokiss Dr. Hertzman said, blowing Nicki a kiss. "Just open your mouth and...here, watch me."

I watched as he opened his mouth wide and plunged the novacaine needle into his gum.

It worked. I was numb.

"Okay, Philip, you know the drill. Well, actually you don't know *this* drill," Dr. Hertzman said, his jaw looking like he had a chaw of tobacco in it. "Not yet anyway."

He showed me the drill. It was a shiny black monstrosity that, from the huge drop of saliva on it, looked like its shine came from being freshly spit-polished. Anyone could see it was Dr. Hertzman's pride and joy. Anyone could also see there was a small *swastika* on it.

"Just got it," he said proudly. "It's a 1939 *Luftwaffe* drill. I had to redeem three books of Top Value stamps for it. But it was worth it. After all, it was used by Johannes Blaschke himself!"

"Joanna Blaschke?"

"Not Joanna Blaschke, *Johannes* Blaschke. What, you never heard of Johannes Blaschke?"

I shook my head.

Dr. Hertzman explained during the war Johannes Blaschke was the personal dentist to Hermann Göering, the Nazis' bombastic *Luftwaffe* chief, who invented the *Gestapo* before he got to bombing Poland.

"They say Göering cried before he even got into Blaschke's chair. A big man like that? A leader in the party? I never heard of such a thing! Horrible. He's crying like a baby, bawling, even though Blaschke told him he'd give him prosthetics. You know what prosthetics are, right?"

I shook my head.

"False teeth. They had to be made for Göering, and they had to be ready on the same day his teeth were pulled. You can understand why."

I shook my head.

"Philip, Philip, you can't very well run around as the head of the *Luftwaffe* with missing teeth now can you? How would that look in a staff meeting with the *Führer*?"

I had no answer. Besides, my mouth was clamped shut.

"There's a photograph over there on the wall of Johannes Blaschke."

I looked at the wall. There was a photo of Dr. Hertzman with Lucy and Desi, a photo of Dr. Hertzman with Wilt Chamberlain, a photo of a smiling Dr. Hertzman handing what must have been a dental bill to J. Edgar Hoover, who looked like he'd been mugged. There was a group photo of Dr. Hertzman with Frank Sinatra, Montgomery Cliff, and Ernest Borgnine on the set of *From Here to Eternity*—Burt Lancaster should have been in it too, and would have if he hadn't been on the beach playing touchy-feely with Deborah Kerr. And set in a dark Red frame was another group photo, this one taken at the Kremlin. It showed Dr. Hertzman right up there with Malenkov, Khrushchev, and the rest, toasting Stalin on his seventieth birthday party.

"I wasn't that big a deal to party regulars that year," Dr. Hertzman said with a sigh. That's why it's not signed by everybody."

I nodded.

"The photo above J. Edgar and me, that's Doctor Blaschke with Göering."

I studied the photo. Dr. Blaschke's face was smiling. Göering's wasn't.

"Impressive, isn't it?"

I nodded.

"Think that's impressive? I've got Blatschke beat. Look over there, behind you."

I twisted my neck. I was looking straight at a photo of Dr. Hertzman shaking hands with The Mick! And it was signed *Thanks for your crowning achievement—Mickey Mantle*

My mouth fell open. *"Holy bull shark, you know The Mick?"*

"Of course," Dr. Hertzman said. "We go way back. I did his *1* and *8* when I was team dentist for the Joplin Miners. That's where Mickey played his second year in the minors, you know."

"I know," I said. "They were Class C. Mickey won the league batting title hitting .363. He had twenty-six homers too."

"What are you, a smart guy?"

"Except for Biology."

Doctor Hertzman ignored my comment. "But the one right below that photo is actually the one I like best. It's the newest too."

I looked. It was a photo of a beaming Dr. Hertzman, his arm around Annette Funicello.

90

CANNOT PREDICT NOW

IF I HAD TO DO IT all again I would have taken the short-cut past the Clean Clothes Laundromat. That way maybe I wouldn't have got caught in the rain. Maybe I would have got home earlier.

I didn't...but I should have.

When I opened the front door Linnie rushed into my arms and hugged me. Her eyes were red from crying. Grandma Bessie came running down the stairs, her face streaked with tears.

"Am I glad you're home! We've been waiting for you! Where have you been all this time?"

"I took the long way home from Dr. Hertzman's. What did I do now?"

"Nothing...but we have to get going!"

"Going where? What's the matter, Grandma?"

"We need to drive to the hospital. Your mother and father are already there."

"Oh my God! What happened?"

Linnie had been holding Linnie Junior. She dropped her, buried her head on my shoulder, and sobbed.

"What happened?"

"It's your Uncle Harold," Grandma Bessie said. "He's had a heart attack."

I grabbed Linnie's hand, Grandma Bessie grabbed her keys, and the three of us rushed out the door to her car.

"Linnie, wait!" I shouted. *"You forgot Linnie Junior!"*

She stopped and looked at me. *"Who needs a stupid doll?"*

91

"IS HE GOING TO BE okay? Tell me the truth, Mom, is Uncle Harold going to be okay?"

"We don't know," Mom said. "It's too early to tell. Your Dad's in his room right now with the doctor."

"He never listens to me." Grandma Bessie was trying hard not to cry in front of me. "Thinks he's Gene Kelly. I keep telling him if he's going to dance in the rain he needs an umbrella."

Grandma Bessie explained Uncle Harold had stopped by the house with three or four rain-soaked bags of Coney Islands from Skyline. "He'd already eaten most of one bag. He was sitting at the kitchen table with your mother, Linnie, and me when…when…."

"When what?"

"He started complaining about his stomach, then shooting pain in his shoulder traveling down his arm. He got up from the table, staggered, and threw up. Then he fell to the floor."

With that, she burst into tears right there in the cardiac care waiting room.

At the desk across from us sat a nurse working on a crossword puzzle. The phone rang. With a sigh, she picked it up on the third ring.

"CCU...Cardiac Care Unit...hold, please." She put her hand over the mouthpiece as she saw me standing there.

"Yes, young man?"

"Uncle Harold—" And I caught myself. "Harold Greenberg, can you tell me what room he's in, please?"

"*Two-fourteen.* But you can't go in there."

"Why not?"

"No one under sixteen is allowed on the floor."

I told her I was almost sixteen.

"Almost?"

"Well, I will be in just three more years." And I gave her what I thought was my best *almost sixteen-years-old* smile.

"You have to be sixteen *now.* Hospital rules....Excuse me." She took her hand off the mouthpiece of the phone. "Sorry, Joanie....So what time will you be home tonight?....No, that's too late....Because I'm your mother, that's why....I don't care what Cookie's mother lets her do....No, I won't be home early. Today's Wednesday....Yes, I'm sure. Wednesday, Joanie....No, I'm working till five in the morning....Uh-huh, that's right, five. Then we're going for breakfast....Who? What difference does it make?....Okay, Ola. Ola and I are going for breakfast....Not Lola, Ola. *Ola*! You met her at...."

But I was no longer listening to the problems of Joanie's mother. I'd sneaked past her and pressed the button on the wall. The double doors swung open, and I darted through.

"Hey, kid, where do you think you're going?" An orderly was rushing down the corridor after me. *"You can't be in here!"*

Dad had just stepped out of *Room 214.* "It's okay, he's my son. I'll take full responsibility."

The orderly stopped, shrugged, and continued down the corridor.

"C'mon, Skip, let's go in," Dad said. "But you have to be real quiet."

"I promise, Dad," I said.

Uncle Harold was propped up in a hospital bed, a nurse leaning over him adjusting the pillow. On the table next to him was a heart monitor. All sorts of tubes and wires were attached to him. He even had a tube in his nose.

"What's that for?" I asked.

"To help him breathe," she said.

Uncle Harold's face was pale and puffy, his hands tied loosely to the bedside.

"We do that so he won't disconnect anything when he's sleeping or restless," the nurse explained. She carefully checked the monitor. "It's safer than having to replace lifesaving tubes."

I nodded.

"He's pretty weak...been drifting in and out of consciousness. Right now he's a bit hazy and has trouble speaking. There's difficulty understanding what he says. But you can talk to him."

"I can?"

Dad nodded. "He'll recognize your voice. He did mine."

"Just keep it short," the nurse said. "And don't say anything that might upset him."

"I won't."

I walked quietly to the bed and looked down at Uncle Harold. His eyes were closed, his eyelids fluttering. I kissed his forehead. Suddenly, he stirred. There was a low groan. I looked at Dad. I was trembling.

"It's okay," Dad said. "Don't be afraid."

"Uncle Harold?" I said.

His eyes slowly opened. "Skip?" he murmured.

"It's me, Uncle Harold."

"Closer."

I bent down over him, putting my hand on his. He mumbled something that sounded like *earthday*.

"My birthday…"

"January," I said. "Mom told me. Don't worry, I won't forget to give you a present."

He smiled. "Birthday..." I could tell he was struggling to speak. "Lucky…" he murmured. "Lucky…."

"I think he's had enough for now," the nurse said. "Doctor Groelich says he needs rest."

I nodded, sniffling.

She handed me a tissue. "Oh, here's Doctor Groelich now."

Dr. Groelich had walked into the room, his eyes studying Uncle Harold. He turned to the nurse. "How's he doing?"

"No change, Doctor. We're closely monitoring him. He's getting loop diuretics now."

"Good."

"He is going to be okay, Doctor, isn't he?" I asked.

Doctor Groelich looked at Dad.

"It's okay, Doctor," Dad said. "You can talk in front of him."

"It's too early to tell," Dr. Groelich said. "He's had a massive coronary. We've got him on a cardiac monitor. We'll be able to tell immediately if his heart rhythm suddenly becomes disturbed."

I nodded.

"Sometimes patients have setbacks or another heart attack. That's why we keep them in CCU."

"Thanks, Doctor," Dad said.

Doctor Groelich went on to explain to us that Uncle Harold's heart monitor would allow a nurse to check his heartbeat, blood, breathing, and other vital signs from a central station.

"I'll be back a little later to check on him."

In minutes he was hurrying back.

92

I DON'T REMEMBER how long Dad and I stood there in the hallway outside Uncle Harold's room until Dr. Groelich came out. But I do remember the first thing he said to us.

"He's gone."

Dr. Groelich put his hand on hand on Dad's shoulder. "I'm sorry."

Dad slowly nodded.

"We did everything we could. I'm sorry, Mr. Kleinmann."

"NO!" I screamed. "NO!"

Dad held me tight.

"Dad!" I cried. "Dad!" I buried my head on his shoulder. I stood there shaking in his arms and sobbing.

"He's gone, Skip. He's gone, and we can't bring him back." Dad wiped my tears with his hand. "He's with God and the angels now."

I looked up at him. "Why, Dad? Why Uncle Harold? It's not fair. Doesn't God have enough angels?"

"I don't know, Skip."

Dad held me tight against his chest. I remember the wetness of his cheek, can still hear his voice quivering....

"Maybe God needed a specialist."

93

IT HAD BEEN a huge funeral. Over three hundred people crowded into the Weil Funeral Home, all three rooms filled with tears. Just about everyone who knew him was there to pay their final respects and offer their condolences. That's how well-liked Uncle Harold was. Mayor Bachrach was there. So was the entire HUC baseball team, Myron, Natalie the operator from Cincinnati Bell, Mrs. Guttman, Mrs. Fatuzzi, the Sklafers, Dr. Hertzman, Izzy Kadetz from the delicatessen, even Charmaine. Those who couldn't make it sent flowers. There was a beautiful arrangement sent by Hubie Suvpansky.

The shovel was sticking out of a pile of newly dug earth.

"*Al mekomo yavo ve shalom*...." Rabbi Breitzig paused. "May Harold Milton Greenberg go to his place in peace."

Rabbi Breitzig motioned to Grandpa Albert. Grandpa Albert shoveled a little soil from the pile, emptying it slowly into the open grave, the echo of earth falling on the wooden coffin.

It was a terrible sound—haunting.

Grandpa Albert stuck the shovel back into the pile and stepped back. Dad was next.

Philip Schlaeger

Then Rabbi Breitzig nodded to me. "It's a Jewish tradition," he said. "Helping to fill the grave means you've left nothing undone."

Rabbi Breitzig took the shovel. He turned toward Mom and Dad, Grandpa Albert and Grandma Bessie, to all the friends, cousins, neighbors, and school classmates who'd followed the hearse to the cemetery. His voice was calm and clear. "In Judaism, after you have emptied a shovel onto a loved one's casket, there is no denying death. That makes it possible for healing to begin."

Linnie looked at me. "When does it start

"What?"

"What he said...the healing."

Rabbi Breitzig mumbled something in Hebrew. "Would anyone in the family like to say anything?"

Mom nodded. She started to say something, then broke down, sobbing.

"*Ado-nay Hu na-chalato, v'yanu-ach b'shalom al mishkavo...* May his resting place be in the Garden of Eden. Amen."

Rabbi Breitzig motioned to the two grave diggers, who'd been standing quietly in the background.

I bowed my head. "Good-bye, Uncle Harold."

The sky had darkened. I took Linnie's hand, and together we trudged from Uncle Harold's grave...no need to say anything. There was a sudden clap of thunder. My tears were quickly mingled with the rain. There was another clap of thunder. I lifted my head to the sky.

"This is for you, Uncle Harold."

And I hummed *Singin' in the Rain.*

94

IT HAD BEEN a week since the funeral and Linnie had returned to being abnormal. On the fifth ring, she picked up the phone. "It's for you, Penis Breath."

I pushed George into his gerbil cage and walked downstairs, reminding Linnie on the way to the hospital she'd said she wasn't going to call me Penis Breath any longer.

"That was last week," she said. "The week's up."

I looked at Turkey Lips and rolled my eyes. "So, who is it?"

"I don't know. It sounded like he said *Pressert*." She shrugged and handed the phone to me.

"Hello?"

"Hello...is this Philip Kleinmann?"

I told him that was me. "Sorry, I was rolling my eyes at my little sister."

"Oh? Have I interrupted anything?"

"No, sir."

"Philip, this is James Reinert from Esso Gasoline....Congratulations, Philip. Your entry was the winning one last week in Esso's Mickey Mantle Tape-Measure Home Run Derby.... Are you still there?"

I nodded my head.

"*Philip?*"

"Oh, I'm sorry."

"*1-5-0-7*…am I right?"

"Yes sir," I said. "That's my Uncle Harold's birthday."

95

"HOLY BULL SHARK! It's him!"

Dad frowned at me. *"Bull shark?* And use your knife to push the peas, not your finger."

I couldn't tell you what Mickey Mantle was pushing his peas with because photographers from the *Daily News, Post,* and *Herald-Tribune* were clustered in front of him, snapping pictures for their papers' front pages.

Dad and I were sitting at a big, round, white-clothed table in the middle of the room, along with The Schneid, his father, and a couple of other kids who'd also brought their fathers. Our table was Number 7, which just happened to be the number The Mick wore. It was my lucky number.

All the weekly winners of Esso's Mickey Mantle Tape-Measure Home Run Derby were gathered there. We'd all been invited to the historic old Roosevelt Hotel in New York for the contest's Final Award luncheon. The tables had been cleared, the waiters had wiped up puddles of ice cream, and we were ready for the luncheon's piece de résistance. Soon we would learn which one of us would get to be the Yankees' batboy for the last home game of the season...which one of us would be the lucky one to kneel in the on-deck circle with Mickey Mantle. Mel Allen was there to announce the name of the Grand Prize winner, The Mick was there to make the presentation, Mr. Reinert was there to taste Mr. Essovitz' dessert for him since Mr. Essovitz was allergic to anything that had been near peanuts, and Hyman H. Essovitz II was there to drone on forever about Esso gasoline.

"...And finally...yes, finally, I come to octane...."

There was a loud groan. Mr. Essovitz held up both his hands, saying he was just kidding. I knew he wasn't.

"Okay, and now it's time for Mel Allen to announce the Grand Prize winner of Esso's Mickey Mantle Tape-Measure Home Run Derby. As you all know, one winner will be chosen from all the weekly winners to be the batboy of the Yankees...."

He paused for effect. There was none.

"And if that wasn't enough, our Grand Prize winner will be given absolutely free, one hundred gallons of Esso Gasoline, which as you know—"

There were more groans...which suddenly turned to wild cheers. Two busboys, staggering under the weight of their trays, had dropped dishes. Throughout the room there were cheers of encouragement as more busboys started staggering.

Mr. Essovitz rapped his water glass with a spoon, and the busboys stopped dropping trays.

"Now then, I have Mr. Sheldon Lumpkin here from the *Baseball Encyclopedia*. He will read one question, which has been selected by a vote of the Esso board of trustees from the statistics on page 1322 of the *Encyclopedia*. No one other than the board members—and their wives—has seen the question. All of the wives have been sworn to secrecy. Not even their hairdressers know."

The kid across from me snickered. His father gave him a stern look.

"Mr. Lumpkin, will you stand please?" Mr. Essovitz looked at the little man sitting at the end of his table. "And everyone hold your applause."

Everyone gladly did.

Mr. Lumpkin stood and waved. Mr. Essovitz motioned for him to sit back down.

"You've all been given an Esso pen to write down the answer to the question on your napkin," Mr. Essovitz said.

"And their name," Mr. Reinert whispered to him. "Tell them to make sure they put their name on the napkin too."

"Yes, print your name on your napkin. That's first *and* last name. We will be collecting the napkins." Mr. Essovitz smiled. "And the pens, of course."

A kid near the front raised his hand. "My pen won't write!"

"We'll see if we can find you one to replace it," Mr. Essovitz said, reaching for a glass of water. "And I'm going to waive the ten cents we would normally charge."

There was applause from the kid's father.

"Anybody else before we start?"

A hand shot up.

"Yes?"

"May I go to the bathroom?"

96

"I'VE BEEN TOLD we have a   special person seated in the room," Mr. Essovitz announced. "Before Mr. Lumpkin reads the important question that will decide the Grand Prize winner, I'd like him to stand and be recognized."

There were moans throughout the room. Mr. Essovitz ignored them.

"Sitting at Table Number *13* is Richard L. Slefavitch, the president of..." Mr. Essovitz turned to the waiter standing behind him and whispered, "What did you say he's the president of?"

The waiter leaned over. "I didn't," he whispered. "It was him." He pointed to James Reinert, who as Mr. Essovitz's right-arm man was sitting to his left. "Sir, he wants to know what Slefavitch is the president of."

"My church brotherhood," Mr. Reinert whispered to Mr. Essovitz. "I belong to Saint George and the Dragon."

"Mr. Slefavitch, of course, is president of Saint George and the Beast," Mr. Essovitz announced to the audience.

"Not Beast...Dragon," Mr. Reinert whispered.

"Beast, dragon, what's the difference," Mr. Essovitz whispered back. He rapped his water glass again. "Now if everyone will take their seat, we will proceed with the question. Mr. Lumpkin, if you please."

"Well, as some of you many know," Mr. Lumpkin began, "the tape-measure home run started with the man sitting right up here on the di-is."

The Schneid leaned over and whispered. "He means da-is."

"Uh, Mr. Lumpkin, that's *day*-is." Mr. Essovitz grinned as he corrected him.

"What did I tell you?" The Schneid said.

Mr. Lumpkin's face reddened. "April 17, 1953.... Mickey was twenty-one, in just his second full season with the Yankees when he hit the granddaddy of all home runs. It came in the fifth inning at Griffith Stadium.... Chuck Stobbs pitching for the Senators. Well, since Stobbs was a lefty, Mickey was batting right-handed...right, Mickey?"

Mel Allen nudged Mickey, who'd started to doze off. He nodded and cleared his throat. "Uh...yeah."

"Mickey's being modest," Mr. Lumpkin said. "Anyway, he hit Stobbs' second pitch to him like a shot out of h—" Mr. Lumpkin caught himself. "Well, Mickey hit it with such explosive power that...well, you know what I'm saying?"

No one did.

"Well, the ball rocketed towards the big scoreboard in left-centerfield.... grazed the Natty Boh beer sign above the words *Oh, Boy, What a Beer* and cleared the 55-foot high bleachers....Well, that's a distance of 460 feet from home plate...and the ball was still climbing!... Finally it landed in a backyard on Oakdale Place. It's still the longest home run ever measured!"

"But it wasn't really measured!"

I turned and looked at The Schneid. So did everyone else in the room.

"They never used a tape measure!" The Schneid shouted at Mr. Lumpkin. "It was stepped off by somebody with the Yankees front office. He had a size 11 shoe…11-B."

Mr. Lumpkin glared at The Schneid. "Always has to be someone with technicalities. Tape measure, shoe, yardstick…doesn't matter with what. Well, point is the distance *was* measured. You can look up what the distance was in the *Baseball Encyclopedia.*" He smiled. "I have copies available for sale… *after* the answer to the Grand Prize question. And now here's the… question. *Ready?*"

"FINALLY!" someone yelled.

Mr. Lumpkin ignored him, reveling his moment in the spotlight.

"You have fifteen seconds to write down your answer on your napkin. Well, let me remind you, the one who comes closest to the correct answer wins Esso's Mickey Mantle Tape-Measure Home Run Derby and all that goes with it."

He paused for dramatic effect. There was none.

I looked at The Mick. My knees were shaking.

"Using a size 11-B Cordovan Oxford to measure it, how far did Mickey hit that home run?"

97

MY PALMS WERE SWEATY, my stomach churning. There was screaming and wild cheering—and it wasn't because the busboys had resumed dropping trays.

"Mel, if you will, please." Mr. Essovitz handed Mel Allen the envelope. The Voice took out his reading glasses.

"The Grand Prize Winner of Esso's 1957 Mickey Mantle Tape-Measure Home Run Derby is...Philip Kleinmann!"

My mouth fell open. *I did it! Holy bull shark, I really did it!* I pushed my chair back from the table, my heartbeat racing as I stood, beaming.

"Philip's answer was..." The Voice stopped as he was given a note.

"Looks like we have TWO Philip Kleinmanns here....You boys know each other?" Mel laughed, then turned and looked at Mr. Reinert, who nodded his head. *"The winning Philip Kleinmann is in the back...table number 22!"*

What? I slumped back down in my chair as Cousin Philip stood up, basking in thunderous applause. I buried my head in my arms, sobs trapped in my throat.

"Philip...will you come up please and meet Mickey Mantle, who will present you your award!"

357

I looked up through a flood of tears. Cousin Philip was marching up to the dais, his head held high, pie crumbs on his chin. He stuck his tongue out at me passing my table. Flash bulbs popped as the photographers snapped picture after picture.

"Philip's answer was right on the money...565 feet...almost two football fields!"

Mr. Lumpkin nudged Mel Allen aside. "You can look it up in *The Baseball Encyclopedia*."

The Mick presented Cousin Philip the award, then shook his hand. "Congratulations, Philip."

The room erupted in applause as Mickey and Cousin Philip posed for the cameras.

Mr. Essovitz smiled and shook hands with Cousin Philip, then turned to the crowd. "Mickey says he has to go. But I want to thank him for being here today to present the award, and to wish him luck for the last games remaining this season."

There was a standing ovation. Mickey waved and rushed through the *Exit* door to chants of *"Mick! Mick! Mick!"*

"I know, I know," Dad said, sadly shaking his head. "It hurts."

It sure did. I covered my face with my hands and cried.

"Here, son, take my handkerchief." Dad was trying to sound soothing. It didn't help. He lifted my chin up. "Skip...Skip...listen to me...."

I shook my head and ran out of the room.

98

THE EXACT MOMENT when I decided to go ahead and do it remains kind of hazy. But I do remember standing at the sink in the men's room, splashing cold water on my face. All I could think of was Cousin Philip up there instead of me, shaking hands with Mickey Mantle.

I decided to stick my head in the toilet bowl and flush my life away. But the toilet door was locked and...well, there was just that one stall. Most Kleinmanns would have given up right there. Not me. I knew there had to be another way to quickly end it all.

That's when it hit me…gas.

Whoever was sitting there on the toilet wasn't mincing any grunts. There was no telling how long he'd stay in there, not when between grunts he was singing *Take Me Out to the Ball Game.*

"...if they don't win it's a shame..."

Perfect! I really needed to hear how I felt standing there, head up my butt, as Cousin Philip was announced the winner.

Suddenly, there was a grunt, then a loud flush, and *ahhh!* The toilet stall's door opened and, zipping up his fly, out walked The Mick.

99

I STOOD THERE unable to move, unable to speak, unable to do anything but gawk.

"You okay?...Hey pard, you okay?"

He talked to me! Me, Philip Morris Kleinmann! Mickey Mantle looked right at me and called me 'PARD.'

"You okay?" And then he saw I'd been crying. "Say, pard, what's happened? It can't be that bad, can it?"

I nodded.

"C'mon, tell me. Maybe I can help. What's wrong?"

And I told Mickey everything. I told him about the Magic 8 Ball, and that no matter how many times I asked, it always said this was the year I was going to meet him. "This morning I got IT IS CERTAIN. Yesterday I got WITHOUT A DOUBT. The day before it said YOU MAY RELY ON IT."

I told him all I went through when Mel Allen announced the name of the Grand Prize winner.

"It should have been me shaking your hand. Not my stupid Cousin Philip."

"How 'bout me making it up to you?" The Mick smiled and stuck out his hand.

But I didn't shake it.

"Uh, Mick, maybe we shouldn't shake hands just now." I blushed. "I mean, you just got off the toilet and—"

"You're right, Skip. You're right. I should wash my hands." Mickey threw his head back and laughed.

Which got me laughing too.

The Mick and I stood there laughing and talking for what seemed forever. We talked about baseball and movies and school and Wheaties and *Playboy* and phosphates and little sisters—all the things idols and idol worshippers talk about—until Mickey said this time he really had to go.

"I promised Mervyn I'd be home in time to take the dog for his walk." Mickey rinsed his hands and shrugged. The only paper towel was in the waste can. He stood there, trying to shake his hands dry.

"Hey, it's been great talking with you, Skip. Anything I can do for you?"

Anything he could do for me? I gulped and told him I'd be the happiest kid on Earth if he gave me his autograph.

He smiled. "You got it." He reached a still-dripping hand into his jacket and pulled out a pen. "Skip, you got some paper I can write on?"

I didn't have any. Neither did The Mick.

"Darn, I guess no autograph," he said. Mickey put his hand on my shoulder. "I'm sorry, Skip. Wish we had some paper."

"You can write on my sleeve!"

Mickey shook his head. "I do that and your mother will kill me."

I wasn't about to give up. I rolled my sleeve up. "You can write on my arm!"

"Yeah, but it would come off in the shower."

361

"Who says I have to shower?"

The Mick smiled. "Your mother."

I sniffled. "No one's going to believe I met you. How do I prove it?" I told Mickey ever since I was six, I dreamed of meeting him someday and getting a special autograph. "The Magic 8 Ball said this year it would happen."

"I'm really sorry."

"The Schneid told me it was stupid." I wiped my nose on my sleeve. "I'm smashing my Magic 8 Ball when I get home."

100

THE YEARS FLEW BY, and we all went our separate ways. We moved to places like Syracuse, Fayetteville, Worcester, Omaha, Santa Fe, and San Quentin. And then we moved again, to Atlanta, Dallas, Seattle, New York, Rome, and LA. Some of us did well, very well. Some of us didn't.

Ryan Rappaport is an executive producer at one of Hollywood's major studios. He's working on a blockbuster film to be released next year. It takes place on the East Side of Antananarivo, the capital city of Madagascar. I'm not permitted to tell you the title or where Madagascar is.

Jeannette Moskowitz lives in Nepal and now owns a very prominent logo design agency. It's supposed to be the biggest in the Himalayas.

I lost contact with Lenny Gordon, Alice Waxman, Peter Carella, Diane Beitler, and Maureen Levenson…oh, and Harvey Meshugana too. If you know anything as to their whereabouts, please contact me. I'd appreciate it.

Steven Sklafer lives in Scarsdale and was on the board of directors of the Pepsi Bottling Company until he got caught sniffing Coke.

Ziggy Zagsky was sent to prison for insider trading.

Ira Luwis became a composer-songwriter. His new hit, *I Saw Daddy Kissing Santa Claus,* topped the charts in *The Village Voice* last Christmas.

Stanley Kaplan was recently nominated for a Pulitzer Prize for his work in teaching Pig Latin to illegal immigrants.

Tommy Salamo never became a professional wrestler. He was walking down Hollywood Boulevard when he was jumped by a couple of gang bangers, who busted his nose and kicked him in the scrotum. He failed to survive a testicle transplant.

Porky Babirusa went to Hebrew Union College and became a rabbi. At present he's the head of the Central Conference of American Rabbis and doesn't go by *Porky* anymore.

Gordon Hymandinger has an online yo-yo tutorial. If you're interested, the website is imayoyo.com.

I haven't seen Aaron Levy since he dropped out of MIT in his sophomore year and, with the money he got from selling his baseball card collection, bought a one-way plane ticket to Tibet. Rumor is he convinced the Dali Lama to take him on as an understudy.

Howard Kodesh followed in his brother's footsteps and flunked out of law school at Ohio State. His memoir about his semester there, *Eighth Amendment for Dummies,* can sometimes be found at Barnes & Noble.

Elaine, I hear, is now on her fifth husband and teaches a remedial course on marriage at some online community college in Florida—I forget the name.

The Schneid scored 1605 on his SATs—getting extra credit for penmanship—and accepted a full scholarship to the

University of Bialystok, where he studied Polish culinary arts. I think about him every time I boil water.

Fenny no longer stuttered by the time he was a drill instructor in the Army. He fought with the 173rd in Vietnam, and his name was in all the newspapers when he threw himself on a grenade to save his men. That the grenade was a dud didn't matter to the Army. They awarded him the Medal of Honor anyway.

My cousin Philip left Bellmore. Actually, he did live in Baltimore for a while. I'm not sure, but I think he lives in Bryn Mawr now. Or maybe it's Tribeca. Frankly, I don't care.

Like I said, some of us did well and some of us didn't. But not one of my old friends and classmates, the kids I knew in Cincinnati and the Bronx, has lived the life I have.

Spielberg couldn't have scripted it better.

101

MY SUCCESS DIDN'T COME easily. There were major bumps along the way. And I came close to living on the street.

Sometimes life is hard.

The year after I met The Mick, I lost Grandpa Albert to prostate cancer. I didn't know it at the time, but he'd been diagnosed shortly before my bar mitzvah. I wish I had known. I would have included him in my thank-you speech. Grandpa Albert was only sixty-four when he died.

Yogi was hit by a car five years later while chasing a poodle. He was nine.

By then I'd flunked out of college and was slinging hamburgers at McDonald's up on North Bend Road...that is until I got a letter from the draft board.

When I got out of the Army, I went back to school, finished with a degree in advertising from Syracuse, and proceeded to lose job after job on Madison Avenue. No one seemed to remember *You don't know shit from Shinola*, which I always explained was inspired by Uncle Harold.

Doors kept closing on me.

I tried selling ad space for a weekly community paper and making telemarketing calls. I was let go after leading the company in hang-ups. I pushed an ice cream cart around Greenwich Village. I bagged groceries and walked door-to-door selling Fuller brushes.

And whenever it rained I'd think of Uncle Harold.

I'd think of the bogies at six o'clock, the mad dashes to the men's room, and the loose-boweled Peregrine falcon. I'd think about his pursuit of Charlene, Charmaine, or whatever her name was. I'd think about him dancing joyfully in the rain without an umbrella. And I'd find myself humming *Singin' in the Rain*.

Then one day a registered letter came that wasn't from a collection agency. It was from Probate Court and must have been lost for years by the Post Office.

"You have to sign for it," the man who rang the doorbell said. So I pulled my Yankee ballpoint pen from my pocket and scribbled my name. Then I rushed downtown to the Probate Clerk's office and showed them my ID.

I used half the money to open a small discount store. And since the money came from Uncle Harold, I named the store after him. I did well enough to open a second *Uncle Harold's*, then a third and fourth.

I kept expanding and expanding.

Today, I live in what some say is the largest estate in Cincinnati. The house has seven bedrooms, two of which are for the live-in help. I forget how many bathrooms there are...who's counting? All I know is Gordon Hymandinger has his own whenever he comes to visit.

There's a six-car garage, which gives me more than enough space for Mom's old '57 Riviera, which I always drive on her birthday. There are two tennis courts and two swimming pools. We haven't decided yet where to put a pickleball court. I'm open to ideas.

Before you ask, no, I haven't forgot those not as fortunate as I've been...and I never will. I give all I can...often anonymously. I like it when my stocks go up. So does United Way.

Besides United Way, I sit on the boards of the Cincinnati Symphony, CET-Public TV, St. Aloysius Orphanage, the University of Cincinnati, and Skyline Chili.

My home life couldn't possibly be any better.

I have a wonderful wife, who's as charming and bright as she is gorgeous. I guess sometimes the ugly duckling does become a beautiful swan. Madeline sure did. I fell in love with her way before she was first runner-up in Miss Ohio—Madeline, of course, had long been in love with me. Our marriage has truly been a blessing. We've been happy together all these years and do just about everything together—except practice *ushiro mawashi sushi* and eat broccoli.

Madeline has given me two wonderful, loving kids. Both are tremendously successful, and for that I'm very thankful.

Our son Jeff is making a handsome living as a canine psychologist. He specializes in treating dogs with Attention Deficit Disorder. Jeff's married to a lovely lady and has three beautiful girls. Two years ago, they all moved to North Carolina. Madeline and I are planning a surprise visit there this winter.

Our daughter Nan gave up a promising career as a literary agent to become a sous chef in Manhattan. If you've ever dined at *Bouley, Jean Georges,* or *One If By*

Land, Two If By Sea, you've probably raved over her cupcakes. Nan and her husband have a cute little boy and spend summers on Cape Cod. I love taking them all sailing to Nantucket with Madeline and me.

I've been lucky to see the world as few people have. If you want my opinion, I recommend you see Prague and Africa...yes, Africa. I've been to fourteen countries there so far. I think it's one less than my friend, Barbara Lowenstein.

But my favorite spot on the planet is right here in my study. I have it filled with memories.

On one wall there's a photo of me with Vladamir Putin. It was taken when we broke ground for our *Uncle Harold's* in Sochi. There are photos of me with Netanyahu, Hillary, and Bill O'Reilly; photos of me with Jay Leno and Yogi Berra. One with LeBron James too. Next to LeBron is a photo of me with Uncle Harold. It was taken that day at Yankee Stadium.

On the wall behind my Victorian desk are certificates of appreciation and honorary degrees, plus thank-you notes from the White House, the Pentagon, NASA, and Michael Jackson. I've also put my bar mitzvah certificate up there.

The third wall is mostly reserved for family pictures. I've hung my favorite Picasso there. A Georgia O'Keefe too.

But my most treasured possession hangs on a wall all by itself, a light from the ceiling always shining directly on it. Inside the gold frame is a wrinkled brown paper towel, fished out years ago from a wastecan in the men's room of the old Roosevelt Hotel in New York. Over the years the writing on it has faded, but if you stand close enough you can still read it....

To Skip — Never give up your dreams. And always have pen and paper with you — Mickey Mantle

EPILOGUE

"LADIES AND GENTLEMAN..." You could hear Mel Allen's unmistakable voice throughout the Stadium. *"A MAGNIFICENT YANKEE...THE GREAT NUMBER SEVEN...MICKEY MANTLE!"*

More than 60,000 fans were on their feet. *"MICK-EY...MICK-EY...MICK-EY!"*

It was June 8, 1969...Mickey Mantle Day at Yankee Stadium. I was twenty-six years old then.

The Mick finished that 1957 season with 34 home runs, to Willie's 35. But he outhit Willie, leading the American League in batting again, this time with a.365 average. That was more than enough to beat Willie's .333 and keep me from losing my $500 bet with Cousin Philip.

Mickey won the American League's MVP award in '57 too. It was his second in a row—something Willie Mays never would match.

"The way Mickey was in '56 and '57," Mel Allen would remember, "there was nothing like him in baseball history."

Running all out to first base on a drag bunt...slamming a fastball to where no ball had gone before...racing across the outfield to snare a sinking line drive...throwing a runner out at home with his cannon of an arm—that was Mickey Mantle.

In 1958, The Mick hit 42 home runs despite an injured shoulder that robbed him of some of his left-handed power. The next year, he finished with 40 homers, sometimes playing in terrible pain.

His greatest home-run season came two years later.

Nineteen sixty-one was the year he might have broken Babe Ruth's single-season record of 60 home runs, a record that had stood for 34 years. The Mick wasn't the only Yankee chasing the Babe. So was Roger Maris, the other half of the M&M Boys. By the start of September, it was neck-and-neck, with Roger at 56 home runs and Mickey at 53. But a serious infection, one that hospitalized him, forced Mickey out of the race. He finished with 54 home runs, leaving it to Roger to hit Number 61 on the last day of the season.

Though he lost the race, The Mick became solidly entrenched as the most popular player in baseball.

Two years later, on May 22, 1963, Mickey hit the hardest ball he ever hit, a tenth-inning home run that slammed into the façade in Yankee Stadium and bounced back into the infield...734 feet.

But The Mick was a shadow of what he was...and he knew it. Years of aches and pains—and hard living—had taken their toll on the once magnificent body. Mickey's last home run came Sept 20, 1968 in Yankee Stadium. Future Hall-of-Famer Jim Lonborg, a right-hander, was on the mound for the Red Sox. It was home run Number 536.

On March 1, 1969, Mickey Mantle announced his retirement from baseball. "If I knew I was going to live this long," he told the press, "I'd have taken better care of my body."

On that day, his famed number 7 was retired by the Yankees.

The Mick finished his career playing in 2,401 games. But he sat out 400, most due to injuries.

He left baseball, a living legend.

He hit more balls over 500 feet than any other player in baseball history.

Four times he captured the AL home run title. He won three MVP awards and the Triple Crown once. Ten times he batted over .300. In World Series play, he hit 18 home runs, still a record.

And he did it all playing on only one good leg.

"On two legs, Mickey Mantle would have been the greatest ball player who ever lived," said Nellie Fox, the great White Sox second baseman whose plaque hangs in Cooperstown.

In 1974, Mickey was elected to the Hall of Fame…on the first ballot.

In June of 1995, doctors at Baylor University Medical Center in Dallas told him he had inoperable liver cancer. He received a liver transplant. On July 28, he checked back into Baylor for the last time. His liver cancer had rapidly spread throughout his body. The doctors said it was the most aggressive cancer they'd ever seen.

Mickey died sixteen days later. He was sixty-three.

Mickey Charles Mantle was the greatest natural talent to ever play the game. Sports writers who saw him play will tell you he was better than Willie Mays.

Sometimes I wonder what kind of numbers The Mick would've put up if he hadn't been plagued by all those injuries, half his body taped up like a mummy, his knee in a bulky brace.

Eight hundred home runs isn't inconceivable.

"AND NOW, MICKEY MANTLE, YANKEE STADIUM IS ALL YOURS!"

There was a thunderous ovation for what seemed like eternity. From the upper deck in right to the box seats along the third-base line, fans stood on the seats, shouting deliriously.

I was sitting in the upper deck with my three-year-old. I held him high to see.

"Daddy," he said. "Why is everybody cheering that man?"

I brushed away a tear. "Because," I said, "he's Mickey Mantle."

ACKNOWLEDGEMENTS

It was the seventeeth-century English poet John Donne who said, *"No man is an island."* That's certainly true when it comes to writing a book.

Mickey Mantle Doesn't Eat Broccoli would not have been possible without the support of many people. A few deserve special mention.

Barbara Azrialy, Leah Silverman Gales, Beth Goehring, and Richard Armstrong are writers whose early feedback encouraged me. So too did Patty Duffey, Jeane Harvey, James Logsdon, Scotty Curran, and Bob Meadows at Anthem Authors in Henderson, Nevada.

Authors M.A.R. Unger, Donna Mabry, and Dianne Hahn are my critique partners. Skip's story is much better with their weekly input. M.A.R. and Donna were also instrumental in formatting the manuscript for publication, M.A.R. even lending me her talent in book cover design.

Finally, a huge thank-you to the adorable woman I travel life with. I would never have come this far without Marni Graves at my side.

In memory of Dr. Stanford M. Goodman.
You will always be my hero.

CPSIA information can be obtained
at www.ICGtesting.com
Printed in the USA
BVHW041255061220
595043BV00022B/1430